D1156482

HOW TO

Almost

MAKE

A

MILLION

DOLLARS

Copyright © 2004 by Robert X. Leeds
All rights reserved under the Pan-American
and International Copyright Conventions.
Printed in the United States of America
Published by
Epic Publishing Company

This book may not be reproduced in whole or in part in any form or
by any means, electronic or mechanical, including photocopying,
recording, or by any information storage and retrieval system now
known or hereafter invented, without written permission from the
publisher. For information, address:

Epic Publishing Company
1027 S. Rainbow Blvd. - #236
Las Vegas, Nevada 89145-6232
www.epicpublishing.com

ISBN 0-9674025-6-5

Publishers Cataloguing
Robert X. Leeds, 2005
How To *almost* Make A Million Dollars
First Edition
Includes index.
1. The Heritage of Great Failures 2. One Hundred Proverbs For
Success 3. Humor 4. Motivation 5. Think Big! Act Big! Do Big!

Mainland China rights acquired by:
Jiuzhou Publishing House, Beijing, P.R. China

Manufactured by Cushing-Malloy, Inc., Ann Arbor, MI

Cover design by George Foster
Photograph by Martin Sullivan

Also by *Robert X. Leeds*

Build A Better You - Starting Now (26 Volumes)
        Don Dibble, Editor - Robert X. Leeds Co-Author

How Santa's Best Friend Saved Christmas

All The Comforts Of Home

Doctor Leeds' Selection of Popular Epic Recitations -
                        for Minstrel and Stage Use

Christmas Tails

Love Is A 4 Legged Word

TO ALL WHO TRIED
AND TRIED AGAIN
UNTIL THEY SUCCEEDED

"What is it that confers the noblest delight? What is that which swells a man's breast with pride above that which any other experience can bring to him? Discovery!

To know that you are walking where none others have walked; that you are beholding what human eye has not seen before; that you are breathing a virgin atmosphere. To give birth to an idea - an intellectual nugget, right under the dust of a field that many a brain-plow had gone over before. To be the first -- That is the idea.

To do something, say something, see something, before anybody else -- these are the things that confer a pleasure compared with other pleasures are tame and commonplace, other ecstasies cheap and trivial. Lifetimes of ecstasy crowded into a single moment."

The Innocents Abroad   Autobiography of Mark Twain
Mark Twain's Notebook   Speech 3/30/1901

FOREWORD

There must be a million magazine ads, books, tapes, radio commercials and television infomercials out there begging to tell you *"How To Make A Million Dollars"* or *"How To Get Rich Quick."* Add to these another million telephone, Internet, and mail order seminars, and you begin to wonder why everyone isn't already a millionaire. Well, some of them are; the people who sold you their tapes, programs, magazines, books and seminars.

Now, I haven't read all the books, listened to every tape, or attended every seminar, but I have engaged in enough moneymaking ventures to realize there are certain considerations rarely (or never) found in these enticing reservoirs of entrepreneurial wisdom and they are not taught in any college classroom.

To establish the fact that I speak from experience, let me offer some of my credentials. By the age of sixteen, I figured I knew the important things in life so I dropped out of school in the eleventh grade. I got my GED when I left the Air Force and eventually went back to school. After acquiring an undergraduate degree in Industrial Engineering I earned a Master of Business Management from Wayne State University. I went on to teach Business

Management in undergraduate studies at Harper College in Palatine, Illinois and in graduate school at Wayne State University in Detroit. With all due modesty, the classes I taught were "standing room only."

In addition to being president of Sigma Iota Epsilon (the Business School's honor fraternity), I was president of the Student Division of the Academy of Management.

My work experience covers a diverse array of entrepreneurial ventures, many of which were abandoned or failed. (Oh, if only someone had written this book for me!) While some of my efforts were modest and some temerarious, others were of such consequence they threatened to change entire industries. In 1987 and again in 1988, I was nominated for the "Entrepreneur of the Year" by Venture Magazine and Arthur Young Accounting Services. I was beaten out of first place by a woman whose innovative accomplishment was to set up a company that imported sweaters from China. (So much for ingenuity.)

What I will reveal to you in the following chapters is why some of my successes and some of my failures were due more to the insidious influences that impinge upon our lives than to the ordered strategies of the textbook.

In the course of my endeavors, I met and enjoyed the company of many leaders of industry and even started a business with a guy named Ray Kroc, founder of McDonald's. I even partnered in a movie venture with the great actor and director, Orson Welles.

You don't remember my name? (Oh sure, everyone knows that Michelangelo painted the ceiling of the Sistine Chapel, *but does anyone remember the name of the guy who painted the woodwork?*)

CONTENTS

CONTENTS

HOW TO
Almost
MAKE A
MILLION
DOLLARS

I *almost* did it. You can almost do it, too!

ROBERT X. LEEDS

Forbes

60 FIFTH AVENUE NY, NY 10011

"Have you seen the Money & Investments Section?
It's all 'Robert X Leeds this, Robert X Leeds that'
and nothing about us."

©2004 Stu Heinecke, Inc.
Permission Granted

PROLOGUE

I awoke from a deep sleep and everything about me was strange and eerie. The room was filled with puffs of white clouds and as my eyes became adjusted to the scene before me I was able to discern the shapes of cherubs and other celestial beings. In the midst of these figures was one towering figure dressed in a long white flowing robe. I knew it was **GOD**.

And **GOD** *spoke to me in a voice so deep and resonant that my very flesh trembled, and* **HE** *said, "Robert, what is it that you wish to know?"*

*And I answered, "***GOD***, how much is a million years to you?"*

And **GOD** *smiled and said, "Naught but a minute."*

*And I asked again, "***GOD***, how much is a million dollars to you?"*

And **GOD** *smiled and answered, "Less than a penny."*

*And so I asked again, "***GOD***, would you give me a million dollars?"*

And **GOD** *smiled and replied, "Sure Robert, in a minute."*

PROVERB # 1
Even with important friends,
you don't have a million years.

CHAPTER 1

THE HERITAGE OF GREAT FAILURES

In doing some research, I totaled up thirty different reasons that are always given for most new businesses to fail within their first three years. I'm sure you're familiar with all of them, i.e., inadequate funding, inadequate experience, inadequate bookkeeping, inadequate marketing, etc., etc., etc. Every damn fool already knows these things. Even me! But, I'm going to give you a hundred more reasons that are rarely mentioned in these get-rich-quick offerings.

The fact is, there are many additional forces out there that can cause you to fail (or succeed). So, don't stop reading now! I am going to reveal these pitfalls and save you the trouble of experiencing them as I had to do.

First, let me introduce you to a little business parable:

Once upon a time, four very close friends sailed their boat out on the ocean to go fishing. Their names were *Ambition*, *Doubt*, *Fear*, and *Failure*.

1

When they reached the middle of the ocean, a squall came up and they lost their sails, motor, oars, and all their fishing rods.

Doubt, Fear, and *Failure* did nothing except predict their demise, but *Ambition* instinctively knew there had to be a way to survive. He attached an open safety pin to a piece of string, threw it overboard, and lo and behold, felt a strong tug on the string. He pulled in his line and to everyone's amazement he found an ancient oil lamp attached to the end.

Ambition started wiping the lamp when to his surprise a magic genie appeared.

"Thank you, thank you," the genie bellowed, "and for freeing me from this watery prison I shall grant each of you one wish."

He turned to *Doubt* and asked him what he wished for and *Doubt* replied, "I doubted the wisdom of this trip from the very beginning. I wish I was in my nice dry home" Whoosh, his wish was granted.

Then the genie turned to *Fear* who said, "I was afraid something would happen. I wish I was back in the safety of my home." *Whoosh*, the wish was granted.

The Genie then turned to *Failure* and asked for his wish.

"Even before we started I knew we couldn't succeed. Send me back to my home and I will never go sailing again," said *Failure* and whoosh, his wish was granted.

Finally, the genie turned to *Ambition* and asked his wish. *Ambition* lamented, "I'm sure we would have made it, but now I'm all alone and lonely. I sure wish my friends were with me now." Whoosh!

If there is one lesson I learned in life, it is not to invite *Doubt, Fear,* and *Failure* back into the boat!

Don't surround yourself with "friends" who have a negative attitude. Develop a small circle of real friends that will support and motivate you.

Let me assure you that what I am going to tell you is the gospel truth. For over sixty years, I have been smitten with the desire to live like a millionaire. Of course, I wanted to be a millionaire but since the prospects appeared so slim, I decided to settle for the goal of being able to live like one. If there is some enterprise I didn't try in my quest to become a millionaire, it wasn't my fault. There are only so many years in a lifetime.

After meeting all kinds of entrepreneurs, I have come to believe there is a rare biological gene possessed by the genuine entrepreneur that sets him/her apart from all other individuals.

Look at your history books. Thomas Edison, Henry Ford, Abraham Lincoln, Thomas Adams, and Walt Disney, all great men who were great "failures" and yet they ultimately succeeded. They didn't give in and they didn't give up. Persistence, intuition, and providence, an act of GOD, what ever you want to call it, greased the rail on which they glided uphill to success. They never stopped when they failed. They picked themselves up and went right on (often to another failure).

The cliché says, "Success is ten percent inspiration and ninety percent perspiration."

That isn't what I learned in life. The truth is, success is ten percent inspiration, thirty-five percent perspiration and persistence, and fifty-five percent providence. Some prefer to call it luck or heavenly intervention.

Let's take the case of Abraham Lincoln. He sure didn't make it on good looks. He began in 1832 when he opened a store with his friend, William Berry. The following year the store failed leaving Lincoln and Berry heavily in

3

debt. The following year Berry died and Lincoln's indebtedness doubled. He owed everybody.

In 1834, Lincoln received his license to practice law (and all this time you thought he was a nice guy.) The year after that, he proposed marriage to Mary Owens and she turned him down. He even failed in love.

In 1843, he ran for the nomination to the United States Senate and lost. In 1849, he tried his first case before the United States Congress. Yep, he lost again. Interestingly, that year he was granted Patent Number 6,469 for "Buoying Vessels Over Shoals." To this day Lincoln remains the only American president to have ever been granted a patent. There's no record of him ever making a penny on his invention.

In 1854, he actually won an election to the Illinois Legislature but turned it down to run for the United States Congress. Unfortunately, the Illinois Legislature didn't want to run a loser so they refused to place his name in nomination. He had failed again.

In 1858, Honest Abe participated in the seven famous Lincoln-Douglas debates. His performance was so stellar the Illinois Legislature chose Stephen Douglas as their candidate instead of Lincoln. (I think they were scared off by his nickname, "Honest" Abe.)

On February 23rd, 1861, Lincoln finally won an election. He was elected president of the United States! He didn't give up and he didn't give in.

Now take Thomas Alva Edison. Edison was something that most of us are not. He was a genius. Contrary to popular belief, Edison did not invent the light bulb. What he did do was find the right filament that would not burn up in an evacuated light bulb. He took someone else's idea and improved on it. Everyone knows he invented the phonograph, the telegraph, and the motion picture camera, but few people know about his numerous failures.

One of Edison's failures was to make a motion picture projector that combined sound and picture. After numerous disappointments he proclaimed that it was impossible to ever make motion pictures with sound and moved on to another idea.

If you want an example of great failure consider the Edison Portland Cement Company. In 1890, Edison invested most of his money in his own cement company. He started building everything out of cement including furniture, pianos, and even his phonograph cabinets. He even tried building houses out of cement. His venture was a total failure. He lost a fortune. Building concrete structures was a losing idea until a guy with some wooden clubs and a lot of balls hired the Edison Cement Company to build a concrete baseball stadium in the Bronx. It is still standing and it's called Yankee Stadium. (Actually, Edison's stadium was remodeled several times and finally torn down and rebuilt. However, Edison wasn't going to pursue the failed idea of concrete structures, so he unloaded all of his stock in the Edison Cement Company before the Yankee Stadium contract.)

Do you think you know what perseverance is? From 1927 to 1931, Edison tried to develop a substitute for rubber out of agricultural plants. He spent four years and tried 16,999 different plants before he succeeded with plant number 17,000. He failed 16,999 times. Can you imagine a married man failing 16,999 times in this day and age? If you or I failed half that many times we'd be dining on frozen dinners in a bachelor pad somewhere.

Have you ever heard of a thing called the telephone? It was invented by Alexander Graham Bell in 1876 and he couldn't give it away. He even got the president of the United States, Rutherford B. Hayes, to make a demonstration call on the telephone. When President Hayes completed his call he remarked, "That's an amazing invention, but who would ever want to use one of them?"

Bell was so short of cash that he offered to sell all his rights and patents for the telephone to Western Union Telegraph for $100,000 but was promptly escorted off the premises. The president of Western Union reportedly remarked that he had "no use for an electrical toy."

A few years later Western Union reconsidered, but to save money, they purchased another inventor's rip off of Bell's telephone patents. Bell won a patent infringement lawsuit and Western Union was frozen out of the lucrative telephone business forever.

Not everyone's a genius and this next example will show you how providence can play a part in our lives.

By the mid 1800s an entrepreneur named Thomas Adams had moved through a dozen different ventures, all of which had failed. He decided to try one more time with a new product called photography. He tried many innovations but nothing developed. Then, about 1860, Mexican General Antonio de Santa Anna went into exile and made his way to Staten Island, New York. As if fate ordained it, General Santa Anna knocked on Adams' door and asked if he could board in his home. Needing the income, Adams agreed.

During one of their conversations General Santa Anna told Adams about the sap of the Mexican sapodilla tree thinking it would make a wonderful synthetic rubber. The sap was called chicle. It had a thick consistency, was elastic, and he had friends in Mexico who could supply him with as much cheap raw material as he could vulcanize.

Adams became enamored with the idea. He envisioned toys, masks, boots, raincoats, and tires, all made out of chicle. He set about experimenting with various vulcanizing processes. Unfortunately, every process failed.

One day in 1869, Adams finally gave up and decided to dump his entire stock of chicle into the East River. On his way out that night, Adams recalled the general mentioning that Mexicans all chewed this chicle like a chewing gum so he broke off a small piece and put it in his mouth. To his surprise he found the flavor both pleasant and longer lasting than conventional chewing gums. It was almost indestructible.

On his way home that night (presumably still chewing the chicle), Adams stopped into a corner apothecary shop and was standing at the counter when a little girl came in and asked for a penny stick of chewing gum.

Adams asked the clerk what the chewing gum was made of and was told it was paraffin wax with some flavoring. A light bulb went on in his head. The next day, he and his son began cutting thin layers of chicle into short strips. He purchased a ream of brightly colored paper and wrapped each stick of gum neatly.

I don't have to tell you that this was the birth of real chewing gum and bubble gum, but I will. In 1871, Adams' New York Gum went on sale in drugstores throughout New York for one penny a stick and they had trouble keeping up with demand. By the end of the century, it was the most prosperous chewing gum company in the country. Seizing the initiative, Adams and his son created a monopoly by merging with the six largest and best-known chewing gum manufacturers in the United States and Canada and became the successful maker of Chiclets Chewing Gum.

These cases happened years ago. Is anybody, besides you, still making mistakes today? You bet they are!

Let's talk about a crazy inventor named Chester Carlson who claimed he had developed a process for electrostatic paper copying. He took his idea to twenty major corporations and was turned down by every one of them. They told Chester it couldn't be done or there wasn't a market for such a product.

Finally, on the twenty-first try, he got a small company named Haloid to purchase the commercial rights for the process. Haloid became Xerox Corporation and Chester and Xerox both became very, very rich.

You probably know that the company Hewlett-Packard turned down an idea proposed by one of its own employees. The employee, Steve Wozniak, went off on his own and founded the Apple Computer Corporation. No one is laughing at Wozniak today.

Do you remember that Hollywood fool, David O. Selznick? Against everyone's advice, he went out and produced a multimillion dollar spectacle called *Gone With The Wind*.

Irving Thalberg told his boss, MGM's Louis B. Mayer, "Forget it, Louis. No Civil War picture ever made a nickel." Gary Cooper turned down the chance to play Rhett Butler and remarked, "I'm just glad it'll be Clark Gable who's falling flat on his face and not Gary Cooper."

Consider what all of these people lost by not trying. Now, the piece d' resistance. Victor Fleming, who was chosen to direct the movie, predicted it would be the "biggest white elephant of all time." He turned down an offer of twenty percent of the profits and demanded a flat fee instead. His warped decision cost him millions.

On a cold winter's day in 1962, four young musicians played and sang in their first record audition for executives of Decca Recording Company. The decision was unanimous. Their sound was "terrible." "Guitar groups are passé." "They'll never make it."

In the next couple months, four more recording companies turned them down. Fortunately, they had an agent who wouldn't give up.

Today, the Beatles are acknowledged as the greatest band that ever played, having had twenty of their songs reach number one on the charts. They brought unlimited enjoyment to millions and millions of fans and they have made many people in the entertainment industry millions and millions of dollars.

If you're not a genius, an inventor, or a gifted musician, it doesn't really matter. The world is full of opportunities, even if they are only to improve an existing product or to distinguish yourself as an expert in some field.

Take the lowly corkscrew. It was nothing but a coiled piece of steel with a wood handle. Even today it can be bought for less than one dollar. But someone realized that upscale wine drinkers would pay a lot more for a fancy corkscrew. Today thousands of wine drinkers take pride in opening a bottle of wine with Le Creuset's "Screwpull," a beautifully crafted, chrome plated, corkscrew that sells for $149. I even own one as do many of my friends.

From my perspective they still haven't invented the perfect salt or pepper shaker but hundreds of people have succeeded in marketing their own unique versions.

PROVERB 2:
Look around you.
You don't have to be an inventor or genius.
The world abounds with opportunities
to improve anything that exists today!

Amusement parks, carnivals, and circuses have existed for centuries. Do you remember Ringling Brothers and Barnum & Bailey circuses? Who thought you could ever improve on them? One man believed he could.

His name was Walt Disney. Here was a man who was already successful but he had grander dreams. He wanted to build an amusement park unlike anything anyone ever dreamed of. The *"Happiest Place on Earth."* He was ready to wager everything he had on the idea, but he still needed several million more dollars.

Three hundred and one investors thought it was a nightmare not a dream and they turned Disney down. He hit pay dirt (and financing) on his 302nd try. No one is laughing at Disney today.

Fried chicken isn't a new commodity. People have been eating fried chicken since the frying pan was invented. But, let's not overlook the late Colonel Harland Sanders and his ridiculous idea for selling dead chickens.

Harland Sanders was born in Otisco, Indiana in the year 1890. His father died six years later and Harland was forced to take care of his three-year-old brother and baby sister when his mother went to work. This meant he was charged with preparing the family's meals.

Instead of treating it as just another routine chore, Harland decided he'd make the best tasting meals their meager income would allow. In time he became a master of several regional dishes, but because chicken was the cheapest meat available, it figured prominently into his menus.

At ten, he got his first real job working on a neighbor's farm for $2 a month. Two years later his mother remarried and Harland left his home in Henryville, Indiana for a job on a farm in Greenwood, Indiana. At 15 he became a streetcar conductor in New Albany, Indiana and at 17 he spent six months soldiering with Teddy Roosevelt in Cuba. After that he was a fireman on a railroad locomotive, took a correspondence course in law and practiced in justice of the peace courts He sold insurance for a time and even operated a steamboat ferry on the Ohio River. He sold tires and finally operated a gas station in Corbin, Kentucky.

Harland never excelled or made a lot of money in any of his work pursuits but although his friends considered him just another worker bee, in the back of his mind he never forgot the delicious fried chicken he used to prepare for his mother and brother and sister.

Being located on a main thoroughfare, motorists frequently asked Harland to recommend a good restaurant. It was then that he saw the opportunity that would propel him into the ranks of the famous.

Not having any financial means, Harland began inviting motorists to sit down at his own dining room table and feast on what he called the best fried chicken in the world. Before long, he had so many motorists stopping for his chicken that he made a deal with the motel across the street and took over their dining room which seated 142 diners.

He was 40 years old and for the next nine years, he and his wife enjoyed the growing success and security of his own business. It was the right time. He had the right location. And it was the right product. He was a very inspired man. What could go wrong?

Providence!

In the early 1950s the government announced plans for a network of Federal highways across America. A major expressway was announced that would bypass the town of Corbin and destroy the transient trade that had frequented his gas station and restaurant.

In an effort to salvage some of his investment, Harland auctioned off everything he owned. After paying off all his debts, he and his wife were reduced to living on his month Social Security check of $105.

Like most people, he could have found comfort in the turn of fortune that we call bad luck. But, instead, he had a dream. He told his friends he was going out and sell his recipe for fried chicken to restaurants all over America. You might imagine what his friends thought.

In 1952, at the age of 62, with the confidence that only a real entrepreneur can know, Harland Sanders began traveling the length and breadth of this country for two years trying to sell his recipe for cooking a dead chicken to restaurants. He was turned down 1,009 times before he sold his first fried chicken concept. The franchise was consummated with only a hand shake and a verbal promise to pay Sanders a nickel for every chicken sold. Two years and 1009 rejections! He failed 1009 times! How many spouses would still be waiting at home with an apron and a hot greased skillet? A skillet maybe, but hot? Not a chance!

By 1964, "Colonel" Sanders had sold more than 600 franchises and at the age of 74 he decided to "semi" retire.

He sold his company to a group of investors for $2 million dollars, but stayed on as the spokesperson for the company. The new owners took Kentucky Fried Chicken public in 1966. When the Heublein company acquired Kentucky Fried Chicken for $285 million in 1971, it had more than 3,500 franchised and company-owned restaurants all over the world.

When Heublein was acquired by R.J. Reynolds in 1982, PepsiCo. purchased Kentucky Fried Chicken for $840 million. During all this time Harland Sanders visited "his" restaurants numbering almost 32,500 in more than 100 countries.

Back in 1976, Harland Sanders was ranked as the world's second most recognizable celebrity!

If you ever thought you were too young or too old to become an entrepreneur, think about Harland Sanders.

There is another reason to strive for success. Individuals, who are achievers, benefit all mankind. We live in a wonder-world that could just as easily been a universal hell of hardship and disease. Some of these achievers were specially endowed, but many gained their success by refusing to accept the mantle of mediocrity.

An example that comes to mind is a fellow named Robert Jarvik.

From an early age, Jarvik possessed a self-confidence not shared by most of his peers. Above all else, he wanted to become a doctor. However, his friends, teachers, and others judged him unworthy of the effort.

To others, Jarvis lacked the natural ability to ever master the requisites for a medical doctor. In his quest to become a doctor, Jarvis was turned down at least three times by every medical school in America. It didn't keep him from going back for a fourth try. Providence served Robert Jarvik well. He was finally accepted to the University of Utah School of Medicine in 1972. Medical school was not easy for Jarvik. In fact, one of the professors in a class he was failing urged Jarvik to transfer to the dental school.

By existing standards Jarvik never should have achieved worldwide acclaim as a medical genius, but he did. Ten years after beginning his studies, Doctor Robert Jarvis invented the world's first artificial heart and achieved a medical breakthrough the likes of which had never been seen before.

He started out as many of us have. He was not an outstanding student in his prior schooling. He lacked a prestigious academic degree and didn't even attain a high score on his medical entrance exam, so to what do you ascribe his success? His ability to succeed and the ability of many like him cannot be measured.

The desire to succeed that resides in each of us cannot be measured on some mechanical device. There is no way to calculate your reservoir of creativity and more importantly, no one can predetermine the persistence you are capable of generating. And, there is one other intangible that no one will ever be able to quantify. Providence! You might just be the luckiest person around.

PROVERB 3:
Action may not assure success
but inaction will always assure failure.

There is a Hall of Fame for almost every conceivable group, but one Hall of Fame is missing; a Hall of Infamy for the real failures, the entrepreneurs who give up and the people who constantly tell you it can't be done or that your ideas are no good.

If you take away one thing from this book, let it be this: Everyone who tries will fail at something but you only become a failure when you give up.

If there is one classic example, it has to be one of the noblest sports figures who should be every young person's role model, a basketball player named Michael Jordan.

One day someone was praising Michael's seemingly natural ability to succeed. He paid Michael the highest complements and in the end, he asked Michael to tell him what he attributed his success to.

Michael paused for a while and then, with a smile, answered the man's question.

"I've missed 9,000 baskets. I've lost 300 games. Twenty-six times I was trusted with the game winning shot . . . and missed. I keep failing, and failing, and failing. And that's why I succeed!"

Remember these words the next time you think about giving up. It is normal to fail, but a champion gets back on his feet and keeps going. The real failure never even tries! In fact, that's the golden rule of life.

PROVERB 4:
Fear of defeat is the parent of failure.

CHAPTER 2

STARTING FROM
SCRATCH

I realize that you are swelling with wild anticipation for the wonderful knowledge I am about to impart. And, while I consider myself the paragon of entrepreneurial spirit and the paradigm of enterprise, I wish to assure you that I arrived at this plateau through personal experience. (Sadly, much of it bad!) It is unfortunate I didn't have the benefit of such a book as this, for had I one, I surely would be among the wealthiest men in the world today.

Before continuing, I have a very important message for you: *Don't do as I did, do as I didn't do. Just follow the yellow brick road of my 100 proverbs and I guarantee you might almost make your million dollars.*

To begin, let me give you an example of the priceless information I am going to share.

It must have been about June, 1944, when my ship, the *SS General Meigs* pulled into the harbor at Biak, New Guinea. I had just turned seventeen and joined the Merchant Marines.

15

In addition to a load of P-63 Black Widow fighters on deck, below deck was stashed about a dozen P-38 Lockheed Lightning intercepter aircraft, tons of canned beer, and cases of an item that promised to revolutionize the canned product industry forever.

To fully appreciate the introduction of this product you need to know that the mosquitoes of New Guinea were alleged to approximate the size of one of our airplanes. It was not uncommon for a soldier to claim he heard two mosquitoes discussing whether they would carry the soldier outside or eat him in his tent. If you've ever seen an Arctic Circle mosquito, consider something twice its size and twice as voracious.

On that momentous day, I was introduced to the first aerosol spray cans. Cans of aerosol propelled DDT, the *"aerosol bomb."* I will never forget this auspicious occasion. At the time, the only thing we were told was that the contents would kill mosquitoes. It was all we needed to hear.

As soon as word of the DDT distribution got around, the small landing area was overrun with soldiers ripping open cardboard cases and running from the area loaded down with aerosol cans.

At that point in the war, we held half the island and the Japanese held the other half. I can only imagine their consternation as they watched hundreds of American soldiers running through the jungles spraying a white fog from little brown cans. The following morning the body count was fifty million enemy mosquitoes killed and zero American troops.

Millions of American soldiers and civilians were introduced to aerosol spray in 1944 and millions never comprehended its potential. One man did. Me! Unlike them, I would never forget it and unlike most people when they discover a new product, I was thinking about the application, not the material in the can.

Five years later, after returning from the Middle East with my new Finnish bride, I was up against the financial ropes. I had worked at a dozen jobs and ultimately, every good job I got degenerated into work and ultimately, dismissal. I needed to make a fast million dollars.

I was flat broke and, to make matters worse, my wife had chosen this fiscally inopportune time to present me with a baby daughter. This was cause for alarm, but not panic. The panic occurred when my wife accepted an invitation to a luncheon and conveyed the impression that I was supposed to take care of the baby. (My wife did not speak English and I did not speak Finnish.)

Crying was out of the question, so I paid attention as she showed me how to change a diaper. I was not impressed. I was distressed. Especially when she insisted that I had to coat the baby's southern hemisphere with a liberal covering of Johnson's Baby Oil. And, there wasn't a single pair of rubber gloves in the house!

I will not relate my emotional trauma to the reader other than to affirm that changing diapers is strictly a woman's chore. Smearing baby oil on the naked private parts of a scrawny, squirming, screaming baby is definitely not within this man's sphere of competence.

I was halfway through the chore, my eyes clinched tightly and my face all scrunched up, when it came to me: **AEROSOL!** Baby spray in an aerosol dispenser.

I couldn't wait for Peggy to arrive home. When she did, I sat her down on the sofa and tried to explain all the virtues of a baby lotion dispensed from an aerosol can. No muss. No fuss. No bother!

She could hardly contain herself.

"Crrrrazy!"

Instinctively, I knew she was wrong. This wasn't just a million dollar idea; it was a mega-million dollar idea. After the war everyone was having babies. In our own group of friends I could count a half-dozen babies that absolutely needed this product.

The next morning I began calling all our friends to sound them out on the idea. Not surprisingly, the verdict was unanimous. It was a "crrrrazy" idea. "If it was such a good idea, someone else would have done it." "The spray will soil everyone's clothing." "It can't be done." Over and over, I heard the same argument I had encountered on all my other great ideas: "It's not practical!"

When successful entrepreneurs get a good idea, it is expected they will mention it to their spouse and friends and then ignore their negative input. (Unfortunately, this book hadn't been written yet, so I usually gave up.)

The next morning, I telephoned the headquarters of the DuPont Company, producers of the DDT aerosol spray for the military.

After several transfers, I finally got to speak to someone in their product development department. My message struck a chord.

The following is a vital lesson for you. DuPont, General Electric, Dow Chemical, and hundreds of other companies engage in pure research. In other words, they let many of their scientists experiment and develop products and processes for which they have no immediate use. Indeed, they are not even sure the product will have any future use. In hopes that someone will find a commercial use (and therefore a commercial value), these companies will spend their own money to help you develop a marketable item using their product or process. And, it's free for you! General Electric even used to have a newsletter in which they offered all kinds of new products to anyone who could develop a use for them.

A few days after my call, two DuPont scientists knocked on my door. I bid them to be comfortable on the sofa behind our three-legged coffee table and I drew up my own chair after inserting a grocery carton under the damaged corner of the coffee table.

Setting down a huge brief case, one of the men withdrew a lined yellow pad of paper and a massive 3-ring binder full of technical data. Then I heard the sweetest words of all:

"Mr. Leeds, how can we help you?"

I explained what I wanted to do while they made notes and conferred back and forth. When I was finished, the older scientist said "OK, we need a nonstaining and nonirritating vehicle and product." He looked over at his partner. "We'll need a lotion that is an excellent emollient so we'll add Vitamin A. That will prevent and cure any diaper rash."

At this point his partner interrupted, "You'll want a nice aroma to this product won't you?"

"Oh, absolutely," I responded although I hadn't even thought of the prospect.

"What aroma would you like? Roses, evergreen, baby powder, lilac? We can give you any smell you'd like."

"Roses!" I replied in a tone that suggested I had already considered this aspect. Actually, I had considered "new car" aroma, but passed on the idea.

With that the meeting was over and the two men left after promising to return with the formula and specifications for manufacturing it.

I was ecstatic. I knew this was the beginning of something big. BIG!

A few days later, one of the scientists called on me again and handed me the formulas for "RASH-A-WAY," one of the first home aerosol products in the world. In addition, he gave me the name and address of a fellow who had the equipment to can aerosol products in his garage.

Within two weeks, I had arranged to have six-dozen cans of my secret formula, RASH-A-WAY, canned and delivered. Against almost overwhelming opposition, I withdrew eighteen dollars from our meager budget and paid for the material. My wife was furious, but I was confident this was one venture that would justify my state of euphoria.

I immediately telephoned each of our friends and asked them to test my new product. Nonstaining, sweet-smelling, it would be a product that would eliminate diaper rash forever. Being good friends, each of the wives agreed to try the *RASH-A-WAY* for one month. I personally delivered one can to each of the six families with the stern warning to "Hold the can at least twelve inches away from the baby because, as the gas leaves the can, it expands and becomes a frigid blast of air! After the gas travels through the air for twelve inches it warms to the air's temperature." I didn't only warn them once. I repeated the warning a dozen times. Doesn't anyone read labels or listen to warnings?

I couldn't sleep that night. I lay awake dreaming of the acclaim I was certain would be forthcoming.

My first call went to Doris because her husband Ron was my best friend and I knew they'd support me. Instead, there was an ominous silence when I asked her how the spray was working.

After a respectable pause I heard Doris mutter, "It made him cry and shriek and his balls turned blue. Wait, I'll let you speak to Ron."

"Robert. . . ? I know we've been friends for a long time but I've got to warn you, if my son can't produce any heirs after he's married, I'm going to sue you!" My dream was turning into a nightmare.

My next inquiry went to Betty. "Betty? How's little Patricia doing?"

"Robert! My daughter almost jumped off the bassinet. Her skin turned all blue and we thought she'd never stop screaming."

Ruth, Eleanor. Shirley. Pat. Dorothy. All of them. The calls were very much the same.

If the results weren't disappointing enough, I was also subjected to all sorts of recriminations. As if it was a proven fact that if a baby lotion spray could have been made, someone would already have done it.

To top it off, I had parlayed eighteen dollars of our hard earned cash into seventy-two cans of useless refrigerant. I heard this continuously even though I insisted it would make a great hand and skin lotion for adults. And, it did. I think I finally used the last can eleven years later.

But that wasn't the end. I began to see an endless variety of products that could be dispensed with an aerosol spray. Disinfectants, medications, cleaning solutions, shoe polish, suntan lotions, and paints were only a few products on my list. Despite my enthusiasm for the concept, without exception, my wife and all of my friends refuted the merits and urged me to "come down to earth."

In view of such overwhelming and recurring pessimism, I conceded the point that there was no future in aerosol spray products.

That was 1949. Last year, Americans bought 3.3 billion cans of aerosol-type spray products. The number sold worldwide reached 10 billion! Over 50,000 people are currently employed in the pressure can industry and 1,500 different aerosol products now account for over $10 billion in annual sales.

Obviously, someone didn't listen to his or her spouse, relatives, and friends. Instead, they boarded that inimitable little choo-choo train and kept repeating, "I know I can. I know I can. I know I can!"

PROVERB 5:
Critics are the eunuchs in the harem of success.
They all know how it should have been done.
All have seen it done by others.
None are able to do it themselves!

Before going on, let's dispose of one widely accepted myth. "The best way to succeed is to inherit wealth." The facts do not support this fallacy. You might inherit some things, but motivation, success and persistence are not inherited traits. In fact, most inherited businesses fail within a few years because the heirs are more motivated to spend their inheritance than they are motivated to build their business. Most inherited wealth is squandered. If the heir of a successful person distinguishes his/her self, it is because they developed the drive, determination, and effort to succeed, and along the way they had some luck. Their own mistakes and failures did not stop them in their own effort to become a success.

If you take away one thing from this book, let it be that everyone who tries will fail at some time, but you're only a failure if you give up. The worse kind of failure never even tries! In fact, that's a cardinal rule.

PROVERB 6:
Providence may move the player
but not the goalpost.

CHAPTER 3

ADVANTAGES OF BIRTH

I was born in Detroit, Michigan in the year 1927, the last of five children to an Irish immigrant father and a second generation American mother. I had a great advantage over most of you. I was born at the time of the great depression. I was born poor and raised poor. I had only one way to go. Up!

My father was shipped to this country when he was three years old and grew up in the back room of a relative's tavern in Cleveland, Ohio.

Without much formal education he decided to start his own business. With only a ladder, some paint, and a few paint brushes, he turned his efforts into a small but successful painting company. He never owned a computer or even an adding machine but would sit at his old rolltop desk in our basement and with a pencil and lined yellow pads of paper, estimate the cost to paint a house, library, or even a huge factory.

We lived in a large two-story frame home that was built for my father by a general contractor who bartered the house in exchange for money he owed my father. At the time of the Depression, bartering was a common practice for settling debts.

In those days, an allowance for a child or gift of money, even a few pennies, was a rare treat and almost nonexistent in my family.

I am sure this was one of the factors that influenced my early excursion into the realm of entrepreneurship. Those were the days before gas furnaces and every house and apartment building burned coal. As a result of burning coal, there remained a large accumulation of ash that was usually collected in wooden bushel baskets.

While the apartment buildings had janitors who carried the ashes to the alley for collection, the residents of many homes were senior citizens who depended on someone else to carry the ashes up from the basement and into the alley.

At nine or ten years of age, without realizing it, I formed my first business. *Robert Leeds Ash Carryout Service.* If I was starting that business today, I suppose I'd have business cards and a large sign reading, "I'LL HAUL ASH FOR YOU."

I went around the neighborhood and asked neighbors if I could carry out their spent ashes every Saturday. When I got so many clients that I couldn't service them, I hired some of my friends to join my company. As I recall, I was charging five cents a bushel and didn't make anything off my friends.

I didn't save the twenty-five or fifty cents I earned. Instead, I went to the movies. I like to think I was investing in the movie industry. While I enjoyed Westerns, I was really fascinated by the newsreels. Almost every week, the newsreels showed a segment on movie stars and socialites wining and dining in fancy restaurants or boarding transatlantic steamships in their tuxedos, evening gowns, and fur coats.

One thing in particular caught my attention; the monogrammed shirts the men wore. To me, that was the epitome of success. I wanted to live that lifestyle. I wanted to be rich. I didn't care if I was a millionaire, I just wanted to look and live like a millionaire. I wanted to wear monogrammed shirts!

I had another dream. Those were the early days of aviation and I dreamed that one day I would fly. The only thing holding me back was school. It was taking up a disproportionate share of my time.

Life, however, is not something you can predetermine. Fate, or whatever you want to call it, may have other plans for you. It did for me.

PROVERB 7:
**Youth and innocence provide
a veritable cesspool of life's goals.**

In the seventh grade, I became paralyzed from the waist down. I was diagnosed with rheumatic fever and immobilized in bed for a full year.

In retrospect, maybe this was one of my luckiest breaks. One day, our milkman pulled his horse drawn wagon in front of our house and carried in a huge carton of old books. With nothing else to do, I picked up my first book and began reading. If it hadn't been for that milkman, I would have missed the greatest adventures a person can imagine.

Jack London, Mark Twain, Charles Lindberg, Wally Post, Roscoe Turner, Eddie Rickenbacker, Admiral Byrd, and even Upton Sinclair and Karl Marx were introduced to me. I thought I hated poetry until I read a book by Robert

Service and another by Rudyard Kipling. Strangely, it was Cervantes' *Don Quixote* that affected me the most. I thought Don Quixote was the noblest man I'd ever read about. Heroes and despots, I devoured their histories and went out each day with them on their fateful journeys. I couldn't change the outcome, but I could remember and learn from the results. Each page was a lesson and each chapter a magic medicinal bullet.

Another book that impressed me was Osa Johnson's *Four Years In Paradise,* about her and her husband's adventures exploring Africa. At the time I never dreamed that one day I would come face to face with her. Her book still occupies a favored spot in my library.

A year later, when I was pronounced cured and had learned to walk again, I had my future all planned. I knew that my life was going to be different. I wanted something good out of life! I wanted adventure, I wanted my own virtuous Desdemona, and I wanted to live like a millionaire. I was going up to the Yukon and discover a gold mine. Then I'd sail to Africa where I'd explore jungles where no other person had ever set foot. I'd scoop up a treasure in diamonds and rare jewels and, along the way, I would become a famous aviator.

I could envision myself seated in the open cockpit of my bright yellow Stearman biplane, my leather helmet in place and a pair of goggles protecting my eyes. A white silk scarf around my neck would stream behind me in the wind just like in the movies. I'd be adventurous and I'd be rich.

I would feast on half-pound, pecan-laden Hershey bars in a huge house with double entry doors, a gigantic swimming pool and garden, and two Jaguar automobiles, one for my Desdemona and one for me. I'd have a fancy tuxedo and white silk shirts with diamond cuff links. I'd be rich, rich, rich! Oh God, at the ripe old age of thirteen I was ready. I guess God wasn't.

PROVERB 8:
Enthusiasm is the engine of success.
Youth is the hole in the gas tank.

On December 7, 1941, a lot of people's dreams were shattered, but for some it was the beginning. America went to war and many of the barriers to youthful employment were relaxed because of the manpower shortage. It was a perfect opportunity to quit school and make some big money. I decided to go to sea. Well, I didn't exactly go to sea, but I did go down to the Detroit River.

It was June 26, 1942, that I got my first shipboard job sailing on the Great Lakes as a coal passer on the *SS Put-In-Bay*. The *Put-In-Bay* was an excursion boat owned by the Ashley and Dustin Steamship Company. The ship was an ancient side-paddle wheeler powered by a coal fed steam boiler. The important thing was the pay. I was hired on at the impressive wage of ninety dollars a month, plus food and lodging. I was on my way.

What they neglected to tell me was that the crew's food was leftovers from the passenger's meals. This food was often moldy or sour and all of it was served cold. The lodging turned out to be anyplace on deck when there were no passengers on board.

As a coal passer, I would shovel tons of coal out of a chute and across the steel floor plates to the fireman who would scoop up the coal and shovel it into the cavernous mouth of the furnace. It seemed like the coal hardly made it through the opening before a huge belching flame would reach forward and consume the coal like some kind of monster. In addition to the thick coal-dust laden air, the temperature was over one hundred degrees and there was rarely a breath of fresh air. At the end of my first four hour shift, I was certain it was one job I would never become accustomed to.

However, the thought of the ninety dollars sustained me. At the end of the month, I lined up in front of the purser's office to collect the huge sum for which I had labored so hard. I watched eagerly as the purser counted out and handed me three twenty-dollar bills.

"Where's the other thirty dollars?" I asked.

"That's for your room and board," he replied.

"Room and board?" I queried. "What room and board? Do you mean that moldy food and sleeping outside on the deck?"

His reply was to take it or leave it. If I didn't like it, I could quit. Although the practice of kicking back thirty percent of my wages was a shock, I learned that it was not an uncommon practice among the non-unionized shipping lines plying the Great Lakes.

PROVERB 9:
Every new skill you acquire
is another rung up on the ladder of life.

In any case, if I couldn't make my million dollars sailing, I figured the least I could do was get a more comfortable job. Shortly afterwards, a job opened up in the Rathskeller, a beer garden area of the ship that served beer and wine and also contained about two dozen slot machines. I immediately applied for the job and was accepted providing I could get the appropriate Coast Guard rating. This required nothing more than filling out another form and having it approved. When all was said and done, I received my official United States Coast Guard Certificate of Seaman's Service rating me as a "Barkeeper" from June 26, 1942 to September 7, 1942. I was fifteen years old.

PROVERB 10:
The dreams of youth are written in chalk.
Life is an eraser.

As it turned out, my new boss rarely let me draw beer. My job was to be a "nickel-nurser." I had to run around and make change for the slot machines. When someone hit a jackpot they won the amazing sum of twenty nickels. More often than not the customers lost. When a machine jammed, my boss, Paul, never came out on the floor and repaired it. Instead, I had to carry the heavy machine about forty feet to the bar where he would fix the machine in less than a minute. Then I would have to carry it forty feet back to its stand.

The last trip of the season was made on Labor Day and I departed for home with the feeling that this was not the way to become wealthy. I should add that in those days my goal was to someday earn ten thousand dollars a year. That was a princely sum in the early forties.

My next job was a short employment with Excello Corporation in a factory making parts for the landing gears of military aircraft.

In addition to a nice workplace and good wages in a unionized shop, my job was wonderfully easy. All I had to do was sit on a stool, place a small hollow screw over a holding tool, and rotate the threads in a buffing wheel to remove any burrs. In less than an hour, I developed a rhythm that permitted me to exceed the production standard by fifty percent. This achievement earned a visit from the union steward who told me in no uncertain terms that I was producing too many pieces and to slow down. I was not entirely clear on their logic. There was a war on and we were producing parts to aid in the effort to win.

The following day, I would learn there are varying degrees of virtue to a union shop. That day, I produced double the production standard. Upon leaving the shop that afternoon, I was accosted by three burly union employees. Their message was all too clear. If I didn't stop overproducing, something unpleasant was going to happen to me. According to them, every man and woman working in the factory was going to have to double their output just because of me. It was specious reasoning to say the least.

The following day, I deliberately produced more than I had ever done before. As I was about to leave my workplace, all of my production was returned to me. The quality control inspector said they were not deburred adequately and I'd have to do all of them over.

I inspected several pieces and they appeared just fine. Then I looked up at my critics. The quality control inspector was a union member, the foreman had belonged to the union prior to his promotion to foreman, and both of them had been among the men who threatened me in the parking lot the night before. It was a lose-lose situation. The wages were good but the conditions were wrong. I needed a situation where I could exercise my own initiative.

I tried a few other jobs, even selling shoes for Baker's Shoe Store. I didn't want to do it but my good friend, Marvin, convinced me there were all kinds of benefits to commission selling in a lady's shoe store.

I soon learned what Marvin meant. I think he would have paid them to let him work there. He would get down on one knee to fit a shoe while trying to look under the customer's skirt. He would then turn his head toward me and render the most ridiculous grin.

Occasionally, there was a customer that just could not be satisfied with the fit of any shoe. I remember the first time I had one of those customers. In the thousands of shoes in our inventory, I couldn't find one pair that would fit her properly. Noting my predicament, Marvin took over. He picked up the pair of shoes the lady liked most and assured her we had equipment in the back room that could expand the shoes to her satisfaction. I was really surprised because no one had ever mentioned that we possessed such amazing equipment.

I followed Marvin into the back room where he went through some twisting contortions and then pounded the shoes on a wooden bench several times, so that the noise could be heard throughout the store. Then Marvin winked at me and proceeded back out to where the lady was seated. Glowing with satisfaction, Marvin struggled to slip them onto the woman.

"Now! Do you feel the difference?" Marvin asked with a big smile.

The lady took a few steps and nodded her approval.

"Much, much better," she said.

I wrote up the sale and concluded I could never be a successful shoe salesman. During that year, I came to the conclusion that working for someone else, or at least the wrong employer, was not going to contribute to my long term objective. I was born to be an entrepreneur. I was born to be an economic engine and not just a human utility.

About this time the tide of war was turning and my penchant to do something useful for the war effort motivated me to take some unorthodox steps. The first was to lie about my age and become a Red Cross blood donor. Although we were supposed to wait several weeks between donations, I simply acquired two cards and donated two pints of blood in the time that other donors were giving only one pint.

Each time I donated blood they would take one of my little identification cards and stamp the date on it. All I had to do was make sure I presented the right card each time. The consequences of this oblation will become apparent in a later chapter.

The other thing I did was join the Civil Air Patrol Parachute Squadron. This was a group of aviation enthusiasts that traveled around the country performing in air shows, war bond rallies, and Army recruiting drives.

On my first airplane ride, at three thousand feet altitude, I calmly stepped to the door of a Stinson monoplane and stepped out into space. I counted to three and pulled the rip cord. It was an exhilarating experience for this fifteen year old.

As part of our training we learned to pack and repair all kinds of parachutes and participate in overnight maneuvers which usually turned into coed beer parties. Within a short time, I achieved the rank of warrant officer. Except for the insignia the suave uniform was identical to an Air Force officer's uniform, . It was worth every cent I wasn't getting paid.

Suddenly, I got an inspired idea. The public always turned out in droves to see our parachute jumps when we performed at military air bases and stadiums, why not form a small group and do it commercially? Air circuses were a phenomenon of the time and several of us had already specialized in "death defying" jumps and mid-air plane-to-plane transfers.

Like any good entrepreneur, I began by choosing a name that would bait the public's appetite for excitement, *Death's Angels!* Next in order were business cards and a large cloth patch sewn onto the backs of our flight jackets. The emblem was a skull and crossbones between two parachute canopies.

The way my program worked was to visit various airports around Michigan, Ohio, and Indiana, offering to put on free spectacular parachute jumping exhibitions. In exchange for taking us up, we would schedule an intermission between jumps during which the airport owner could take spectators up for plane rides. He would keep the money from the passengers and we would take up a collection from the audience after each jump.

On the Thursday before each show, we would run a large display ad in the local newspaper advertising a "free" air show. We always drew a good turnout. At the end of the show, we would cover our expenses and divide the balance equally. The show would include several really unusual stunts, including a *one-mile-delayed-opening jump*, a *race-to-the-ground* between two jumpers, and a *pull-off*, where the jumper sat on a swing ten feet below the plane and opened his parachute in front of the crowd at two hundred feet above the ground.

One of the sure thrillers was the *cutaway jump*. One of us would open our reserve chute first and, after a few seconds, we would release one of the risers so it would look like the parachute had come apart. After plummeting for one or two thousand feet, we would jettison the disabled chute, open our main parachute, and descend safely to the ground. The *death-defying-batwing jump* would close the show. By saving it for last, we insured that the crowd hung around until the end.

I recruited three other parachutists to join me. Elmer Kanta and I each had special canvas bat wing suits specially made with webbing sewn between our arms and legs. With our feet spread apart and our arms outstretched, we resembled huge bats. It was an act that had killed most of its performers, but it wowed the crowds and our collections were always gratifying. It really didn't permit us to soar horizontally to any great extent, but the audience swore they saw us travel back and forth through the sky covering several hundred feet. Jimmy Moll and George Manuzak would perform any of the other specialty jumps.

Another special show we did was to try and set a world's record for the most number of parachute jumps made within a 24-hour period. It made a good show, but I don't recall ever getting more than thirty jumps in before darkness set in and the event was called a draw.

In those days parachutes were a little more complicated than the ones available today and the facilities were also less accommodating. In fact, on most occasions we had to spread our parachutes out on the grass and pack them using beanbags to hold the canopy folds in place. When the wind turned gusty, it became a difficult chore to pack your chute and on one occasion it almost became a fatal chore.

On July 6, 1947, during an air show at the Monroe Airport in Monroe, Michigan, Elmer was slated to do the bat wing jump and I was to precede him with a one-mile freefall before opening my parachute. For some reason the show was running late and it was already 6:00 PM when my turn came up.

I had my pilot take me to about 7,000 feet before I climbed through the open doorway and let go. In those days we didn't have portable altimeters; we just counted out the seconds and eyeballed a building on the ground. When you figured the rooftop was getting pretty large you pulled your ripcord. As I recall, we counted to ten for the first thousand feet and then estimated two hundred feet per second after that.

Everything went according to plan until I pulled my ripcord. Instead of the parachute's canopy stringing out and blossoming into a huge umbrella-like canopy, it just went straight upward and remained closed. This fatal malfunction is known as a streamer.

A feeling of panic gripped me, but I knew the problem. Somehow, during the packing sequence, a line had crossed over the canopy preventing air from entering the canopy and inflating it. I immediately grasped the shroud lines and pulled them apart in an effort to get air into the center of the canopy. It wouldn't happen. As a last resort, I grasped the ripcord of my auxiliary chest pack and pulled it with all my might. There was a snapping noise. I watched as the reserve chute seemed to float out of its pack and just hover there, neatly folded, suspended in front of me. I grabbed hold of the folded chute and threw it as hard as I could. To my amazement, instead of opening, it just snaked upward coiling around my main canopy, sealing it in a closed position.

What I said at the time would not be fit to repeat in these pages. I looked down and realized that although I had slowed down a little, I was still hurtling downward at fifty or sixty miles an hour. It is amazing how rational a person can be under extreme circumstances. I distinctly remember asking myself if I wanted to die or maybe spend the rest of my life in a wheelchair. The answer was clear: I wanted to live and be able to walk.

I reached up and started hauling in the shroud lines of my reserve chute. When I finally felt the hem of the silk, I gave a mighty tug and spread the panels of the canopy as far apart as I could. In one giant puff the canopy inflated sending me on a wild oscillation upward so my back was parallel with the ground. A split second later, my body was met by the newly plowed ground of a farmer's field. My reserve chute had inflated at telephone-pole height.

I lay there embedded in the soft earth for several minutes while a large crowd assembled around me. It was kind of eerie. No one spoke. They just stood around me and stared down at me. Afraid to move, I continued to lay there and just stare back. Finally, I tried to wiggle the fingers of my right hand. Then I tried the fingers of my left hand. So far, so good. Little by little, I tested every limb and finally sat up with the help of my buddies. I not only didn't break any bones, I didn't even have a scratch or bruise on my body.

As we were packing up to leave, I asked the fellows how much we collected after my jump. Everyone looked perplexed. We had just given the best air show of our career and no one had remembered to pass the hat.

One of my outstanding memories was meeting world famous aviator, Roscoe Turner, in 1944 at the New Albany and Jeffersonville airshow just outside of Louisville, Kentucky. I was performing the infamous batwing jump for the spectacular close of the show. Apparently my pilot had engine trouble, so Turner volunteered to take me up.

After the show, Turner told me about his early experiences of wing-walking and parachute jumping back in the '30's. Despite our age differences, we became instant friends. Whenever the two of us were appearing at the same airshow, I had only to make it to his hanger in Indianapolis and he would fly me back and forth and always reveal a little more of his famous flying history.

Just by hanging around with him I met some of America's most famous aviation pioneers, men like Bennie Howard, Clyde Pangborn, Reeder Nichols, Eddie Rickenbacker, and others whose names I no longer recall.

He seemed to fill with pride when he reminded me that he was the only pilot to ever win the Thompson Trophy Race three times in addition to establishing seven transcontinental speed records.

He even gave me a guided tour and introduced me to his famous Laird-Turner Meteor airplane with which he won so many of his awards. It still looked brand new.

At the time, I had over a hundred free-fall parachute jumps, yet I was no closer to my million dollar goal than when I began. Still, I never even thought of giving up.

PROVERB 11:
You can bank good wages,
    but impressions are not negotiable.

Actually, the die was cast when I was only five or six years old. The occasion is still fresh in my memory.

It was late in the evening and my father was working at his old rolltop desk in the basement of our Detroit home. The only light was provided by a single bulb dangling from a cord that disappeared in the wood trusses supporting the first floor.

My favorite pastime was to stand a short distance away watching the miracle of entrepreneurship. Usually, he would be turning the huge pages of blueprints, measuring, and writing down long columns of numbers. On this solemn evening, he was just sitting there staring down at his desk and the papers scattered across it.

They were not the usual blueprints. They were unpaid bills and returned checks. Like an inexorable tidal wave, the depression had finally enveloped our livelihood. Among the past-due notices on his desk was notification from the bank advising my father that they were repossessing our home. We were about to lose almost everything we owned. An old Chevy truck, some ladders, and half-filled paint buckets were the golden harvest of years of honest hard labor.

In the dim shadowy setting, my father suddenly became aware of my presence. He turned his eyes to mine and solemnly said, "Just think. . . Someday, all this will be yours."

I was ecstatic.

Someday, I would be sitting at a rolltop desk, covered with important looking papers, pencils, and lined yellow pads. I would be a businessman. My God, what more could anyone want?

PROVERB 12:

Be careful what you wish for. You might get it.

CHAPTER 4

WORKING FOR THE GOVERNMENT

As far back as I can remember, airline piloting was perceived as a noble and well-paying occupation. Even in the military, pilots on flying status were among the highest paid in the armed forces.

Even so, it wasn't the money that motivated me to enlist in the United States Army Air Force; it was a compulsion to fly and a streak of patriotism that ran the length and breadth of my body.

Too young to join when World War II broke out, I had to wait until 1944 to enlist.

Now I realize, not everyone would consider the armed services a vehicle to wealth, but as the old man on the mountain said, "It's an ill occupation that doesn't teach someone a useful skill."

Keep in mind that when I enlisted during World War II, my pay was twenty-one dollars a day, once a month. My grandson, by comparison, just enlisted in the Marines and his starting pay is one thousand dollars a month. Plus, he will receive the rank of private first class and a couple hundred dollars extra each month because he also snookered two of his best friends into enlisting with him.

My point here is that there are other hidden virtues in a brief period of indentured service. For instance, a free college education you could not otherwise afford. You get to travel to places you would never go to as a civilian. You learn rare skills. And, you can learn to disassemble and reassemble a machine gun while blindfolded and, if you keep a good diary and are lucky enough to get involved in a good war (and live through it), you can write a bestselling book or even a movie.

Do you remember the story about the aerosol spray cans? I would never have thought of the idea if I hadn't been exposed to it while stationed in New Guinea.

When I enlisted, my only goal was to learn to fly. I wanted to become a fighter pilot. Unfortunately, I was born one year too late plus the fact I had not considered completion of a high school education as relevant.

I had two obstacles to overcome. The Army Air Force pilot training program required enlistees to be eighteen years of age, and to have a high school diploma. I had just turned seventeen and had dropped out of school in the eleventh grade.

As I would often do, I began researching my prospects. I looked into every military branch I could think of until I finally found one I could almost qualify for. It was the Army Air Force's *Army Specialized Training Reserve Program*. The *ASTRP*. This program placed seventeen year olds into a college training detachment until they turned eighteen. Providing you completed the program successfully, you went directly into a pilot training program.

I lacked two major qualifications. I didn't have a highschool diploma and my highschool grades placed me at the far left end of the Bell curve.

I could have given up like thousands of other young men, but I didn't. I resorted to a practice that would benefit me numerous times during the rest of my life. I asked someone to help me. My personal philosophy of *"Ask and You May Receive."*

Too embarrassed to tell anyone what I was going to do, I closed my bedroom door and secretively wrote a plea to General Hap Arnold, the commanding general of the United States Army Air Force.

In my letter, I told General Arnold that more than anything in the world, I wanted to be an Air Force pilot. I admitted to being less than a serious student and promised that all that would change if I could just get into the Air Cadet Program. I closed by promising General Arnold that, if given the chance, I would be the best fighter pilot in the United States Air Force! (Hey, *Think Big! Act Big! Do Big!*)

A few weeks later, I received an official-looking letter from the Army advising me to appear in one week for an eight-hour testing session to qualify for the ASTR Program.

The hall was filled with hundreds of applicants, all of whom had at least a highschool degree if not one or two years of college.

I was literally shaking when I opened the test and found that almost all of the questions were on algebra, geometry, chemistry, and physics. These were certainly not my strong suits. In fact, they weren't even in my cerebral wardrobe. A few of the questions required a true or false answer, but the majority were multiple-choice.

I knew some of the answers, but I guessed at an awful lot. I didn't leave one question unanswered. What the heck, I had one chance in five of hitting the correct multiple-choice answer.

The hall was pretty well empty when I turned in my papers and I did so with a sinking feeling in my heart. Unless there was some heavenly intervention, I figured my test score would be posted only to give everyone a laugh.

Two weeks later, to my surprise, I received another official-looking letter from the Army. I was to report in two weeks to the ASTRP college training detachment at Knox College, Galesburg, Illinois. By some miracle, I had passed the examination.

During the next nine months, I attended college classes eight hours a day with an enforced study period for another four hours. The airmen in the bottom ten percent of the class were washed out each quarter.

Not having the education of the others, it was especially difficult for me. I didn't study only four hours a day. After bed check, I stuffed pillows under my blankets and took my papers into the closet where I inserted a towel into the space at the bottom of the door to prevent the night duty officer from seeing the light coming from the single sixty-watt bulb. I would study that way until I finally passed out from fatigue. While my companions spent their Saturdays and Sundays away from the campus, I spent my time studying.

When my friends teased me about all the extra tutoring I solicited, I would remind them that I was valedictorian of my eleventh grade class for three years in a row. The hazing soon passed.

If anything, the fact that I survived is a testament to what you can accomplish when you set your eyes and heart on your *impossible dream*. By design and hard work, I completed almost two years of college work in less than a year. I wasn't going to let the train leave the station without me!

Circumstances will sometimes overwhelm your best laid plans. By late 1944, it was apparent that the war would end soon and I wasn't going to get my wings in time. I decided I had to take extraordinary steps to personally participate in the war. Still, at seventeen, the only active service that would take me was the Merchant Marines. I had to think of a way to get a leave of absence so I could sail with the Merchant Marines!

Subterfuge, the resort of scoundrels and desperate men, suddenly had an overwhelming appeal.

I sat down and wrote another letter, only this time to the local Red Cross chapter. In the letter, I stated that my father had become very ill and with my two brothers in the Air Force, I was needed at home to help my mother.

Apparently they must not have checked because in a few days I received a six-month leave-of-absence. I packed my duffle bag and took off for the War Shipping Administration in New Orleans.

PROVERB 13:
Ask and you may receive.

Glad to get any able-bodied man, the War Shipping Administration sent me to Panama City, Florida, where I joined the crew of the *SS General Meigs*, a custom-built Liberty ship designed to carry aircraft and other cargo.

I have already related the experience I had with the aerosol sprays, but military life also provided me with a great deal more. It opened a vista of the huge world that was out there. These weren't wasted days; they were classrooms for some of the biggest lessons of my life. I was able to visit Hawaii, and half the battlefields in the Pacific.

Our ship eventually rendezvoused with the invasion fleet for the Philippines at Eniwetok Atoll. A short time before, this chain of thirty islands had been a Japanese fortress. American Marines landed on February 18, 1944, and two days later controlled the entire Marshall Island chain.

Not only did we build several huge airfields on Eniwetok to accommodate our heavy bombers, our Seabees constructed new docking areas out of the abundant hard coral. In one area of the adjacent ocean, over one thousand huge barrel tanks, connected by a system of piping and holding over 146,000 gallons of aviation fuel, floated on the ocean's surface. Still, the most staggering sight of all was the modern armada of ships.

As far as the eye could see the ocean was filled with every type of ship from small cargo carriers to giant warships. Overall, there must have been several hundred ships riding at anchor. Realizing that only a few years before, the US military was totally impoverished by the voices of pacifists and the Japanese sneak attack on Pearl Harbor, I stood spellbound by what American determination and perseverance had accomplished in only a few short years. A strong sense of exhuberance and pride overcame me as I surveyed the scene before me.

My newfound enthusiasm was dampened when we received orders to break off from the invasion fleet and proceed without any navel escort to Biak, New Guinea.

The orders meant sailing without any protection through an area infested with Japanese submarines and aircraft. On our voyage to Eniwetok, I was one of many crew members who took turns on deck all night trying to catch sight of survivors from a torpedoed ship or a downed aircraft. Now we were going to sail at a snail's pace through these same perilous waters without any escort. Despite several submarine alarms and two fly-overs by a Japanese aircraft, we arrived at Biak safely.

Military service provides unique perspectives for those who are willing to learn. Unfortunately, some of the lessons are taught the hard way and I was a recipient of several of these painful lessons. Foremost, was a big money career in boxing.

PROVERB 14:
Life is a classroom.
All you have to do is show up.

When we landed at Biak, the last items unloaded from my ship were tons of bottled beer and it was disbursed without any accounting of age or degree of inebriation. It was 110 degrees in the shade and some of these soldiers had been in the Pacific theater for months without a cold drink. Suddenly there was all the beer we could drink! I think the fact that it was free motivated much of the consumption. Let me assure you that my two roommates and I weren't going to let that warm beer spoil, so we made repeated trips to the wharf to replenish our supply.

Late that night on our last trip for beer, we found the entire dock area filled with cheering and screaming military personnel. On closer inspection, we could see that one of the ship's hatches had been roped off and a prizefight had just concluded. Only one man was standing in the ring. We were told that the Navy was conducting open matches to determine the best boxer on the island. According to our inebriated source, the last fighter standing was going on tour and if he ended up the grand fleet champion, he'd be set for life.

Now, I wasn't particularly impressed by this revelation, but I had friends who were.

"Leeds, this is your golden opportunity." "You can beat that guy." "Get up there and take him!" Almost everyone was in agreement. I don't remember voting. Even spectators who didn't know me shouted for me to "take that two hundred and eighty pound weakling." The fact that I was only five foot eight, one hundred and fifty pounds and had never boxed in my life didn't seem to be a consideration to them. In my inebriated condition it wasn't a consideration to me.

PROVERB 15:
Be wary of advice and encouragement from altered minds!

I'm not excusing my friends, but we were well back in the crowd and the man in the ring did appear smaller than he actually was. Maybe it was the promise of money or maybe the promise of fame. I'd always been enamored by both. Who wouldn't seize the opportunity to be in show business? On the other hand, maybe it was the fact that I had indulged on free beer to the extent that their drunken persuasiveness was able to convince me I could win the fleet boxing championship without any boxing experience.

There was very little explanation of rules or procedures. I stripped off my shirt and wandered to my corner just in time to hear a bell ring. I turned around and took a few steps when someone hit me in the face.

I'm still not sure who did it, but from my position on the deck, even with only one eye available, I could tell I was up against a very formidable opponent. As I rolled over and tried to focus my one working eye on the half-naked figure standing over me, through the wavering vision I actually beheld two or three boxers looking down at me. From the perspective of the deck, I suddenly realized that this black Amazon was at least twelve feet tall, had arms six or seven feet long, and probably weighed in at two or three tons. I don't remember how I survived the rest of the round, but my friends assured me that the bell saved my opponent from an unmerciful beating.

I vaguely remember being helped to my corner where these same friends gushed encouragement. Despite my suggestion (and that of the referee) that I concede the fight, my loyal comrades persuaded me to teach this novice a lesson. I certainly did! I was about to bleed all over his nice neat boxing gloves.

At the sound of the bell, I took three steps forward into a bombardment of blows landed to my face and head. I even think the referee was punching me.

I desperately tried to cover my face with my arms only to have the low life seize the opportunity to turn the lower portion of my body into a punching bag. I tried to yell out, "Only one man at a time," but my mouth kept filling with leather. Unable to even get off a single blow, I sought sanctuary in my corner. When I could retreat no further, in desperation I tried to remove my face from my opponents' gloves by making a swift turning motion and attempt to bury my face in the forged steel take-up drum of the deck winch that anchored the ropes in my corner.

That strategy made quite an impression on the take-up drum and on my forehead. When I turned around blood was squirting from a three-inch gash above my left eye. It ran down my face and across my chest. For the first time the response of the spectators was an eerie silence. I heard nothing.

When I came to the next day I asked who had won and learned that I'd of had a good chance if only that winch hadn't gotten in my way. So much for the deliberations of an intoxicated jury. I have come to believe the promise of fame and fortune by means of physical confrontation should only be entertained by those with sparser cranial mass and an overwhelming bipolar manic depressive desire to suffer debilitating encounters. I concluded I would never enter a boxing ring again unless I was armed.

PROVERB 16:
Matters of consequence should never be considered while under the influence of a mind numbing stimulant!

During our trip back to the States on May 7, 1945, I was sitting in the mess hall when the announcement came over the loudspeaker that Germany had just surrendered. Only Japan was left and I still didn't have my wings.

When we arrived back at Oakland I found two letters waiting for me. Each had a bright orange border and was from the Army. In bold letters was printed the warning: "CONFIDENTIAL. DO NOT FORWARD." Each envelope was stamped with half a dozen Army Post Office addresses the envelope had been forwarded to before being returned.

The first letter gave me a long past date on which I was supposed to report for active duty. The second letter advised me that I was AWOL (Absent With Out Leave), and warned me to surrender to the nearest military installation. Having faith in the written word, I hastily dispatched a letter to the Army explaining that I had just arrived back in the States from six months in the South Pacific war zone with the Merchant Marines.

A response was waiting for me when I arrived home in Detroit. In the new letter were two dates. I was due to report to Fort Sheridan in Chicago on the first date, and on the second date I was to report to Keesler Air Force Base in Biloxi, Mississippi.

CHAPTER 5

GOING BY THE BOOK

Processing at Fort Sheridan, Illinois was more confusing for the Army than it was for me. Upon presentation of my Merchant Marine discharge papers and certificates awarding me the Merchant Marine Atlantic War Zone and the Pacific War Zone Medals, a perplexed captain decided that since I had been in the active reserves at the time, I was also eligible for the Army's American Campaign Medal and the World War II Asia Pacific Campaign Medal.

I think I was the first private to go through basic training with more combat ribbons than my instructors. One thing is for sure, it certainly didn't hurt when it came to assignments.

From Fort Sheridan I was sent to Keesler Air Base in Biloxi, Mississippi, and from there to Chanute Field in Illinois.

Since the men in my squadron had enlisted specifically in the pilot training program, the Army gave us a choice. We could reenlist for a four-year term or we could take a discharge and most likely get drafted for occupation duty in Europe. They were quick to encourage us to reenlist by telling us there was still a good possibility of completing our flight training.

I did a little reasoning and figured that with all the trained pilots coming back to America and no wars on the horizon, there wasn't much chance for any of us to get back into flight training. As it turned out, every other man in my squadron signed up for another four years and ended up doing occupation duty in Europe or Japan. I was the one exception.

PROVERB 17:
Every story offers a message.

If I couldn't get a guarantee of completing flight school, I would gamble on the discharge. On November 5, 1945, I received an honorable discharge.

My discharge papers were arranged by a "shavetail" second lieutenant and fortune certainly did not smile down on me that day. In looking through my papers, the lieutenant concluded that since I had been in the reserves at the time of my service awards, I would not be eligible for them.

With a scratch of a pen, I lost my American Campaign Medal, and my World War II Asia Pacific Campaign Medal, and to add insult to injury, he even took away my Good Conduct Ribbon. He did let me keep my Marksman badges. I figured I was lucky to get my discharge in writing. Cest la vie!

Following my discharge from the Air Force, I still had a patriotic streak so I volunteered to work on a troopship bound for Germany to bring the troops home. I was still young and had plenty of time to delay my million-dollar quest.

However, I was not indifferent to earning more money and a search of the possibilities provided an opportunity. In order to make more money sailing in the Merchant Marines, you had to advance in rank to a higher rating. To do that you needed a certain amount of service in your present grade, plus pass the Coast Guard written exam.

Due to a manpower shortage, the Coast Guard kept reducing the service time required. I had no desire to sail as a wiper again, so I went to the local library and searched for books that would help me pass the examination for an oiler's rating. I found the right information in a set of books called the Audel Marine Manuals.

Each book contained a series of sample questions and answers for almost every marine classification. I selected the oiler's text and found the questions and answers identical to the test questions on the Coast Guard examination. I passed the test. Within a short time, by repeating the process, I acquired the classifications of fireman, watertender, electrician, and ultimately, junior engineer. I'm sure that had I remained in the Merchant Marines, and an Audel text was available, I would have achieved the rank of captain and had my own ship within a very short time.

Anyway, I sailed out of New York Harbor as a newly licensed oiler, the guy who oils all the moving parts in an engine room.

PROVERB 18:
**If you are at the bottom of the ladder,
look around for an escalator.**

PROVERB 19:
**Don't be reluctant to research available resources.
Be assured someone else has been where you
are going and has left a trail of crumbs.**

As we neared the Cape Hatteras area, we ran into a violent storm that caused the ship to pitch sharply in every direction. Visualize an open version of a two or three story automobile engine. Mammoth connecting rods cranking up and down turning the mammoth crankshaft that turned the mammoth propeller. Actually, the crankshaft was immersed in a pit of oil, but certain parts of the connecting rods had little drip-jars that needed to be frequently refilled with oil.

During the storm, the pitching of the ship caused the connecting rods to splash oil out of the pit onto the metal deck plates creating a very slippery surface. Fortunately, the ship had a ready supply of shredded rags for just such an occasion. I was mopping up the oily deck plates when the Scottish chief engineer accosted me. He was one of many very senior citizens who had been brought out of retirement. Normally, I don't like to characterize anyone by his or her birthright, but I do submit that this man reinforced the stereotype of Scotsmen as a wee bit stingy.

"Hoot mon, air ye deft? Ya can no use up all the rags on board while the ship is bobbing around in this storm! Wait until the storm is over, and then clean up the oil. Now put those rags away!" he commanded.

My military instinct was to obey my superior. I put the unused rags away and made my way across the oily floor to the crank pit. I leaned forward as the huge connecting rod was about to be in position for me to fill the oil reservoir, when the ship lurched and my feet separated from the deck plates. Fortunately, or unfortunately, the connecting rod came around and struck a glancing blow to the back of my head, fracturing my skull and sending me to the opposite wall of the engine room in a horizontal position. I say fortunately because, had I fallen into the oil pit and been struck by that five ton crank shaft,, I would have become a long and very thin specimen of a sailor.

I can't recall everything, but I do know I woke up on a couch in the purser's office because he was the only person on board with a Boy Scout's first aid kit. There was an audience present and I heard the purser tell someone that he could only stitch each end of the torn scalp because the skull was protruding out too far to permit sewing the whole tear.

At Bremerhaven, Germany, I was given a cursory examination at a clinic, and handed a huge supply of Phenobarbital pain killers. I was sent back to my ship to do "light work" until the ship returned to America and I could be hospitalized in the Marine Hospital on Ellis Island.

Now let me give you an example of why we have unions in America. A representative from the National Maritime Union visited me in the hospital and told me they weren't going to stand for what happened. He gave me the name and address of a lawyer and when I was finally discharged from the hospital, I went to see him.

His office was in a seedy area near the docks. As I entered, I encountered the figure of an emaciated man slumped over a table with a hypodermic needle protruding from his bare upper arm.

He withdrew the syringe from his arm and put it into a drawer. "Are you Leeds?" he asked looking up at me. "Sit down. We're going to teach those bastards a lesson!"

I didn't really have to do anything. He located the proper documents, filled them in, and I just signed them.

A few months later, the lawyer and I appeared before a judge who advised me that the ship's owners had agreed to settle my claim for the auspicious sum of seven hundred dollars.

The judge then looked at my lawyer and asked how much of the settlement he was taking.

"Forty percent, your honor," was the reply.

"Don't you think that's a little steep?" the judge asked. "I think twenty percent would be more reasonable. Don't you?"

The lawyer paused a few moments and answered, "I guess so."

Then the judge turned to me. "Is this settlement satisfactory?"

"I guess so," I replied. I was eighteen years old and had never sued anyone. Anyway, million dollar settlements hadn't been invented yet. I just nodded my head.

My net share of the proceeds was five hundred and sixty dollars. In retrospect, I'm not too sure we "taught those bastards a lesson." Should you think I was snookered, you have to remember that I also got thousands of dollars worth of free pain killers over the next ten years to treat the horrible migraine headaches I endured. Any damn fool will agree that had to be worth something.

PROVERB 20:
Justice isn't blind.
She just can't stand to see what is going on.

On the other hand, if you think getting injured will always get you your million dollar settlement nowadays, let me give you a more contemporary example.

Recently, an old friend of mine was shopping in a Kmart store and neglected to see a pallet display in the middle of a main aisle. His foot hit the edge of the pallet and he ended up on the floor.

Real, or imagined, every part of his body began to ache. Even though his shoulders and knees had been operated on (due to an automobile accident) the previous year, he claimed the fall aggravated those old problems. He hired a law firm on a contingency basis. Despite several offers to settle his claim, my friend had his heart set on a seven figure prize.

To prove the seriousness of his injuries, he had many of his body parts reoperated on. His medical bills exceeded eighteen thousand dollars and his expectations rose with the rising tide of medical bills. He expressed confidence that if he continued to drag the matter out and continued adding to his medical bills, Kmart would agree to a higher settlement.

The other day he received a "final" offer from Kmart's attorneys; ten thousand dollars! While my friend was turning down all the offers Kmart made, the company had filed for bankruptcy. What about the insurance company? Kmart was self-insured and apparently the insurance division was included in the bankruptcy.

PROVERB 21:
**Don't fall for an insurance windfall until you
have confirmed the defendant's financials.**

PROVERB 22:
**The Phoenicians invented money in 900 B.C.
The next year the first lawyer appeared.**

I, at least, would gain something from my accident. While I was recuperating in the Marine Hospital, I began to think about Osa Johnson's book, *Four Years In Paradise*. What a great life it would be exploring the Dark Continent. I was still a teenager, so spending six or seven years in Africa wouldn't hurt. Besides, Africa was full of financial opportunities; diamonds, gold, oil. My mind was set.

All I needed was a release from the draft board, a passport, and a South African visa. The draft board release and the passport were no problem, but to obtain a visa, South Africa required me to have someone in Africa guarantee my care, possess a round-trip ticket, or post a seven hundred dollar cash bond. I knew no one in Africa and neither of the other two options was viable.

Suddenly I had an inspired thought. I would go to New York and ask Osa Johnson for a job.

Without considering that a lot of time had passed since she roamed the African jungles and wrote her book, I took off for New York. Her office was a beautiful suite of rooms decorated with every kind of African artifact imaginable. Our meeting was very brief. I told her I wanted to go to Africa and work for her and she just stood there and stared at me.

When she finally spoke, she called my attention to the fact that African life in the twenties and thirties was far different than in the late forties. There wasn't anything left to explore.

It was apparent that she wasn't impressed by my desires and wasn't about to be persuaded. Other than meeting this great lady explorer, I left empty handed.

With no place to go, I checked into a YMCA hotel. That very evening they held a dance where I met two lovely young ladies. During the course of the evening, I related my plans to go to Africa. To my surprise, one of the girls told me she had relatives living in Uitenhaig, Africa, and asked me to visit them when I got there. By agreeing to do so, I acquired the name and address of someone in South Africa.

On Monday, I applied for a visa and listed the girl's relatives as my own relatives and guarantors. A few days later the consulate called to tell me my visa was ready.

The next thing I did was ask the America-South Africa Steamship Company if I could work my passage to Africa. That was a big mistake.

Unfortunately, the National Maritime Union had already closed that possibility. Apparently, in the "good ol' days," captains could discharge an employee in any port he desired, leaving sailors stranded all over the world. Now, the Articles of Employment required the shipping companies to bring every American sailor back to an American port. Conversely, it also obligated every sailor to stay with the ship until it returned to an American port.

There was only one solution, I would sign Articles and then jump ship when we got to Africa.

I went to the union hall and took a job on the America-South Africa Steamship Company's ship, the SS *South Africa Dawn*. I signed Articles and was on my way.

Apparently, someone in the company had recognized my name and advised the captain that I had been seeking one-way passage to South Africa. As we were coming into the basin at Cape Town, the captain summoned me to his cabin. He informed me he was aware I planned to jump ship and added the stern threat that it was a federal crime punishable by imprisonment. Also, it was a very personal goal of his to insure that no member of his crew ever evaded punishment.

I assured him that I fully understood and was relieved to be released from his gaze.

Seamen were allowed to draw fifty percent of their earned wages at any time, so I thought I would do that in each port we docked. In Cape Town and East London I was watched like a hawk, but when we arrived in Port Elizabeth a few days before New Years, apparently they figured I wasn't going to jump ship until we were coming back down the coast. The observations had stopped and the gangplank was frequently unmanned. With the advent of Christmas and New Years just a few days ahead, everyone was in a holiday mood.

On January 30th, I went to the train station and purchased a one-way ticket to Uitenhaig for that evening and then headed back to the ship to await nightfall.

That night I picked up my duffle bag, and when the gangplank was unattended, walked off the ship and caught my train. After a brief ride, I arrived in Uitenhaig at about 10:30 PM.

The entire town was dark. The few hotels in the area were locked up for the night and the only source of light was a police station. Rather than risk anything, I found a quiet corner in the park next to a statue of King George and went to sleep.

I woke early, waited until 8 AM, and then found my way to the Kalmin residence.

I was welcomed like a long lost relative. I tried not to impose on them but they insisted on treating me like royalty. After two weeks, I begged their forgiveness and gave them a date for my departure. I had found an ad in the newspaper seeking someone to share automobile expenses on a trip to Johannesburg, the major gold mining city in the north.

I placed a few ads for employment in the national newspapers and gave a post office box in Johannesburg as my return address. I hoped that short periods of employment would allow me to not touch my pocket money.

On the morning of my departure, Mr. Kalmin asked to see me in his study. He looked across his huge desk and asked me who I really was.

Deception, when it affected other people, wasn't something I could easily live with. Terribly embarrassed, I was relieved to tell him the whole truth.

When I finished my story, Mr. Kalmin burst out in a big grin. "I was sure we didn't have any Leeds in our family," he commented.

Then he asked me if I needed any money for my trip and I told him no. Over the previous couple weeks, they had fed me and treated me like a king. Not one day had gone by without them making my stay wonderful. In a way, I was sorry to be leaving, but adventure was calling.

Mr. Kalmin shook my hand and wished me a pleasant trip. He gave me one last instruction, "Please don't tell Mrs. Kalmin. She was really quite thrilled at having an American relative visit us."

PROVERB 23:
Everything ventured, everything gained!

CHAPTER 6

AFRICA, LAND OF OPPORTUNITY

My share-the-ride companion was a jovial, slightly overweight, gentleman of about forty years of age, who would only give his name as Daniels. The car was 1941 black Ford sedan that looked like it had just come out of the showroom.

Huddled in the corner of the rear seat was a small native boy of about twelve years of age. Aside from his ragged clothes, the only unique features were an ear-to-ear grin and a tattered, wide brimmed, dark brown hat that was pulled down to his ears. The trip took us to Middelburg, Bloemfontein, Winburg, Kroonstad, Colesburg, Parys, and finally, Johannesburg.

When we stopped for fuel, the boy would jump out of the car and pump the gasoline. We made two overnight stops, one at Colesburg and one at Parys. Most of the time was passed with small talk. Mr. Daniels seemed to be very interested in my past and future plans.

Whenever we approached a town where we planned to stop for some refreshment, Mr. Daniels would stop the car at the outskirts and the boy would get out and walk through the town while we ate. When we were done eating, we would pick the boy up on the other side of the town.

When we stopped for the night, Mr. Daniels and I had comfortable separate rooms at each hotel, but again the young boy was dropped off before we entered the city and in the morning we would pick him up on the opposite side of town. He would walk all night and sleep in the car during the day. Apparently, he carried his own food in his crude cloth knapsack.

Of course, this aroused my curiosity and when I inquired about it, I learned more than I bargained for.

Mr. Daniels responded to my inquiry with a question. "Would you be interested in making some real money?"

"How?" I replied.

Then everything became clear. Mr. Daniels was a smuggler. He would pick up the diamonds in Johannesburg and deliver them to a contact in Cape Town. As a precaution against being caught with the diamonds, he would give them to the little boy, who would carry them through the town with little notice from the police. I never learned how the boy ate or took care of other necessities but he seemed to have been well schooled for his mission.

When I asked what would happen if the boy just took off with the diamonds, the driver just smiled, and said, "He wouldn't want to do that." The tone of his voice conveyed some sort of ominous punishment.

In America, I never would have considered such an illegal venture but this was Africa, and this was just adventure with the promise of "living" money.

Mr. Daniels introduced me to two men who operated a law office in downtown Johannesburg, after which I went to the local YMCA and rented a room. The YMCA was unlike anything I'd ever seen in America. It was really an old one-story home with about a dozen rooms. An elderly couple managed the hotel and lived there with one of their aged grandmothers. It was quite apparent that the prim and proper wife ran the whole show. Most of the young boys residing there were serving apprenticeships in the area and paid scant attention to the new roomer. My room was quite large and was shared with two other boys.

Each morning, breakfast would consist of two slices of toast, a small portion of jam, a soft-boiled egg, cheese, and tea to drink. I was impressed at the silver service. Even the toast came enclosed in a covered silver serving dish.

A major problem soon surfaced when I was informed that the doors to the hotel would be locked between 9:00 PM and 7:00 AM which meant that my nightlife would be severely limited. Fortunately, I was able to persuade the manager to loan me her key for a special occasion. That was the only time I ever had to borrow her key because I went right out and had a duplicate made. Although it was obvious that I was coming home at all hours of the night, the elderly couple would only look at me kind of funny, and the question they wanted to broach was never asked.

About a week after arriving, I received a call from one of Daniel's lawyers asking me to come to their office. Once there, I was briefed for my mission. I suppose, to make the arrangement more palatable, my employer stressed that the diamonds were not stolen. Instead, they had simply been purchased from various natives, who had found them in the bush. I knew it was still illegal to possess them.

Everyone was aware that the diamond trade was rigidly controlled and anyone caught with illegal diamonds faced a harsh sentence under South Africa's Roman-Dutch legal system.

Feeling that it would be impolite to question the veracity of his disclaimer, I remained silent. I would have accepted the assignment anyway, but his next offer clinched the deal. I could accept my payment in cash or in uncut diamonds. According to him, I could end up a very rich young man. Dreams of wealth swarmed through my mind. Of course, I would choose to be paid in diamonds!

I was provided with a map and a schedule for the trip and told to study them. On the following morning, I was given a small amount of South African rand and a weathered leather pouch about six inches long, secured at the top with two leather laces bound together by a metal band.

My car was parked about two blocks away and when I arrived, I found the same little boy crouched in the corner of the rear seat.

Over the next several weeks, I averaged about three trips every two weeks and my stash of precious diamonds kept growing. I had no safe place to keep them so I cut the lining in my leather shaving kit and inserted the diamonds between the lining and the leather bottom.

I think things would have turned out better if I hadn't met a young raven haired beauty named Sheila, who worked for the American consulate in Johannesburg. My erratic schedule only allowed for an irregular courtship and, since I was not really accumulating any cash, sometimes Sheila had to pay or help pay a tab. It was only a matter of time before I confided in Sheila about my diamond enterprise, but I had the foresight not to reveal where I hid my diamonds.

While the rewards were good, the driving started to become wearisome. The only interesting break in the monotony was when a pack of wild animals blocked the road and I could sit in my car and watch them, sometimes for hours, before proceeding on an otherwise mundane journey.

There was one constant highlight of every trip; an overnight stop at the Central Hotel in the small village of Colesburg. Daniels had introduced me to this wonderful lodge on our first trip.

I would try to arrive towards dusk and just in time for dinner. Over a large glass of brandy I would contemplate the sequence of entrees I would indulge in. I would usually begin each meal with a large bowl of soup and follow that with an order of a fresh local fish. After the fish I would have roast veal, lamb chops, steak, cottage pie or a roast of the local game. All of this would be accompanied by different kinds of potatoes, green mealy, and a variety of vegetables. My brandy glass was never allowed to remain partially empty.

The main course was followed by a huge bowl of lettuce, tomatoes, cucumbers and assorted African greens. Following the salad course they served a large dish of sweets. Dinner included as much as you could eat, as well as all the deliciously rich, locally grown coffee you could drink. When I thought I was finished, the waiter would set a huge wooden bowl on the table containing every kind of fruit and nut you could think of, and I would conclude the evening's meal.

At about 6:00 am the next morning, a small native boy would steal into the room and deposit a steaming hot cup of coffee. On his way out, he would take my dusty shoes with him and return a short time later with my shoes looking like new. Most often, I would be sleeping when he returned.

Including the cost of my room, my entire bill was one pound and two shillings, the equivalent of four dollars and forty cents American!

Another favorite stop was Parys, just two hours south of Johannesburg. There I would stay at the Parys Hotel and enjoy the same kind of amenities. One difference was that the town had a movie theater. I still remember two of the movies I saw there; *Four Feathers* and *Gone With The Wind*.

While the courier's job was extremely rewarding, it soon became monotonous and I decided to seek fame and fortune in more remote areas of Africa.

My plan to hike across Africa to the east coast was changed after a variety of hardships, not the least of which was an encounter with a male lion in a dried-up river bed. I beat a hasty retreat to Johannesburg to take a train.

While back in Johannesburg, I read in the newspaper that a giant airshow was being planned on May 3rd, 1946, to celebrate a visit by the King and Queen of England. I called around until I finally reached a Mr. Kelly who was in charge of putting the show together. He became quite excited when I told him I did wing walking and parachute exhibitions, and he insisted I meet him right away at the Johannesburg airport. Apparently, while I was on my way to the airport, Mr. Kelly and his staff discussed how they could make my act a star attraction of the show.

Although I urged them to consider a one-mile delayed parachute jump trailing a visible stream of flour, the planners had already decided on another feat. I was to go aloft in a World War I Tiger Moth aircraft that had one landing wheel painted green and the other painted red. While the pilot flew back and forth only a hundred feet above the ground, I was to climb down underneath the airplane and, while hanging by my feet from the axle, remove the wheels and replace them on opposite sides of the axle.

To their surprise, I broke out laughing. I had listened spellbound while they explained their request and I immediately wanted to recommend that they have plenty of spare wheels and gasoline in the airplane, but I restrained any attempt toward humor. Instead, I just looked down at the desk because I couldn't wipe the smile off my face.

Finally, Mr. Kelly spoke up, "We're prepared to offer you fifty pounds if you'll agree." That was equal to two hundred dollars and the most money I had seen in a long time. I agreed to the deal.

It was confirmed with a handshake and plans to meet some weeks before the show, to work out the details of the act.

PROVERB 24:
In the end, easy money is difficult.

The air show was a couple of months away and I wanted to see more of Africa in that time. The one city I wanted to visit more than any other was Mombasa in Portuguese East Africa.

Mombasa reminded me of an old Western frontier town. Most of the buildings were single story frame structures. Except for the eastern edge, which boarded along the Indian Ocean, you could walk a very short distance in any direction and find yourself out in the jungle. If you were hungry, it was a simple task to climb one of the many fruit trees and eat to your heart's content.

In the dock area, I met an Indian named Rahman Ismail at a little coffee shop facing the waterfront. He was extremely friendly and asked me all kinds of questions.

Over and over, he assured me of his high regard for America and Americans. His questioning seemed to center on my mechanical skills and my political philosophy. At that time, Indians were treated as poorly as blacks, and I had no problem convincing him that I abhorred the prejudicial system imposed by the colonial rulers of Africa.

Encouraged by my frankness, he then confided to me that things were going to change in Africa. I shook my head from side to side when he suggested that perhaps I could help. How could I possibly help?

"Soon the natives of Madagascar are going to revolt against their French rulers. Even now they are accumulating guns, but the only place they can get them is from the mainland. Right now there is a boat in the harbor ready to take these guns to Zanzibar and from there they will be smuggled into Madagascar. All they need is an engineer to tend the engine. It would be a simple task for you."

When he finished, I tried to suppress a smile. He was assigning me much more credit than was due. Still, Rahman went on in an almost secretive voice.

"It would only take you a few hours and you wouldn't be required to do anything illegal. All you have to do is make sure the engine keeps running."

"What happens if we get stopped by the police?" I asked.

"Don't worry, they will never find anything. Everything will be hidden under a false deck which will be covered by tons of coal."

Rahman was still wearing his friendly grin when I finally agreed to help him out just this one time. I was given directions to the boat and assured him that I would meet him at the boat as soon as it was dark.

PROVERB 25:
Never seek trouble, it will find you.

CHAPTER 7

THE GREAT ESCAPE

I had no difficulty locating the ship that night. My only surprise was seeing its size. It must have been eighty feet long, with two cargo holds up forward and the engine room in the stern. The pilothouse sat between the second hold and the engine room.

Below deck, I found a huge diesel engine and several auxiliary pumps. The toolbox held an assortment of antique wrenches and parts totally foreign to me. While I was familiar with the principles of the diesel engine, I had never worked on one in my life. I was strongly tempted to take a walk, but instead decided to fake it.

The crew consisted of four men, none of whom could speak enough English to converse with. I think they gained a measure of confidence when I wiped off the top of the engine with a rag and then proceeded to go through the motions of tightening as many bolts as I could access. By seven o'clock we were chugging out of the harbor.

Things went smoothly, but every time the engine hiccupped or groaned, I had a panic attack. To make

67

matters worse, it seemed like we were only chugging along at three or four knots an hour. At that rate I figured it would take us a week to reach Zanzibar.

It was a hot, moonlit night and the crew didn't appear to have anything to do except keep a watch for approaching police vessels. It was not a comforting thought.

After a few hours, one of the men arranged a few bricks on a metal plate and built a little fire. He set a large concave metal dish over the fire and filled it with rice, vegetables, cut up fish, and God knows what else. It may have looked gross but it smelled heavenly.

On his command, we all gathered around the dish and sat down. I noticed there were no eating instruments but the mystery was solved when the men started dipping their hands, or their own wooden spoon into the food and stuffing their mouths.

I'd have given anything to find an excuse for leaving, but each of the men persisted in motioning me to join in. One of them even threw me a dirty rag so I could wipe my hands when the residue got too thick.

As we finally approached the coast of Zanzibar, the captain bid us to be silent. He peered into the darkness, very carefully examining the shoreline and maneuvered the boat accordingly.

Suddenly, he produced a flashlight and blinked it on and off twice. From the shore came a similar signal. The captain revved the engine and we proceeded toward the source of the light.

We found a small inlet just wide enough for our boat to access and shut the engine down. Immediately, a number of men came out of the darkness and began unloading our cargo. The coal we were carrying was packed in burlap sacks and the men formed a human chain and unloaded the boat in very little time. Apparently, it wasn't quick enough for the captain, who kept pointing to his watch and yelling at the men.

It was beginning to get light when we finally departed. The captain was constantly harping about something that apparently hadn't gone right but there was no way I could learn what. Perhaps it was the absence of two of our crew but I never found out.

PROVERB 26:
Luck is like a rabbit.

Hare today. Stew tomorrow.

Having been awake for almost sixteen hours, I finally dozed off sitting in the stairwell to the engine room. I wasn't conscious of anything until I heard a voice over a loud speaker. I stood up and in the morning light saw a military ship off our port bow. Another military ship was just off our port stern. In front of us, I saw a sand beach with about a hundred soldiers with guns waiting for us.

Once ashore, the captain and the other two crew members were waving their hands and pleading their innocence to an officer. A search of the boat apparently revealed no contraband. They even found the concealed compartment, but it was completely void of any incriminating signs.

My interrogation was different. An English speaking officer asked me all kinds of questions to which I pleaded my innocence. I kept telling the officer that I didn't really know these people. I had just agreed to sail with them because I didn't have anything better to do. As far as I knew, all we did was take some coal to Zanzibar.

Everything was going fine until another officer asked to see my passport. I had several visas but none for Portuguese East Africa. I did point out that I had a valid visa for South Africa and assured them that no one gets a visa when they travel back and forth between South Africa and Portuguese East Africa. They expressed surprise at the news and then exchanged smiles.

Apparently, since I had a visa for South Africa, the officers decided that I should be sent back to South Africa. Two officers placed me in a jeep and drove me to the South African border.

Things might have gone better with the South African border patrol if I hadn't arrived with an armed escort.

The two groups discussed the situation and I suspect the Portuguese police prejudiced my situation with some ridiculous cockamamie story about gun smuggling. The South African soldiers went through my duffle bag, wallet, and passport. Everything appeared in order and they finally let me pass. In a week, I was back in Johannesburg and the first thing I did was call Sheila with the good news.

PROVERB 27:
Good intentions are not always good currency.

There was bad news and there was worse news. Apparently Sheila thought I had left for good because she had already embarked upon other social arrangements. The situation became more awkward and I soon got the feeling that I was intruding. It became more and more difficult to get a date with her even after telling her about my hair-raising run in with the Portuguese army.

My romantic persistence was resolved a week later when two men from the Criminal Investigation Department (CID) came to my room in the YMCA and arrested me. It was almost comical the way the manager, her husband, the elderly grandparent and all the students lined up to watch the event. They stood there with their mouths wide open as if this was the most shocking thing they had ever seen. It probably was. I couldn't help but smile as they stood there like a reviewing stand while I was paraded out of the building.

What I have always wondered about was how the CID men knew about my diamond running and gun running episodes. *Chercher pour le femme!*

At the Marshall Square Jail in Johannesburg, I kept asking why I was arrested, but no one would give me the satisfaction of an answer. You have to understand that South African law was modeled after the Roman-Dutch legal system; totally opposite from most western cultures.

According to the law, an accused person was guilty until proven innocent. Even worse, they could incarcerate you for years without charging you or bringing you into a courtroom. Moreover, it seemed the Dutch jail administrators and police were openly hostile to foreigners, and especially to Americans and Australians. It was probably their revenge for having lost the Boer War to the English.

I had several ideas on why I might have been arrested, but not the slightest clue of what they knew or on what charge they were holding me.

After checking my passport and visa, someone discovered the fly in the ointment. Although I had a valid visa to enter South Africa, I was lacking the stamp showing I had passed through customs when I entered the country through Port Elizabeth. I had entered the country illegally. I was designated an illegal immigrant!

They verified their suspicions by making calls to Pretoria and then Port Elizabeth. The clerk drew two parallel red lines diagonally across the visa with the word "CANCELLED" in bold letters between the lines. Underneath the visa he carefully wrote, "Authority: Telegram No. 2829, Department of the Interior, Pretoria, and dated the note. Underneath, he stamped the authority,

J. Rituf, Principal Immigration Officer, Hogofimmi-grasiebeampte, Johannesburg.

After confiscating all my possessions, a guard took me by the arm and led me to an outdoor courtyard surrounded by fifteen-foot high walls topped by rows of barbed wire.

At about one o'clock, I was given one well burnt pork sausage, a boiled potato, some squash, and a tin cup of a watered down version of coffee for lunch. I then sat in the courtyard until about five o'clock when a supper was served. Supper consisted of a piece of corned beef which had the consistency of shoe leather, a boiled potato and another tin cup of a watery coffee.

Shortly afterward I was taken to an interior holding room, approximately twenty feet by forty feet in which five cots were set up. There were already two men residing in the room. Each of us was provided with three blankets that obviously had been used many times before and never cleaned. A single light bulb burned night and day, and every hour during the night a guard would come into the unheated room, wake us up, and ask if we were allright. My most frequent complaint was that the room was damp and freezing cold. I don't think they heard me.

Breakfast was two hard-boiled eggs (one rotten), two pieces of bread, and the tin cup of watery coffee. Shortly after breakfast, we were all taken to the outside courtyard for the rest of the day.

The following evening, I was put on a train for Cape Town with a CID escort of two six-foot officers named Rieks and Jacobs. Although they had paid for a four-person compartment, the conductor let us use a vacant six-person compartment. The police paid for my food allowing me two shillings, three pence. This was more than adequate to purchase a meal of bacon, eggs, potatoes, and coffee. For lunch and dinner, I would order two hard-boiled eggs, sausages, a loaf of bread with a jar of butter, and some assorted cold cuts. I suspect my escorts pocketed their food and bedding allowances because they carried their own packed lunches, dinners, and bedding. My only personal expense was four shillings (eighty cents) I paid for sheets, blankets, and two pillows.

At Cape Town, I was taken to the police station where an immigration officer met us and transported me by taxi to an immigration holding-compound on Chippeny Street. The compound was located on a half-acre site. A gate was attached to a long building forming the front barrier. A lengthy barracks for Europeans (Caucasians) ran the length of the left side and a separate barracks for blacks ran along the rear of the compound.

The right side of the enclosure consisted of an eight-foot concrete wall topped by seven rows of barbed wire. Except for the bathrooms, the barracks were single rooms with double rows of cots running from one end to the other. There were windows running along the outside wall but they were barred securely to prevent escaping. I was registered, and given three blankets, two pillows and pillowcases.

The detention center was run by two elderly army veterans, who operated the site very casually. After registering, I was told to order my dinner from four different selections; fish & chips, stew, steak and potatoes, or curry and rice. I thought they were joking with me but it was true.

Over time, I found out that while the selection process was fine, the quality of the ingredients was lacking. Two or three times a week we would complain about the rice being rancid or little worms crawling around in the food. It is surprising how you can grow to tolerate things when you are incarcerated.

Finally, an official told me that I was being held as a prohibited immigrant, but that I could return if I left the country and reentered legally. I hired an immigration lawyer to secure a visa to Rhodesia but the Rhodesian government responded that South Africa was empowered to issue Rhodesian visas, and that I would have to obtain the visa from them. The issue went back and forth but without any visa issuance. It was a *"Catch 22"*.

The main obstacle turned out to be Captain Studer of the SS South Africa Dawn. Despite the captain's personal warning that "No man has ever jumped one of my ships," I had dared to do so. He was insisting that the immigration department hold me until the *Africa Dawn* reached port and that I only be allowed to leave South Africa aboard his ship when it was bound for America. He was not about to tarnish his reputation and hoped to teach me a lesson.

From the time I arrived in Africa, I had been answering employment ads in the *Rand Daily Mail* and other newspapers. Now, after incarceration, I received two intriguing offers. The first reply was from William C. Ker in Livingstone, Northern Rhodesia. Ker was running a river transport business on the Zambezi River.

At the time, many people were immigrating to South Africa and he was transporting their household goods down the Zambezi river to Southern Rhodesia from where it was taken overland to sites in South Africa. I wrote and advised Mr. Ker of my current indisposition and assured him that the matter was only temporary. I was certain that this job offer would enable me to obtain the needed visa. I was wrong.

The second really intrigued me. I had answered an ad titled "COCOS ISLAND" appearing in the Cape Argus newspaper. It read as follows:

Attempts are being made to form a syndicate to go "treasure-hunting" on the above island. Anyone (particularly yachtsmen) interested, and able to put up a small capital, invited to write for further particulars to XYZ-1119, Argus.

In his reply, Donald Klopper related that he was a direct descendant of the famous explorer, Captain Cook who roamed the seven seas from 1768 to 1771. It was also rumored that Captain Cook had somehow acquired untold wealth, "salvaged" from unfortunate treasure-laden civilian ships. It has always been rumored that prior to his death, he buried his treasure somewhere in the vicinity of the Cocos Islands. Although there were many attempts to find the treasure, no one had been successful. This descendant of his claimed that he had come across private records of Captain Cook in the family's heirlooms that indicated the approximate location of the treasure.

In our correspondence, Mr. Klopper informed me that in order to seek the treasure, a grant must be obtained from the Australian government. If the treasure is found, ninety percent of its value must be given to the government. Anticipating that the treasure of gold, silver, and diamonds would be worth several hundred million dollars, the effort appeared economically worthwhile.

Mr. Klopper estimated each member's expense at three hundred pounds ($1,200.), plus their own travel expenses. The best part was that I wouldn't have to advance any money until we rendezvoused in the Cocos Islands. Since the expedition of not more than six individuals wasn't scheduled to meet until January 1948, I decided to try and stay in Africa for another six months. If all efforts to remain failed, I could still look forward to the treasure hunt.

On the following Thursday, I learned the *SS South Africa Dawn* was in the harbor and I was to be taken on board at seven o'clock for the return trip to America. If I didn't do something, I was going to be the Captain's guest on a trip to America and possibly prison. I had to develop a plan and do it quickly. My plan was to escape.

My immediate solution was to break a hole in the bathroom ceiling and escape via the roof. It was mid-afternoon when my head poked out of the West slope of the roof, and I found myself looking at an assembly of spectators on the street below. With total disregard for my audience, I climbed out on the roof, slid down to the edge and dropped to the sidewalk. Since everyone seemed too stunned to do anything, I simply picked myself up and beat a hasty retreat to a lofty and discreet area of shrub up on Lion's Head Mountain where I spent the remainder of the night.

I wouldn't be joining the *Africa Dawn* after all.

PROVERB 29:
Escape is only a temporary situation.

CHAPTER 8

THE WAGES OF SIN ARE BAD AND THE BENEFITS ARE LOUSY.

The following morning, I walked to the Cape Times Building where the American Consul's office was located.

Vice Consul Anderson was the only one in and appeared shocked when he learned what I had done. He told me that I would have to be deported for sure now, but that he would personally intervene to have me put on a coastal freighter so I could return to South Africa and make a legal entry. The important thing was for me to return to the detention barracks so a legal process could proceed. I actually believed him.

Over the next few weeks, it seems I spoke with every immigration lawyer in South Africa, as well as every officer in the immigration department. Each person told me they would see what they could do and then returned with a story explaining that the last person I had spoken with was the one refusing to let me go. I even called the Sturrock Agency, agents for the America-South Africa Steamship Company, and offered to buy my release. They said they were quite agreeable but Captain Studer was adamant on my returning to America on the *South Africa Dawn*.

One day, two Swedish sailors who had missed their ship were brought into the detention barracks. For reasons of their own, the two guards forcefully warned them to stay away from "the American." They even detailed how I had escaped from the detention barracks. That was a big mistake.

The very next day, the two Swedes failed in an attempt to duplicate my escape. Their escapade resulted in collapsing two huge sections of the ceiling and the crushing of two toilets in their fall to the ground floor.

Within minutes the barrack's door opened and the two guards entered along with a half-dozen men from the Criminal Investigation Department. An inspection of the bathroom confirmed the worst. The Swedes were ordered to get dressed, and then one of the guards addressed a CID man in Afrikaans. I could sense what was going to happen and it did. The CID man walked over to my bed and pointed his club at my face.

"You too!" he shouted.

Although I was innocent of any collaboration, nothing I could say prevented me from being arrested, and then incarcerated in one of South Africa's most infamous prisons, Roeland Strat Goal.

PROVERB 29:
**Problems arrive by the pound
and leave by the ounce.**

The name may mean nothing to you, but if you ever lived in South Africa you would know that Roeland Strat

Goal was a condemned prison and one of the worst prisons in South Africa. (With the demise of Apartheid, one of the first acts of an enlightened government was to tear down Roeland Strat Goal.)

I will save the descriptions of the horrible conditions of a South African prison for another time, but let me just give you a brief description of life inside Roeland Strat Goal.

First of all, you were held under the Roman-Dutch legal system which meant you were guilty until proven innocent (an unlikely event). What is worse, they may not even tell you why you are being held or when you are likely to have a hearing. I met men in that prison who had been there for several years awaiting a hearing.

It seemed that the courts reasoned you wouldn't be in Roeland Strat Goal unless you broke a law, so you are guilty to begin with. To make it worse, if you are a foreigner the trial is most likely conducted entirely in the Afrikaans language without the benefit of a translator.

Punishment appeared to vary with the whims of the court, but few young prisoners escaped the bamboo lash in addition to a lengthy incarceration. It was easy to distinguish repeat offenders by the long linear scars borne by their backs and buttocks. Lashes were meted out with a length of knurled bamboo. To import his own sadistic nature, as the bamboo rod reached the flesh, the guard was likely to draw it quickly so it acted as a saw blade on the offender's flesh.

The prospects for any kind of a tolerable existence were enhanced only by meekly obeying the whims of the guards. For a young American, there was a limit.

I honestly don't remember how long I spent in that prison. It seemed like a lifetime but it was probably only several months. During that time, I collected poems and songs from the passing parade of prisoners. Years later I would include these poems in a 332 page anthology of previously unpublished verse. I also had the opportunity to enjoy the brief quietude of solitary confinement which presented itself when I threw a bucket of cleaning water at the feet of a guard and told him I was not going to help clean my cell or the courtyard any more.

"I didn't do anything to get in here, so I'm not going to do anything to get out!" I shouted in an unreasoned outburst of frustration. Would you believe you can gain weight in solitary confinement on a diet of rice water?

PROVERB 30:
**The wages of sin are bad
and the benefits are lousy.**

Early in April 1947, I was again called into the warden's office.

"Your American Consul called and wanted to know if you were ready to go back to America? Yes or no?"

I had had enough. I answered, "Yes."

That afternoon, two escorts came and took me to the American Consulate. For half an hour I listened to Consul Carol H. Foster tell me how fortunate I was not to be further imprisoned by the South African government, due to the intervention of the Consulate. I was certain the consul was lying because I knew no one had ever been tried or sentenced to prison for an immigration offense. Foster finished by telling me how lucky I was that he happened to find a ship heading for America that had an opening for a galley man.

His summary of the benefits that had accrued to me was interrupted when a secretary announced that the captain of the *SS Nira Lukenbach* had arrived.

The captain was a short, slender man, probably in his fifties, who walked hunched over and apparently in great pain. He and the consul exchanged pleasantries and the captain related how his old back injury was bothering him again.

It was obvious that the *Nira Luckenbach* was not affiliated with the America—South Africa Steamship Company, but I chose not to question what was going on.

The captain asked me several questions and finally told the consul that he would accept me. I would be working the day shift in the galley in exchange for my food, lodging, and transportation. As an aside, he added that I would also be paid one dollar a month compensation. Of course I could earn more if the occasion arose. Oddly, the signing of articles was not mentioned. The reason would become apparent the next day.

I was told that I would be picked up from the prison at 4:00 PM the following day. The meeting adjourned and I was taken back to Roeland Strat Goal.

The next day I was more than ready and at three in the afternoon a guard took me to a room with several long wooden tables placed end to end. A policeman was standing behind one of the tables on which all my personal belongings were spread out.

Three men, who were obviously with the CID, were lingering in a far corner of the room seemingly unconcerned with my presence.

I began picking up my clothing and books and placing them neatly in my duffle bag. I noticed my leather shaving kit set about a foot apart from everything else and suddenly realized that in that shaving kit were enough diamonds to keep me in prison for another twenty years.

A strange feeling came over me. If I claimed the shaving kit and the police were aware it held illegal diamonds, I would never leave that prison. If I claimed the shaving kit and the police did not know it held any diamonds, I would be a wealthy young man.

I glanced over and caught one of the three men watching me. It was instinctive, but I just didn't feel right. I finished packing the rest of my possessions and closed the duffle bag.

"Isn't that your shaving kit?" the policeman asked.

"No, that's not mine," I replied.

"Are you sure?" the policeman asked in a surprised tone.

"I'm positive." I replied.

There was an unnatural pause, as if no one knew what to do next. Finally, two of the three men who had been witnessing the event came over and announced that they were there to take me to the ship.

PROVERB 31:
Never trade a headache for an upset stomach.

I have rarely felt more relieved than when those huge prison gates closed behind us and we headed for Waterfront Street and the ship.

I was put on board and the CID men waited until the ship was a distance from the dock; before turning and walking toward their car.

On deck, the crew strangely avoided me. During my months in prison, I had never had an opportunity to get a haircut, and now my hair hung in an unruly arrangement down below my shoulders. I had also given up shaving in prison so my entire appearance was short of respectable.

I later found out that a ship's officer had spread the word that I had been a condemned prisoner in South Africa's most infamous prisons. Either he or a crewmember embellished the story by referring to me as a murderer.

As we headed out of the breakwater and into the Indian Ocean, I noticed a short heavy set young man leaning against a railing. I walked over and apparently startled him out of his daydreaming.

"How long before we reach America?" I asked.

He looked at me as if he didn't understand English. "How many days will it be before we reach America?" I asked again.

His expression didn't change.

"Where?" he asked me back.

"America!" I repeated.

"We ain't going to America. We're going to China. This ship's been sold to Chang Kai Shek. Then they're flying us back to America."

Now I knew why they didn't have me sign articles. When we arrived in China, I was going to be on my own.

PROVERB 32:
Behind the bait
        there is always a hook.

CHAPTER 9

SHANGHAIED

I had only to look around me to determine that this ship was on its last legs. The color scheme was a well-worn black, orange, and white; the colors of all Luckenbach ships. In shipping parlance, the ship was referred to as a "hog islander."

Nearly the entire deck was taken up by huge stacks of lumber identified by painted imprints reading, "UNNRA-BRASIL." Unlike most American vessels I had been on, this ship had not been painted in ages and in many areas you could see rust and the remnants of several old coats of paint. The brass identification plate revealed the ship was actually built in 1927, the same year I was born.

The *Nira* had started its current journey on a run from New York to San Francisco, then to Santos, Brazil, then Capetown for fuel, and finally onto China where the journey would end.

While in Brazil the previous galleyman had missed the ship, presenting the opening for my employment.

The crew was the most cosmopolitan I had ever seen. The steward was Indian, the first cook was an African American, the second cook and most of the deckhands were Chinese, the bos'un was British West Indian, the carpenter was Dutch, and the remaining crew hailed from all over the world.

All of a sudden I heard my name being called by a seaman who led me up a flight of stairs to a gangway where we met a tall, fat, gray-haired black man.

The elderly man introduced himself as the first cook and told me that I would be working in the kitchen from 6:00 AM to 10:00 AM, 11:00 AM to 1:00 PM, and from 4:00 PM to 6:00 PM. This was eight hours, but it was stretched over a twelve-hour period.

Still, when you are at sea, there isn't much else to do but work. He led me to a small room containing four bunk beds, five small lockers, and a dresser with four drawers. As the last man aboard, I was assigned the lowest and smallest bed.

Coming into a galley with every kind of food available to me after months of prison rations was like awakening from a bad dream. I ate constantly and I ate everything. It was a dream come true. In two weeks I gained fifteen pounds.

I didn't think there was anything lower than a wiper on board ship, but there was. A galleyman did every menial task in the kitchen from scrubbing pots, pans, and floors, to the basic prep-work of cooking, such as peeling potatoes and cleaning vegetables.

Our voyage took us past the Mauritius Islands into the Straits of Malacca and on to Singapore. We docked on a Friday and left for Shanghai on the following Tuesday.

We arrived at the mouth of the Yangtze River a week later encountering rainstorms and heavy seas. The fog was so bad that we had to anchor out until the following morning and then complete the fifty-mile distance to Shanghai.

Shanghai was a metropolis gone mad. There was a civil war going on and I don't think foreigners realized how near the Communists were to the outskirts of the city.

Cars, trucks, rickshaws, and pedestrians moved helter-skelter in an effort to get to their destination. Crowds of peasants tried to climb onto trucks carrying bales of cotton and were pulling out tufts of cotton while guards riding on top of the bales sought to beat them off with bamboo sticks.

There were old men pushing carts loaded with devalued Chinese currency and the next day you would see the same people transporting double the quantity of paper money than they had the day before.

Chinese currency was no longer the currency of the realm. One American dollar was fetching twelve thousand Chinese Dollars. A carton of American Cigarettes would cost 400,000 Chinese dollars. On my first day ashore, I spent $580,000 Chinese dollars on silk scarves, leather suitcases, and hand-carved curios.

By the second day, I was beginning to get concerned about my long-term welfare and no one on board the ship could tell me what was going to happen. Nobody seemed to know.

I finally decided on a plan. I had always been sympathetic to the Nationalist Chinese cause, so I'd just hire on to the Chinese army as a mercenary. When the fighting was over, I'd use the money I earned to pay for my passage back to America. It never occurred to me that the Chinese Nationalists might lose the war.

The following day, I found a young peasant on the docks to replace me in the galley. This arrangement met the approval of the first cook. I prepaid the man with two pounds of butter and a gallon of black paint. He thought he was a millionaire.

Despite my inquiries, I could not find the military office where I could volunteer my service. Instead, I found a guide who offered to take me out to the battlefront. He was about seventeen years old and named Chen Yi. which I shortened to Chen. I loaded up with several cartons of cigarettes and went with Chen to the train station where we purchased two coach tickets. It was still early morning yet the train was filled to capacity. In fact, I'm sure it was filled well over capacity with almost as many passengers sitting on the roof or hanging onto some exterior bracket.

The passengers in our coach carried bundles of clothing and baskets of food; cooked, raw, and alive. Apparently, there was no prohibition against bringing live or dead animals on-board. There were many of them in our car.

We traveled for hours and hours making numerous stops along the way. It wasn't until almost midnight that the train finally belched to a stop and the few remaining passengers were ordered off the train.

I found myself in a cold, driving rain which apparently had been going on for quite some time. I climbed down and was struck by the scene. As far as I could see, an encampment of tents covered the muddy ground.

All of the smaller tents were quiet and dark, but there were a few much larger tents lit from within and I could make out the movement of people inside them.

The few people walking around were in uniform and carried rifles slung over one shoulder. Many had bandages or wore slings but they either did not notice us or chose to ignore us. I reasoned it was too late to make any contact that night so I asked Chen Yi if he could find us a place to sleep.

He returned a short time later and led me to a small farmhouse where the owner seemed more than willing to accommodate us. The bickering over the cost of the room ended with a payment of two packs of cigarettes.

The house was probably twenty feet wide by thirty feet long and divided into two rooms; a kitchen and dining area, and a large bedroom area with three bunk beds in it. There was a single kerosene lamp at each end of the room, but only one was lit. The floors of the house were just dirt. The farmer's wife and two very pretty teenage daughters lived with him.

When I asked about a lavatory, I was shown a small shallow trench at the rear of the kitchen. The trench led outside through a hole in the wall. I decided I would bust before I would avail myself of the trench. It was especially abhorrent since no one indicated they would take leave of the kitchen while I used the darn thing.

I assumed that I would have the entire bedroom to myself and Chen Yi and the family would all sleep in the kitchen. I was wrong. Before I could get undressed, the farmer came in with his two daughters and started jabbering away and waving his hands. Chen Yi appeared and explained that the farmer was throwing his two daughters into the deal and he wanted payment for that amenity.

I shook my head vigorously and made every motion I could to signify that I wasn't interested and he should take his daughters and leave me alone.

After much arguing, Chen Yi told me that the two girls had no place to sleep except in my room and if I wasn't going to sleep with the farmer's daughters, the farmer would need more money because of what he would lose from me not sleeping with them.

In the end I gave the farmer another two packs of cigarettes and everyone left the room; everyone except the two girls. They stayed on their side of the room just staring at me..

Not knowing exactly what to do, I removed my shoes and stockings and climbed under the covers where I removed the rest of my clothing.

The girls were not so inclined to modesty. In the glare of the lamplight, each girl disrobed and put on something that appeared to be two-piece silk pajamas.

While the younger girl looked on, her sister came to my cot and began to lift the blanket. I pulled the blanket tighter and shook my head "no". She stared at me for a few moments and then just retreated to the other side of the room where the two of them got into their respective cots.

I reached over and turned the lamp down till it extinguished itself. I was dead tired and only looking forward to a good night's rest.

Within minutes I fell into a deep sleep that was abruptly interrupted by a loud explosion and the sudden feeling of several prongs jabbing into my body. A bright light was shining in my face and from somewhere a voice was shrieking orders in Chinese. It took me a few moments to gain my senses and by then the room was filled with light from numerous lanterns.

Standing over me were several uniformed Chinese soldiers with their bayonet-clad rifles probing my body. An officer stood by my head shining a flashlight directly into my face.

He kept yelling something, but I didn't understand a word. His soldiers had stripped off my blanket exposing my naked body to the world. Apparently, they were looking for weapons or secret papers, but a thorough search of all my possessions revealed nothing.

One of the soldiers handed the Officer my wallet and he began examining each picture and paper without the ability to read anything he came across.

I think the most incriminating fact was that I had refused to have sex with the farmer's two daughters. Americans had an international reputation. Except for John Wayne, no real American would ever pass up such an opportunity. Only a spy would obey unnatural priorities.

Not surprisingly, the officer concluded that I was a Communist spy and the punishment for spying was swift and final.

PROVERB 33:
Not every house is a home.

Two of the soldiers grabbed my arms and hoisted me out of bed. Only then did I see the splintered remains of the bedroom door and notice that the farmer, his wife, Chen Yi, and the two girls were also spectators. The farmer's wife was crying hysterically and Chen Yi was cowering in a corner of the room where a soldier had ordered him. A gash on the side of his face left a trail of blood down his cheek and jaw.

Being held in a vise-like grip, I gave up any attempt to conceal my manhood and just averted my glance to avoid any eye-to-eye contact. For a guy who was the last man into the school showers, it was really embarrassing.

The next thing I knew, I was being dragged outside through the mud and and freezing rain to the rear wall of a nearby house and ordered to stay there.

The officer dispatched a couple of soldiers who returned with several more soldiers in full military dress and with rifles. They lined up about twenty feet in front of me and my worst suspicions were confirmed. This was a firing squad and they were going to execute me.

PROVERB 34:
Where you seek honey, you will find bees.

I could accept the rain and the cold. I didn't even feel them any more. I was even ready to accept being shot. But the thing that really bothered me was standing up there and being shot while naked. I stretched out my arms and pleaded with them to let me put on a pair of pants, but to no avail. My God, what could be worse than being shot in public when completely naked?

The officer had just called the firing squad to attention when out of the mist an ancient touring sedan drove up with its huge headlamps lighting the entire area.

Several staff officers got out of the car and began interrogating my captor. Someone produced my wallet and one of the staff officers began pulling out all the documents including my Red Cross blood donor's card with the bright Red Cross emblem printed at the top. Talk about providence.

Some very animated discussion followed with the more senior staff officer raising his voice and pushing my blood donor card into the face of my captor.

On his command, two soldiers came over and took me by my arms over to where they were standing. The senior staff officer held out my card and pointed to the Red Cross emblem.

"Red Cross," he said in broken English. "American?"

"Yes. Yes. I'm with the Red Cross. I *am* an American."

The officer handed me my papers and apologized profusely. "Sorry," he said. "SORRY!" He issued an order to my captor who immediately had me escorted back into the farmhouse.

PROVERB 35:
A good deed is like a rainbow.
You may not see it until it rains.

91

I dried myself off not even noticing my family audience. I crawled under the quilt, took a couple of deep breaths, and again fell into a deep sleep.

In the morning I was jarred awake by Chen Yi who announced that the train was leaving for Shanghai in minutes. It took me only seconds to get dressed and we boarded the train in plenty of time. There were only a few civilians and several wounded soldiers aboard when the train pulled out. I don't remember buying a ticket or even eating anything on the long trip back to Shanghai.

PROVERB 36:
Fate often deals from a deck of deeds.

Back on the *Nira*, I gave Chen a pound of butter as a bonus and abandoned the idea of earning my fare home by service in the Chinese military.

The ship was abuzz with all kinds of rumors about what was going to happen. I learned the answer when I was again called to the captain's cabin. For some reason the Chinese government had decided not to buy the *Nira*, so we were returning to America. Best of all, the Captain was going to let me sign articles. I was going to make the big bucks again. How lucky can a guy be? Don't let your spirits soar; I'm going to tell you how lucky!

By having me sign articles, I had contracted to take the ship back to an American port. What the crew and I didn't know was that the Longshoremen's Union had called a work stoppage in America, pending a strike. If the *Nira* went back to San Francisco, it could be tied up for weeks or months by the strike.

To avoid this, the owners had contracted with the Canadian government to take a shipment of grain from Vancouver, British Columbia to England. This meant I could not get off the ship and would instead be sightseeing in England. It seemed fate was conspiring against my treasure hunting escapade in the Cocos Islands. There was no way I could envision making my million dollars in England.

When it was finally announced the ship was headed for Canada, I headed for the purser's office and gave him notice that I was signing off the ship in Vancouver.

We both walked to the captain's office and the purser gave him the news. Captain Donald pulled a book off a shelf and read the passage spelling out the Canadian law on discharging American seamen in Canadian territory. Other than requiring a physical examination, there was no legal problem. The articles of employment were another matter.

When he brought up the articles, I wisely deferred to my latrine legal education. I advised him that since I was under twenty-one years of age, any contract I signed was not binding. He suggested waiting until we docked to straighten out the matter.

The day after we landed, Captain Donald and I visited the American Consulate. There my legal education was enhanced with the news that Merchant Marines were considered wards of the government and were bound by articles regardless of age.

In any case, they had agreed to release me and the Canadian government had classified me as a prohibited immigrant. I was given twenty-four hours to get out of the country.

I confirmed that I could do it in a lot less time, and I did. I packed my duffle bag, drew down all of my earned wages, and caught the first train across the border to Seattle, Washington. From there I hitchhiked back to Detroit. I had a date to find treasure in the Cocos Islands.

I had gone out to seek my fortune and had returned with approximately half as much fortune as I had started with. Not only that, My world of opportunity was shrinking. I had been kicked out of three countries and told not to come back.. I began to get the feeling that making a million dollars was a little harder than I had imagined.

PROVERB 37:
When logic tells you to give up your dreams,
sometimes you must give up logic.

CHAPTER 10

THE MORE IMPORTANT THINGS IN LIFE

I arrived back in Detroit in late 1947 still wearing my black Eisenhower jacket and black navy pants. The only thing new was a beard and hair that reached down below my shoulders. Only a small scar remained on the lobe of my right ear where I had worn a gold earring shaped in the outline of Africa. My prized earring had been stolen while I was in prison.

After a shave, haircut, and a fresh set of clothes, I telephoned my old friends and arranged to meet them at the Detroit City Airport to go out and do some parachute jumping just for the fun of it.

There were about five of us standing next to one of the hangars when a stranger walked up and asked us if we were pilots. All of us had handled the controls at one time or another so we all answered "yes."

He introduced himself as a member of the Haganah, a Jewish underground organization that was recruiting pilots to fly for their new country when the United Nations recognized them. None of us knew what he was talking about.

"How much are they paying?" Jim Fitzhenry asked.

"Five-hundred dollars a month and expenses, plus a ten thousand dollar life insurance policy," he replied.

Five-hundred dollars a month was big money and the life insurance of ten-thousand dollars made the offer irresistible. In looking back, I don't know why we should have been the least bit enamored by the prospect of earning the ten thousand dollars that we wouldn't be alive to spend.

There was one other problem. Even though most of us flew, Fitzhenry was the only one who had ever received fighter pilot training in the United States Air Force and had enough flying time to honestly call himself a pilot.

It was big money and adventure and I would have loved to volunteer. Unfortunately, while I had handled a plane in the air, I had never landed one or taken one off the ground. Only Fitzhenry was selected..

Before leaving, the man turned and asked me what I did and I told him I did parachute aerobatics and wing-walking at air shows. He paused for a minute and then asked for my name and telephone number.

"Perhaps they can also use a parachute man."

In less than a week, I was contacted and told that the Haganah needed someone to train parachute packers and to set up a system for dropping supplies to isolated villages. He made me the same offer he made Fitzhenry; five-hundred dollars a month, ten thousand dollars of life insurance, plus expenses. Easy money. I jumped at this golden opportunity.

PROVERB 38:
Never bank a promise made under duress.

My itinerary included a stop at a dime store on Five Mile Road where I was given one-way tickets to New York and Rome plus a hotel address in New York. I was also given a letter authorizing me to pick up two uniforms and a pair of paratroop boots from an Army-Navy store in New York city. After a stop in Paris, I arrived in Rome and checked into the Mediterraneo Hotel to await being smuggled into Palestine.

One morning, I went down to the dining room and took a table near a group of young Finnish tourists who were having a riotous time while eating their breakfast. There were thirteen of them, but my attention was riveted on only one. Her name was Peggy but she was my Madeline from the poem *The Face On The Barroom Floor*, by Hugh Antoine D'Arcy.

> *"Boys, did you ever see a woman*
>   *For whom your soul you'd give,*
> *With a form like the Milo Venus*
>   *Too beautiful to live;*
> *With eyes that would beat the Koh-i-noor,*
>   *And a wealth of chestnut hair?*
> *If so 'twas she, for there never could be*
>   *Another half so fair."*

I was in love. I was hopelessly in love.

Now, I was the youngest of three boys in my family, and having traveled a great deal, I always warned my older brothers never to get married until they had made their fortune. I had always planned on following my own advice.

I don't care about the best laid plans of mice and men. From the moment I saw this girl, a major change in my priorities was ordained; love first, wealth second.

A major problem was that she didn't speak English and I didn't speak any language except English. Despite this handicap, and with the assistance of another girl who could translate, I told Peggy that I was on my way to Palestine to fly with the Jewish air force. I didn't know when I would be leaving but I wanted her to join me.

The moment arrived sooner than expected. Two volunteer pilots were killed while taking off from the Rome airport and all hell was about to break loose. Without a chance to contact Peggy, I was hustled to the airport and secreted away in the cargo compartment of a small South African cargo plane.

I arrived at Haifa Airport and was smuggled past the British guards. In the following days I set up my parachute packing school in a vacant gymnasium around the corner from the Hadassah Hospital in Tel Aviv.

Because of a shortage of personnel, I was asked to volunteer as a bombardier in Israel's fledgling air force and thereafter spent my days teaching parachute packing and my nights flying as a bombardier.

I had no experience as a bombardier so I assumed that they would teach me how to use a Norden Bombsight. On my first night I was instructed to arrive at a small airport on the outskirts of Tel Aviv by 10:00 PM. Not wanting to be late for my first class, I set out early.

As instructed, I stepped to the curb and put out my thumb. The first vehicle I encountered stopped and picked me up. I told him I was going to the airport and I couldn't keep the man from going out of his way to take me all the way to the entrance.

I was directed to a building where about a dozen men were receiving instructions. The field officer read off the evening's targets and then the name of the pilot assigned to each target. When every target was assigned, a man came up and told me I was to go with a certain pilot. I was still expecting an instruction class where I would learn to use a bombsight. It didn't happen.

I followed my pilot out onto the coal black tarmac and looked around for the bombers, e.g., B-17s, B-24s, Halifaxes, and Lancasters. . .where were they? As my eyes adjusted to the darkness, I stared in disbelief. Waiting to take off were three or four Piper Cubs, a couple of Rapids, a cluster of Austers, and a single all-metal Beechcraft Bonanza. All were small civilian pleasure aircraft.

"Where are the bombers?" I asked my pilot.

"You're looking at them," he replied without turning his head.

I tried to keep up, but I kept turning around and staring in disbelief. I had been told that the Israelis had all kinds of modern aircraft. Someone had lied.

"This is the Primo Squadron. Sometimes we're a fighter squadron. Sometimes we're a supply squadron. At night we're a bomber squadron," he informed me.

The pilot led me to the nice shiny Beechcraft Bonanza and told me to climb in and sit with my back to the instrument panel. The passenger seat and the luggage door had been removed, so I was sitting on hard metal framework with a gaping hole next to my left leg. Pretty soon a Jeep pulled up and the driver and his helper loaded three homemade twenty-five pound percussion bombs into the luggage space. These were stood upright resting on their flat noses and held upright by my right leg. The next bomb in was a one hundred pounder. That took the two of them to load. It was laid flat with the nose pointing out the baggage compartment doorway. One of the men pointed to a pin inserted in the nose detonator.

"Make sure you pull this out before you shove the bomb out or it won't go off," he warned. Then he pointed to another pin stuck through a spinner between the fins of the bomb.

"Make sure you also pull out this pin," he ordered. "When the pilot tells you to get ready, shove the bomb half way out and wrap your arms around the fins and hold it until the pilot tells you to let go. Then just let go."

The man disappeared and then returned with a large bundle of silver cylinders about sixteen inches long and tied together with a cord tied around the center.

"These are incendiaries. Remove a couple of them from the center and when the pilot tells you to, throw all of them out. They'll scatter on their way down and ignite on hitting the ground. That will light up your target area. You will make three passes. On the second pass you will throw out the three twenty-five pound bombs and on your last pass you will dump the hundred pound bomb. Just wait until your pilot tells you what to do."

I sat there looking at all the explosives around me. When I looked up, the men and their jeep were gone. Congratulations. I had just graduated from the Israeli bombardier school.

Over the next few weeks I operated the parachute packing school for the air force during the day, and every night I would hitch a ride to the airport and fly out as a bombardier.

In a very short time it became apparent that the Israelis did not have any of the modern equipment I had been told they possessed. Even the parachutes were remnants of the English occupation. Many had been found sitting in warehouses or basements and their canopies and thread were so rotted that you could poke a finger through the material. These were sorted out and destroyed.

Not only were they short of boots for their troops, but they also had only one rifle for every seven soldiers. At that time, almost all of their armaments were captured from the Arabs. I found out that the reason we flew only at night was because we didn't have a single plane that could protect us from the Egyptian spitfires flown by ex-Nazi pilots.

After one harrowing flight to bomb a concentration of Egyptian troops outside of Lydia Airport, I came back with the feeling that it was only a matter of time before our luck ran out. On that last mission the anti aircraft fire was so concentrated that I could not believe we survived it.

We were outnumbered a thousand to one and the United States was enforcing a strict embargo against shipping any military equipment to Israel. At the same time, England and France openly continued to ship their latest model Spitfires, tanks, and artillery to Egypt, Syria, Libya, Iraq, and Jordan, while enforcing the embargo of military goods to the Israelis.

As I sat alone in my room that morning, I felt, with certainty that there was no way the Jews could prevail.

I was quite familiar with the stories of what happened to captured airmen and prepared against that event by having a friend buy me the cheapest gun he could find in Italy, an inadequate 25-caliber Beretta automatic. It was usless as an offensive weapon, but it could prevent my being taken alive if I were ever shot down.

After the previous evening's bombing run, I could only believe that it was just a matter of time.

I sat awake the rest of the morning trying to decide whether to stay or get the hell out of there. After weighing the alternatives, the sum of five hundred dollars didn't seem to matter any more. It was one of those times that try a man's soul.

While in the merchant marines I had visited Germany. I knew about Dachau and the Holocaust. It wasn't about money anymore. It was about justice. It was about right and wrong, and I had always preached never to be neutral. A person ought to support what is right.

There was only one decision I could have made. I packed up my pictures and other very personal items and gave them to a friend to mail to my parents. All my dreams of wealth and success were no longer important. Expecting the worst, I decided to stay to the end.

PROVERB 39:
Making a moral decision
is like choosing a color.
But, you must never choose plaid.

Only a few days later I was instructing a class of parachute riggers when a new group of trainees was brought into the classroom. I looked down from the podium and there among the girls was the most beautiful girl I had ever seen, Peggy.

A few weeks later, we were married on July 4th in a wedding provided for us by the State. A Unitarian and a Lutheran were married in an orthodox Jewish wedding ceremony by a Jewish rabbi; the first international event in the new State of Israel. My total wealth, less than a hundred dollars, was in my wallet. The vicissitudes of war.

PROVERB 40:
When addressing affairs of the heart,
always leave a forwarding address.

Six days later, I was on my way to a secret camp in the Czechoslovakian Sudetenland to take a course in sabotage, espionage, and guerrilla warfare. I was to help train a group of young Jewish death camp survivors to be the nucleus of an Israeli paratroop battalion. The Israeli's new secret weapon.

Five of us were flying from Haifa to Czechoslovakia in a newly acquired Lockheed Constellation that had been purchased for its scrap value. While we were violating Albanian air space, the Albanians opened fire on us with antiaircraft guns and struck a vital hydraulic line. We were able to continue on to Zatek Airfield in Czechoslovakia, and crash landed on the runway. We had lost our entire hydraulic system; flaps, landing gear, and steering. It was another miracle, but I walked away without a scratch.

Six weeks later, I returned to Israel and was appointed to set up and command a paratroop training school on top of Mt. Carmel. I was twenty-one years old.

There were events that space does not permit me to relate here, like the time I fought a duel with a Nazi pilot flying an English Spitfire.

I became the first man to make a parachute jump in the new country and the first man to lead a squad of Israeli paratroopers in Israel's first paratroop exercise. These accomplishments are a sort of compensation that few people will ever equal or exceed. There are many things that money cannot buy.

There was another concession, and ironically it involved my military pay. When I returned from Czechoslovakia I was notified that I was officially transferred from the air force to the new paratroop branch of the army and my monthly "hazard allowance" was terminated because jumping out of airplanes was not as dangerous as flying.

Over the next several months the tide of battle turned. Not only did the various Israeli factions meld into a unified fighting force, they had smuggled in or captured enough artillery pieces, guns, tanks, and airplanes to turn back the "invincible" armies of seven Arab nations. What they couldn't buy, they made out of the material on hand.

I lost my job as a bombardier when they replaced me with bomb racks on those little planes. From then on the pilots controlled the release of bombs with two cables running to the instrument panel.

After the capture of Beersheba in late 1948, a "final" truce was agreed to. It was apparent that the war was ending. Like the Israelis and the Western nations, I really believed there would be no more fighting and decided to return to America. A few weeks before Christmas, 1948, Peggy and I boarded a ship bound for New York. It was time to return to the States and begin our lives in normal surroundings.

When we arrived in New York, the people who were supposed to meet us failed to show up. Around midnight I placed a collect call to my sister and she wired us enough money for train tickets to Detroit.

When I asked my parents about all the money supposedly sent to them, they didn't know what I was talking about. There had been no five-hundred dollar payments or even an insurance policy. I didn't care.

Contrary to feeling cheated, I really felt relieved. I would have been embarrassed to have to admit that I volunteered in that fight and received money for it. Instead, I became a volunteer. I fought for what I believed was a just cause. It was the right thing to do. I learned something else. I learned that there are causes in this world that must come ahead of the pursuit of wealth and riches.

I came away with something equally valuable; a couple of medals and citations. One reads:

> *For service above and beyond the call of duty.*
The other citation reads:
> *For heroism and courage without hesitation.*

I would not try to explain my own behavior, but life has confirmed, for me at least, that heros are not born on the battlefield. They possess a trait of character that is born and nurtured throughout one's life. A coward will instinctively flee the arena of challenge while the hero will instinctively face the challenge, even at the expense of his life. Age, sex, race and religion are not factors.

PROVERB 41:
On the scales of life, the gift of liberty
is more precious than the profit of gold.

I have written much about the character of success; the need to share in order to make this a better world for everyone. Almost everyday I see or hear about unselfish acts of individuals whose deeds go unheralded in order to make space for news of the wanton acts of those who abuse the privilege of freedom. These are the stories that reinforce my confidence in our next generation.

One of those stories concerns a little girl named Liz who was suffering from a rare and deadly blood disease. Her only chance of recovery appeared to be a blood transfusion from her five-year old brother who had miraculously survived the same disease and had developed the antibodies needed to combat the illness.

The doctor explained the situation to her little brother and asked the young boy if he would be willing to give his blood to his sister so that she could live.

After only a moment's pause the boy replied, "Yes, if it will save her."

As the transfusion progressed, he lay in bed next to his sister and joined everyone in smiling as the color returned to his sister's cheeks. Then, suddenly the boy's face turned solemn as his smile faded away. He turned his head and eyes toward the doctor and asked in a trembling voice, "Will I start to die right away?"

Being young, the little boy misunderstood the doctor. He thought that in order to save his sister's life he was going to have to give her all his blood.

At that young age, that little boy defined character. He was, and will always be, a hero. He has everything it takes to be a success in business, and our world will be better off because of his generation.

PROVERB 42:
Sometimes the most important things in life
can only be purchased by
the most important things in life.

CHAPTER 11

OFF ON THE ROAD TO SUCCESS

Marriage changed everything except my desire to become financially successful. To many people, success means a steady job with a steady income. To me, success was being able to live like a millionaire while being able to pay the cost of doing so. That's living.

I am reminded of a story about a small town millionaire who passed away leaving explicit instructions on how his funeral was to be conducted. On the appointed day his heirs had the old gravedigger dig a huge pit. They sat the deceased millionaire in the driver's seat of his Mercedes limousine, stuck one of his ten dollar cigars in his mouth, lit it, and had the limousine lowered into the grave. Lastly, they ordered the elderly gravedigger to fill in the grave.

After everyone left, the gravedigger threw two shovels of dirt on top of the limousine and then stopped.

Unable to restrain himself, he jumped down into the grave and stared at the millionaire through the windows.

He shook his head as he ran his eyes over the dead man's fine tuxedo and top hat. He observed the huge diamond ring on his finger and the fine Perdomo cigar burning in his mouth. The old man continued shaking his head back and forth and muttering, "Man, that's living!"

PROVERB 43:
The dimensions of success are best judged by the individual seeking it.

Living means different things to different people. To the born entrepreneur, life is not worth living without being creative. He has to succeed and takes his failures in stride. He doesn't give in and he doesn't give up. I wish I had always abided by this philosophy. Too many times I listened to the timid harbingers of failure. Still, despite these occasions, I never really gave up on my main goal.

In my early days, grown-ups were happy to settle for the steady job with a weekly paycheck. Security was paramount, and it usually came from working for someone else. This was especially true according to my wife. In Finland, most people settled for any kind of steady employment. She had never heard of a mortgage or a credit card. You didn't buy a car or a house unless you paid with cash. You certainly didn't borrow thousands of dollars from a bank to launch a new business venture. Before World War II most Finnish people never owned a car and if you lived in an urban city, you lived your entire life in a rented apartment.

Despite Peggy's objections, I was determined to have my own home and my own business and it was Peggy who gave me my first idea.

One day, I caught her darning the holes in my socks with an unusual tool. The common darning instrument was a large egg-shaped wooden head on a wooden handle.

Peggy's Finnish darning tool was shaped like a large mushroom on a handle and had a groove around the side of the head. She would slide the tool into the sock, center the hole on top of the headpiece, and then slip a continuous metal spring down into the groove. That way the stocking stayed in place without holding it, while she wove the hole closed.

"What a great idea!" I thought. Here was my chance to make a million dollars.

I designed a similar tool and went out for quotations on the wood fixture and the spring. The next step was to have a dozen prototypes made. They worked perfectly. Now I was ready to do some market research.

I learned quickly that I had my priorities mixed. If I had done my research first I would have learned that women didn't darn their husband's socks any more. After World War II they just threw them away and bought new socks made of new types of thread that seemed to last forever. The days of sock darning had gone the way of the buggy whip.

Unfortunately, I think my wife was the last person in America to darn socks. Timing is everything! You've got to know your market.

If you don't think timing is everything, let me give you another example. When we were living in Kansas City, Missouri, I became friendly with a fellow named Lester who drove a gasoline delivery truck servicing gas stations along route 66.

I wouldn't hold Lester up as a paragon of entrepreneurial virtue, but more as a paragon of unprincipled opportunism and an endorsement of the adage that timing is everything.

It was obvious that Lester was either extremely well paid or extremely generous. One evening in a drinking session at a local tavern, I learned Lester's secret for making money.

At most of the gas stations Lester served, he had arranged to install a condom machine and a machine that dispensed little pornographic booklets. Each item required the deposit of a twenty-five cent coin. Now, a lot of gas stations had these machines in the men's bathrooms, but this is where Lester deviated from the norm.

Lester installed his machines in the women's bathrooms and his machines were altered so that the coins went directly down into the coin collection box without discharging any product.

Lester never put any product into his machines and in that day and age, no woman ever confronted the station attendant to demand her product or her money back.

Do you think you could get away with that today? You'd probably end up in federal court facing a class action suit by a million women. Times change. People change. Products change. Above all, women have changed!

PROVERB 44:
Timing! Timing! Timing!
Location is important,
but timing is everything!

Reluctantly, I started applying for different jobs and was at last offered the position of bookkeeper with a small plastics firm called Cadillac Plastics Company.

This is a classic story. During and after the war, Dow Chemical, General Electric, and others were producing more varieties of plastics than they knew what to do with. In fact, there wasn't a market for most of these new plastics. Their interest however, was only in developing and manufacturing the plastics. They needed someone else to distribute and market their product.

A fellow named Jacobs saw an opportunity and procured the distribution rights for as many of the non-competing plastics as possible. Some people thought he was crazy.

Jacobs opened a small shop and made the plastics available to the public. In the beginning most of his business was with children who made rings or knickknacks out of the plastic. Schoolchildren and teachers of manual training classes were the first major source of sales.

Eventually he turned the business over to his two sons who continued exploring markets for Plexiglas and other forms of plastic. Their first big order was furnishing Plexiglas tops for a special model of Ford Motor Company automobiles. It turned out to be another of Ford's great ideas that didn't work.

Cadillac Plastics was the company that hired me as their bookkeeper after Peggy and I returned to America.

The first thing I noticed was their secretary. She was not only a fox, but she also pretty much had the run of the hen house. It seemed apparent to everyone that she had a very close relationship with one or both of the brothers.

The second thing I noticed was that all the stationery and office supplies were kept in the vault with the cash and checks. Everyone, including people from the shop, would walk through the main office and go into the vault for such minor items as a pencil or paper clips.

One of my first acts, over the objections of the secretary, was to bar anyone who didn't have a need, from going into the vault. At the same time I had the pencils and other supplies moved out of the safe and placed in a separate cabinet. From that day forward I wanted the vault door kept closed.

The next day I arrived at work to find the vault door wide open and the stationery supplies back in the vault. When asked why she did it, the secretary replied that she wanted everything in the vault.

I complained to the two brothers who told me they didn't want to be bothered with trivial matters and to take care of it myself. I did. At least I thought I did. When I completed the bank deposit that evening, I warned the secretary not to contradict my orders again.

The following morning, I was called into the Jacobs' office and told that my bank deposit was short by sixty dollars. I simply argued that it couldn't be. My math skills were excellent and I always tallied up the checks and cash twice to insure the deposit was correct. The matter was dismissed. That night I checked the deposit over and over until I was absolutely certain everything was proper.

When I arrived the next morning, I was called into their office again and told that the previous day's balance was over by forty dollars. It was obvious that someone was playing games, and the only people who had access to the completed deposits were the Jacobs brothers, their secretary, and me. Rather than continuing with this game, I demanded that the brothers choose between their secretary and me.

They fired me on the spot.

That was the first and last time I ever gave an employer such an opportune moment.

In time, Cadillac Plastics grew to be one of world's largest distributors of plastic, with offices in almost every major city and country. Eventually, General Electric Company bought them out.

PROVERB 45:
A sexy secretary is like a malady.
You can get better, but you can't win.

My next job was back in a factory as a timekeeper for Saylor-Beale Corporation, a small manufacturer of past-model automobile bumpers for General Motors, Ford, and Chrysler.

The plant was boiling hot due to all the heat treating operations and filthy due to the nature of the work. I was working the midnight shift and my supervisor was a nag of a man, who had probably spent most of his life with the company.

To save money, Peggy packed me a lunch everyday in a little brown bag, accompanied by a thermos full of coffee. At lunchtime each night, the other timekeeper, the supervisor, and I would sit around a wooden table and eat our food. After two months I confided to the fellows that I wanted something better than this job. I told them I was going back to college during the day and get a degree.

All of a sudden my supervisor reached across the table and grabbed my lunch bag. He raised it high in the air and started rattling the bag furiously.

"You hear that, Leeds? Do you hear that?" he yelled. "You're going to hear that sound the rest of your life. You're no different than the rest of us! You'll be eating your lunch out of a brown paper bag for the rest of your life!"

The next morning I went out and bought a metal lunchbox and told my wife never to pack me a lunch in a paper bag again! I never again carried a lunch in any kind of bag! I also enrolled in college.

Next, I applied for a job as a time study operator at the Kaiser-Frazer automobile factory in Ypsilanti, Michigan, and got the job. The nice part was that I worked in clean surroundings with people who were more educated and looking for an opportunity to advance themselves.

Unfortunately, employment was very erratic. I would work for four months and then get laid off for four months. It went on this way for over a year.

One of my coworkers didn't worry about layoffs. He kept telling me how he had built up almost a half million dollars in assets without risking any of his own capital. I couldn't wait to learn how he did it.

"Real estate," he said. "I buy apartment buildings that people can't sell. I offer them a low price and buy the buildings on a land contract with almost no money down! I'll be worth a million dollars in a few years!"

His wasn't a unique idea. Several real estate investors were offering seminars or selling books which told people how to get rich in real estate by doing exactly what he was doing. They offered an almost foolproof plan.

Unfortunately, Norman didn't read their books or buy one of the seminars. He knew the upside, but he never learned the downside until it was too late.

Suddenly, the country experienced a terrible recession. Thousands of people lost their jobs, among them a high percentage of people who lived in his rundown tenements. He didn't buy depressed properties, fix them up, and then sell them at a profit. He just accumulated slum properties thinking the rents would make him a rich man.

Unfortunately, his cash flow quickly went into the negative column and expenses were eating him alive. He couldn't even give his properties away, so he just abandoned them. Instead of becoming an "instant millionaire", he was forced to file bankruptcy and became such a nervous wreck that he even lost his job.

I decided not to get rich by buying distressed properties. That said, over the years I did make hundreds of thousands of dollars through buying and selling my own homes. I think we moved about every three years and, except for one occasion, I used the sales money to buy a much nicer home than the one I sold. This didn't require any brains and involved few risks. For one reason or another, thousands of nice homes are sacrificed each year due to divorce, death, bankruptcy, and a hundred other reasons. It's a great way for young couples to build their equity, but it will only work for people willing to go through the rigors of packing and unpacking every few years.

When the torment of intermittent and uncertain employment with Kaiser-Frazer became intolerable, I started scanning the want ads again. I came across a Ford Motor Company ad for a time study man. I applied and got the job.

The job led to a transfer to Ford's Defense Products Division in Claycomo, Missouri.

This new plant was built to produce the wings for the new B-47 Bombers. Another man and I were assigned to set the standards for manufacturing the wings.

The nice part about the job was that the two of us would be working twelve-hour shifts, six days a week, and everything over forty hours was time and a half pay. I was making more than I ever made in my life and I was spending more than I ever spent in my life. The overtime was only part of it. Every three months we were rated and I always received the top rating and a subsequent wage increase. I wasn't about to let all that money just lay around.

Peggy and I bought a small home on a choice piece of lakefront property and immediately contracted to build a huge addition. Not only did we enjoy it, but my boss did also. Although he lived twenty-five miles away, he still showed up with his wife every Sunday for a barbecue and swimming.

One constant source of irritation was the man's wife. She hated the drive. She hated swimming. She didn't like wasting her Sundays at my house, and I think she hated me for all these reasons. At least she blamed me for being dragged to my house every Sunday.

A few days before Christmas, the plant manager put out a bulletin stating the day shift would only work until noon on the day before Christmas and regular shifts would resume at 8:00 AM on the twenty-sixth.

To me it was apparent that I would not have to work until six AM on the twenty-fourth and then come back and work from 8 am until noon on the same day.

My boss straightened me out. He really did want me to work my six to six shift, go home for two hours and then come back and work from eight AM until noon. It's ridiculous how some bosses can misunderstand a simple communication. In addition, I lived twenty miles from the plant and it took me forty minutes to drive each way.

I tried to reason with my boss, but to no avail. He kept insisting that it would be unfair for only one man in the department to get off. The fact that I was the only man in the department working from six in the evening till six AM the next morning made no difference to him.

I wasn't entirely sure I was correct so I went to the manager's administrative assistant and explained the situation. He agreed with me one-hundred percent and told me not to worry about it, and not to plan on working the morning of the twenty-fourth.

At five PM on the 23rd when I arrived for work, my boss came over and said, "I understand you got tomorrow off. Well, here's something else; I'm giving you the rest of the year off. You're fired."

PROVERB 46:
Your boss' interpretation
is always the correct one.

PROVERB 47:
In a contest, it is the fool who raises his voice
and the wise man who raises his sights.

That was it. A plant protection officer escorted me out of the building and I was never allowed back in to challenge my discharge.

PROVERB 48:
A "secure" position only offers temporary security.

Since then, the legal system has learned to address these types of actions, but be aware, companies have more than one way to skin a cat.

Our ongoing house expansion left us with no financial reserves so it was time to sink or swim. If I couldn't swim I was going to tread water like hell to keep my head above water.

Despite the fact that the state's largest employer, Boeing Aircraft, had just laid off several thousand employees, I landed a job with a small company that manufactured grain storage bins and grain drying bins. Both bins were almost identical except that one had a perforated floor so a blower could blow air up through the grain to eliminate moisture. Government regulations limited the amount of moisture in grain to be sold.

I got one of my brainstorms and designed a grain bin with an interchangeable floor that could be used for drying or storage. It flew like a rock.

My boss, Joe Kornhauser, was a very timid and quiet individual. When he saw my design he started muttering and accusing me of trying to put the company out of business. He insisted that farmers would only buy one bin instead of two and our sales would be cut in half. I didn't agree but he left me no alternative other than to go back to the drawing board.

Nothing was the same after that. Kornhauser would sit at his desk in the front of the room and ignore me completely. He ignored me until the day one of those raucous, loudmouthed salesmen called on him.

Apparently, the salesman knew Joe pretty well. After reviewing some orders, he turned to leave and got as far as my desk when he turned and yelled out, "Hey, Joe, what say we go out tonight and get some strange stuff?"

Joe appeared startled. He started stuttering while he tried to think of an appropriate reply. Finally he thought of something.

"No thanks," he replied, "I've got more than I can handle at home."

As quick as a wink the salesman replied, "OK, let's go over to your house then."

I couldn't restrain myself. I slapped my drawing board and burst out in laughter followed by everyone else in the room. Joe just sat there with his mouth wide open not knowing what to say.

On Friday I was fired.

PROVERB 49:
In the presence of others,
        your superior's humor is superior.

Jobs were pretty tight and it didn't appear that any of the manufacturing plants would be hiring. In fact, no one was hiring and we were getting pretty scared. A solution appeared in the form of my Farmer's Insurance man, John Harvey.

John listened to my hard-luck story and then invited me to become an insurance salesman. He said that Missouri had just passed a state law requiring every motorist to carry liability insurance and Farmer's Insurance Group had the lowest rates in the state. He assured me there was more business out there than he could write and urged me to become an agent for Farmer's.

Since John's brother, Dexter, was the district agent, all I had to do was read a manual and take the test. The idea of being my own boss with an income commensurate with my effort appealed to me. I read the rules, took the test, and became a licensed Missouri insurance agent.

When the weekend came around, I celebrated my new job by taking Peggy to a drive-in movie. Prior to the movie, several short films advertising various products and services filled the screen. What a great idea, I thought. Where else could an automobile insurance message be seen only by automobile owners, than in a drive-in theater? I'd have a captive audience.

The following Monday, John and I contacted several film production sources until we found a short film showing two cars colliding and then some doctors and lawyers. The film ended with the warning that the State of Missouri had enacted a new law requiring automobile liability insurance. At the very end it told the reader to call our telephone number.

It turned out to be a goldmine so we ran the ad in several drive-in theaters everyday for the next month. The cost was insignificant compared to the volume of insurance we wrote. Between the two of us, we wrote more automobile liability insurance than all other Kansas City agents combined.

Unfortunately, after about a month, there were very few motorists left to insure and my lucrative venture began to falter. My problem was, being a new agent, I didn't have enough immediate renewals to cover my contracted home remodeling debts.

Ultimately we sold our home at a substantial loss and headed back to Detroit where we moved into a public housing development.

We were back to square one.

PROVERB 50:
Pleasing your immediate boss
can be fifty-one percent of your success.

CHAPTER 12

CUSTOMERS WANTED

Going back to school under the veteran's GI Bill of Rights provided us with a little money but not nearly enough to live on. I had to find another source of income. A possible solution came when I was walking down Linwood Avenue, a major thoroughfare in Detroit. I was reading the store signs when it hit me. I noticed that many of the neon signs hanging out from the buildings were old and the painted message on the metal had faded or peeled off to the point you could barely read the writing.

I went to the post office and bought one hundred penny postcards and began typing a short message on the backs:

Sir, please take a look at your sign.

I deliberately left off my name and address. On the front of each card, I printed the address of a store whose sign was in disrepair. I attached a stamp and promptly mailed out the hundred cards.

I was so sure of myself that I went out and bought a quart of every color sign paint. The following day I borrowed a couple of paint brushes and one of my father's extension ladders, tied the ladder to the top of my 1937 Chevrolet, and took off.

I stopped at my first prospect's store and introduced myself as the man behind the "Sign Copy Company." I offered to repaint both sides of his sign with two coats of "genuine, long lasting" sign paint. My charge would be ten dollars.

It was a great idea, but not a money making one. I wasn't an artist. In fact, I couldn't even retrace the old letters without going over the lines a few times. Sometimes, it would take me two days just to paint a single sign. In addition, I often had to remove the fragile neon tubing before I could paint a sign and if I broke a piece, I had to pay to replace it. I had plenty of clients. I just didn't have the time or the skill for this kind of work. I ended up doubling my rates and probably could have tripled them, but something happened to persuade me to quit.

It was a terribly hot day and I was working on a fair-sized sign hanging in front of a tavern. It took me about two days to complete the sign, during which time the owner never once offered me as much as a glass of water.

When I was finished, the owner came out to inspect the sign. It was a beautiful job but he found one fault. The neon didn't light up. The owner swore it worked before I took it apart but it wasn't working now.

I put my ladder back up and removed all the neon from both sides of the sign. The next day I took the neon to a shop and had each piece tested. Everything checked out fine. Something else had to be the problem. I replaced the neon on the sign but it still didn't work. The bar owner blamed me and refused to pay me.

Suddenly I got a hunch that the trouble might be with the switch so I drove over to Sears and picked up an inexpensive continuity checker. Sure enough, the switch was defective. Still the bar owner insisted it was my fault and the only way I would get paid was to replace the switch. I drove back to Sears, bought a new switch and installed it. The neon lit up and I finally got my twenty dollars. I found out that it takes three things to make a good business arrangement: a skill, a fair price, and an honest client!

PROVERB 51:
Do not seek to profit where integrity is absent.

Self-employment hadn't worked out as I had hoped. It was once more time to try being an employee.

Actually, I didn't want to just be an employee. I wanted to be something more, something with a little class to the title. I saw just the right ad. It was titled Manager Wanted. Doesn't every employee aspire to become a Manager?

The job turned out to be for a man to manage six drive-in restaurants.

At the time, the H & N System owned and operated twelve fast-food restaurants in Detroit and its suburbs. Coffee sold for five cents a cup and hamburgers were ten cents.

The employment manager, Allen Lambert, was a gruff looking fellow in his forties and apparently I was just the kind of guy he was looking for. Thinking back, I don't think this reflects favorably on my mental proclivities.

The owners of the company were two men named Heinke and Nu. I would never meet either of the men and all I ever knew about them was that they were supposed to be very rich. In fact, they spent their time on a private island somewhere in northern Michigan.

The one thing that Lambert stressed was that H & N was a fast growing company with lots of opportunity.

PROVERB 52:
When an employer tells you
a job has opportunities,
have him itemize them in writing.

If nothing else, I did learn a lot about the fast-food restaurant business. I also learned a great deal about the employees who worked there and the people who ran the company.

For one thing, almost all of our employees were either young women who were on parole, young women who were desperate to make a few dollars just to survive on, or married women out looking for some extramarital relationships. To make matters worse, Lambert kept a photograph collection of most of the waitresses sans clothing. As I said, I learned an awful lot about the employees.

I took the job because I was also desperate and I knew nothing about how this H & N restaurant chain operated at the time.

My day was supposed to begin at eight AM, but I always had to be at the office at seven-thirty so I could call each restaurant and make sure the day-shift employees had shown up. If a restaurant was short two or three employees, and we expected a busy day, I actually had to drive out to the missing employee's homes, physically drag them out of bed and take them to work.

After making sure we were properly staffed, I would head out to visit each restaurant to inventory the stock and balance the cash register.

Now, let me assure you that this restaurant chain had developed a system that could balance our nation's national debt.

Every portion of food and drink was accurately dispensed and accounted for. If my memory serves me correctly, the hamburgers were shipped to the restaurant on trays with twenty little meatballs to a tray. The total weight of ten meatballs was one pound!

Actually they weren't twenty meatballs. They were twenty balls comprised of a certain percentage of pure fat, a certain percentage of tough gristle, and a very small amount of the least expensive red meat available.

I suppose you are wondering how to make a hamburger out of 1.6 ounces of faux meat. Move over Martha Stewart. It's easy. You take your biggest and heaviest counter girl and make her the fry cook. At the appropriate time she presses her spatula down on the little meatball with all her weight until it expands to the size of the bun. Unfortunately, the little pieces of fat melt on the hot grill and disappear, so if you held the hamburger patty up, you could read the *Wall Street Journal* through it. That was why you piled on any combination of inexpensive fried onions, mustard, and/or ketchup.

Buns were always counted, as were the large cans of beans, chili, and soup. In fact, every food item was accurately counted.

Glasses held six ounces of soda and the other food was apportioned out with a specific ladle that held exactly four, six, or eight ounces. I still recall that a large can of beans provided twenty-eight servings.

After a while, I learned to look into any pot and accurately tell how many servings remained.

After I figured out how much food was missing and checking the register, I knew if someone was "knocking down" the register.

If I had too much money or not enough, I knew the employee wasn't smart enough to keep track of how much she should have taken out of the register. Management even had a way of moving girls from one shift to another or even one restaurant to another, to determine who was stealing.

If the cash appeared fifteen or twenty-five cents short a good manager was expected to line all the girls up and threaten to fire everyone if the money wasn't back in the drawer by the following morning.

The money would always reappear. In fact, the drawer would usually have too much money because none of the girls wanted to be fired so several would put in the missing money. I couldn't help but marvel at the system.

Now, a lot of these girls were graduates of classes in the big stone arena and knew how to play the game. They would come to work with their own supply of buns and meatballs and would proceed to sell their own hamburgers and pocket the money. That way, as long as they took the correct amount out of the register, the cash drawer always balanced. For this reason I had to take inventory and check the cash drawer at random times. It wasn't hard to eventually catch a dishonest employee.

Aside from a total lack of scruples by my employers and my employees, there were only one or two problems with this prestigious job. Namely, an eight-hour job took from twelve to sixteen hours to do; I was driving sixty miles a day in my own car without any gas allowance, and I was made to personally feel guilty when anything went wrong.

PROVERB 53:
**Beware of the management position that
entitles you to work all kinds of overtime
without additional compensation.**

PROVERB 54:
**When you work sixteen hours a day in your own
business, you are an entrepreneur.
When you work sixteen hours a day
in someone else's business,
you may just be a fool.**

I also was given the impression that Messrs. Heinke and Nu might not be able to afford their next Mercedes because one of my restaurants came up short fifty cents. When the second Christmas passed without so much as a raise, a card, or a thank you, I decided I had had enough of the restaurant business.

When I gave my notice, Mr. Lambert feigned distress. He reminded me again that we were like a family and how it was really fun to be a part of a growing business and that having fun in life was just as important as making money. I remember my exact response.

"Mr. Lambert, I've had all the fun I can afford. Now I'm going out and make some money!"

PROVERB 55:
In work, given a choice between having fun or making money, take the money.

My next wantad venture was in the television antenna business.

These were the early days of television and what the world needed then was a good, cheap, outdoor antenna. The Vorta Mark antenna was the answer.
Read the merits of this electronic-less wonder:
"The VORTA MARK II with the New Look in Television Antennas. Eliminates costly installations, rotors and unsightly shapes. *Impervious to ANY weather condition.* The TV Antenna for all sets! There's no other like the Vorta Antenna. . . brings in exceptionally sharp, balanced, no-fade COLOR and BLACK & WHITE PICTURES in VHF and UHF! Especially designed for fringe and suburban areas. Powerful FM Stereo Radio Reception. You can install the 8 by 18½ inch dome *on the roof or in the attic* in a few minutes. A completely new breakthrough in TV reception! No change of terminals necessary when switching from VHF to UHF. Available in 75 OHM Co-Axial Cable."

In addition to its glowing claims, the company also listed a distinguished list of users including the U.S. Army Corps of Engineers!

The unit retailed for $49.95 and I could buy them wholesale for only $23.75. Where else could I find a deal like this?

What really impressed me was how particular they were in giving out exclusive sales territories. I figured I just lucked out at getting the entire city of Detroit. But it wasn't that easy. They weren't going to accept me unless I purchased one unit at $32.00 and tested it myself. Boy, I could tell they were a high class operation.

When I received my first unit I connected the antenna wires and, with Peggy monitoring the picture, I walked all over our roof until she yelled "OK." Then, I put the unit down and screwed it to the roof. I climbed down and went inside. The picture was beautiful. I was ecstatic. Unfortunately, when I turned to Channel 7, the picture was all fuzzy. Only then did I realize you had keep walking around until you located a position where most of the channels would be visible.

I climbed back on the roof, unscrewed the unit, and began walking around again. Finally we decided on a location where the reception on most of the channels seemed satisfactory. I didn't think the reception was any better than my rabbit-ears antenna, but it didn't appear any worse.

I registered my business name and became the International Video Signal Generating Company. *(Think Big. Act Big. Do Big.)*

Over the next few months I averaged one sale a day. Not great, but I was just beginning. On the other hand, the more units I installed, the more my doubts grew. The apparent fact was that no matter where I located the antenna, I could never bring in more than one or two channels clearly. I could never bring in the majority. The units didn't appear quite as omni-directional as claimed.

I began wondering what, if anything, was embedded in the plastic that filled the helmet-shaped antenna. I thought of cutting one open, but I was afraid to. I had a horrible feeling that someone was going to open up a unit and find a wire clothes hanger.

I turned once more to the want ads. Fortunately, a job offering steady income made it possible to resolve my dilemma.

A friend told me that General Motors was opening a new plant in Plymouth, Michigan and was hiring. Plymouth was only about twenty miles away so I drove out and applied for any kind of salaried position. I was hired as a time study clerk, the lowest position in the Work Standards Department. For a welcome change, this new job offered me a good wage, health insurance, and most of all, security. We were still living in a public housing development called Herman Gardens.

Herman Gardens was a rent-subsidized community of two-story apartment buildings. Across the hall from us lived a single mother and her twelve-year-old daughter. Both were alcoholics and a disproportionate amount of their welfare money was spent on beer that the two of them shared. Above us lived Kay, the girlfriend of a prominent imprisoned Detroit mobster. She rarely left her apartment and claimed she had a little black book containing all kinds of mob information, including the names and addresses of mob associates. Whenever she alluded to this book, which she did frequently, she would whisper, "They would kill me if they knew I had this book."

Across the hall from Kay, lived Francis. Francis lived with her two young daughters, Dottie, three, and Myrna, nine. Francis was still married to a serviceman who had suffered a head wound in the Normandy invasion and was confined to the mental ward of a local military hospital.

Each child had been born nine months after her husband's last two escapes.

Enterprisingly, Francis ran a sort of free-lance entertainment center for visiting service men. These were not military servicemen, but electricians, plumbers, typewriter repairmen, butchers, and a host of other passing tradesmen. I dare say I don't think she paid cash for anything her family ate or wore. To our good fortune, an ice cream vendor became so enamored with Francis, that she was able to keep us provisioned with a never ending supply of ice cream bars. Francis even boasted of how she had worked out a system of signals using her window shades so two visitors wouldn't present themselves at the same time.

It was pretty much the same story throughout the community. Peggy and I had resolved to escape this social cesspool before our children became aware of what was going on around us. It was an unfit place for adults to live, let alone children. The position with General Motors made it possible and we seized the first opportunity to move to a modest single story house in Franklin Knolls, Michigan.

My new employment had a narcotic effect. I so enjoyed the security and the pay, that I was content to just maintain the status quo.

Working as a clerk for three or four years was fine until I woke up one day and realized that almost everyone around me had been promoted, but not me. Several had advanced in classification, which earned them much more respect and a higher salary. I went to work everyday, but no one noticed me.

It wasn't anything in particular that lit my fuse. I just woke up and decided I wanted more. More rank, more privileges, and especially more money.

Someone once said to me, *"To be successful you have to think big, act big, and do big!"* Then he held out his hands with an imaginary gift and said, "Here, have an oil well."

The more I observed business life, the more I understood what he meant.

That morning I shined my shoes until they sparkled. I put my worn sport coat away, put on a white shirt, red tie, and my black church-going suit, and went to work. People noticed me.

At first there were a lot of jokes from my coworkers, but I just smiled and said I had worn out my work clothes. In a short time the jokes ceased.

Except for the plant manager, I was probably the only man who was seen in the shop with polished shoes, a white shirt, tie, and suit. I also did something else. I stopped being a clown. I got very serious about everything.

PROVERB 56:
Distinguish yourself.
Successful businessmen
do not wear matching uniforms.

To let management know that I desired more, I reenrolled in college for evening classes. After earning my Bachelor of Arts degree in Industrial Engineering, I enrolled for a Master's degree in Business Administration. It wasn't as much for the knowledge as it was to meet management's (and society's) demand for the credentials of a college degree.

PROVERB 57:
A college degree is like a driver's license.
It makes it possible to go places faster.

Shortly after these changes, the union decided to call a strike at General Motors. Unsure if we would have access to the plant, the manager decided we should take most of our cost estimating documents home with us each night so we could work at another location. This entailed carrying about two-dozen heavy boxes back and forth each morning and night. My coworkers made a game of it, selecting the lighter boxes and choosing to leave the heavier ones for someone else.

This provided me with a unique opportunity. To everyone's surprise I asked if it was all right for me to carry the heaviest boxes. They laughed and joked about it and readily agreed. It wasn't easy, but while they were laughing, the department head couldn't avoid taking notice. About one month later I received a promotion to sixth-level supervision. As an exempt employee I was now a member of management.

With the exception of this latest job, my experience of working for someone left much to be desired. It wasn't the work It was the uncertainty of a lasting relationship. I was hired when they needed me and I was discharged when they didn't. We had become almost paranoid about losing my job. When I returned home each evening, Peggy would meet me at the door and ask if I still had a job. We weren't the only ones who lived this way.

This fear was enough motivation for me to continue searching for ways to become independent. I might fail, but I sure wouldn't lay myself off.

One of the major benefits of working for General Motors was their stock purchase program. Although there was a limit, for every dollar an employee paid into to the program, GM contributed an equal amount.

The vesting program required that you earn the company's contribution over a five-year period. In other words, after one year you owned one-fifth of the company's first year contribution and after five years you owned all of the company's first year's contribution.

I realized that a primary objective of the program was to keep employees from leaving, yet I still yearned to divine my own destiny. Therefore, to the bewilderment of management, I periodically withdrew my funds from the program and used the money to secretly finance my private entrepreneurial ventures.

One of my first efforts was to reenter the insurance business. Naturally, the easiest way was to get reinstated with the Farmers Insurance Group in Detroit.

Although the district agent was opposed to hiring a part-time agent, apparently the home office felt I would be a welcome prospect and the licensing was arranged.

It soon became obvious that I needed an office so we moved into a huge two-story, four-bedroom house located on a busy highway, adjacent to the large parking lot of a major supermarket. This old house was zoned residential but its location on a busy street next to a parking lot made it difficult for the owner to sell. My offer of $700 down and the balance of $11,800 payable on easy terms, was accepted by the seller. We were able to borrow most of the down payment on a short term basis.

The huge home was solid brick and had a natural wood burning fireplace in almost every room. It had originally been built for a doctor who set up his practice there. It had also been used for another occupation.

When Peggy first saw the house her reaction resulted in me sleeping in a motel room that night. Finally I was able to reason with her. Our kitchen would remain on the first floor, but we would actually live in the privacy of the second floor. I even prevailed upon her to tend the first floor "office" while I spent the day at General Motors.

She didn't have to speak much English. All she needed to do was answer the telephone and make appointments for me, or have a walk-in applicant complete a form. When I got home from work each night I reviewed the applications, weeded out the unacceptable risks, and sent the good applications on to the district office.

Everything was great until the neighbor living behind us asked Peggy if she didn't mind living in a house where all those dead bodies had been.

That night I worked desperately to convince Peggy that although it had been a mortuary for several years, the mortician was semiretired and did not do a big business. Considering the alternatives, she agreed to go along with me.

Remember the adage, *Think big! Act Big! Do Big!?*

The first thing I did was remodel the first floor. I stripped out the carpeting and refinished the oak floors. Then I moved in six used desks and a dozen chairs to form a waiting room. There was a telephone on every desk but only the ones on the front two desks were connected. The filing cabinets and other office equipment I needed to complete the furnishings were acquired through want ads, auctions, and used office furniture stores.

I should explain that I did not have nearly enough money to pay for the down payment and all the remodeling and office equipment, so I resorted to some creative financing.

First I went to one bank and got a three-year home improvement loan to put in a new furnace. Then I went to the next bank and got another home improvement loan to put in a new furnace. Then I went to still another bank and got a home improvement loan to put in another new furnace. I simply repeated the process until I had enough money to do what I wished. I might have needed to put in several furnaces if they ever investigated but they never did. Apparently, as long as we made the payments they weren't too concerned.

I wouldn't recommend that you try this today. In the *good ol' days* they didn't have computers and networks with real-time reporting, so one bank never knew what another bank was doing. Better yet, they didn't even know what they were doing.

Understand that I had no intention of ever defrauding anyone. I was young. I was poor. I was desperate. My intentions were honorable. There was never a doubt in my mind that I would pay everyone back.

I did one other thing that was a major contributor to my success in the insurance industry. Driving down Ford Road, I came into an area where the road was being widened. At an intersection I saw that they had torn down a gas station but had left a ten-foot by forty-foot billboard standing. I bought the billboard for a few hundred dollars and had it moved to my driveway facing the supermarket's parking lot. It was a magnet for new customers.

There was one unforeseen problem and it was an industry-wide problem. When an agent quit or was forced out of the company, all his renewals went to the company or the district Agent. An unscrupulous district agent or company could work this arrangement to their advantage and many did. My new district agent was one of them.

It so happened that I began just at the start of a contest offering the agent who wrote the most premiums an all-expense paid vacation to Hawaii.

I learned that my district agent had borrowed a substantial amount of money from one of his agents in order to buy the district agency. It soon became obvious that almost all the new walk-in business of the district agency was being credited to the agent who had loaned him the money. There was also some evidence showing that district office renewals were being rewritten by the agent.

As if that wasn't enough, when someone called in and requested an agent to call on them, every referral was being given to the other agent. This came to light when I called one of the prospects I had solicited and learned that the district office had already sent the agent in question to his house. When I complained, the district agent just shrugged his shoulders and denied it.

Irritated by this disadvantage, I wrote a letter to the Farmer's home office explaining the situation and asking for an investigation.

Despite all the business the other agent was getting from the district office, my sales kept climbing to where I threatened to surpass him and all the other agents in my district. Apparently, the realization that a part-time agent was going to produce more than their seasoned full-time agents was more than the district manager could tolerate.

In the last weeks of the contest, I received a notice transferring me to an obscure district office, miles from my office. I had had enough. I assumed that Farmers Insurance Group was an anomaly in the industry, so I would leave them to open my own general insurance agency representing some of the world's largest insurance companies.

It was 1954, and I had heard of a small local automobile insurance firm called Detroit Insurance Company that was selling only automobile insurance with a quarterly premium plan. This made a lot of sense to me. The majority of people I knew struggled to make semiannual or annual premiums, so quarterly premiums would be very attractive. With this new company I could offer complete automobile liability insurance for only eight dollars and sixteen cents every three months.

The one problem with the company was their reluctance to accept certain risks. In fact, they checked the police record of every applicant and even had employees who went out and questioned neighbors. They would not insure divorced people, married couples who argued, gay people, people who drank, ninety-nine percent of black and

Hispanic drivers, anyone who had ever been involved in an accident, etc., etc.

Naturally, I had to pick up other automobile insurers whose underwriting requirements were more lenient, albeit with higher premiums. In addition, I picked up several excellent mutual and stock insurance companies for fire, life, and other coverage.

Although I was making a lot of money and developing a wonderful retirement fund from renewals, the memory of what happened at Farmers Insurance Company continued to bother me. When you develop a lot of premiums with a single unscrupulous company, your future is the only thing that remains uninsured.

Almost immediately I qualified for the Detroit Insurance Company's Millionaire's Club. In fact, I qualified every month for thirty-five consecutive months. I paid back the seven hundred dollars I had borrowed for the down payment of our house and every one of our home improvement loans.

The insurance commissions plus my General Motor's salary soon permitted us to live far beyond the modest means of my General Motor's peers and it was duly noted.

Every year we would throw a great New Year's party for all our insurance clients. One year we even rented an excursion steamer and gave away mink stoles for door prizes. Our parties were legend and often included over two hundred guests and dancing to a live orchestra. A specially built grill roasted three sixty-pound rounds of prime beef and there was more beer, wine, and liquor than could be consumed.

Life was good. It was going to get better.

I arrived home one night from General Motors and found a notice from the city announcing they planned to widen the street in front of our house and take twelve feet of our frontage. This meant we were going to lose most of our porch and the stairs that led to our front door. In exchange, the city was offering us $2,500.

I hired an architect to design a new entrance. The estimate was about five thousand dollars. I also wanted to put a big neon sign in front, but there was a huge oak tree growing right in the place where the sign pole would go. Since the tree wasn't in the right-of-way, the city declined to pay for its removal and I didn't have the several hundred dollars a tree removal company wanted to do the job.

When a city representative came out to have us sign the necessary papers for the city to acquire the easement, I was at work and Peggy was alone in the office.

Now you have to remember that Peggy still didn't read or speak too much English. When the man explained the documents to her, she didn't understand one word he said. Peggy's natural instincts were to shake her head "no", throw her hands up in the air, and look in the other direction.

Apparently, the agent assumed that Peggy was being obstinate and wanted more money. Actually, she didn't understand what the man was talking about and wouldn't sign anything unless I was there.

On the next trip the agent offered us a thousand dollars more and received the same response. Over the next several weeks, the man continued to raise the offer until he insisted that $12,500 was the final offer. This time he left the papers with Peggy.

When I arrived home and learned what had happened, I had Peggy sign the papers with me. I think I even bought her dinner. It was enough money to remodel the entire front of the building and buy the neon sign I wanted.We could certainly splurge on a pizza.

PROVERB 58
A response delayed may provoke a better offer.

The large oak tree was still a problem, but nothing a good methods engineer couldn't solve.

I arrived home one Friday evening and saw that every tree along Greenfield Road had been painted with a huge red X. I correctly assumed that every tree with a red X was going to be removed by the City. Unfortunately, the tree on our front lawn was not marked because it sat ten feet back from the marked trees in the condemned area.

That night I purchased a can of red paint at the local hardware store and, at midnight, I went out and painted a large red X on my tree.

The next morning I went out to review my handiwork. Shock set in. My X was perfect but the paint had dried orange. There was a marked contrast between the two paint colors and I couldn't count on the city employees to be colorblind.

Fortunately, it was Saturday and the tree removal crews weren't working. That night I stayed awake until 2:00 AM when there was almost no traffic on Greenfield Road. Then, with my can of paint and trusty paint brush, I went out and repainted the X on every tree for two blocks on either side of my home. Now there were more orange X's than there were red. I figured the majority would have to win any decision.

On Monday evening I arrived home to find my tree gone along with all the others. It created a perfect place for the pole that would support our new sign.

The new professional appearance of our building, together with the new two-sided neon sign, doubled the traffic into our office. I have to tell you about one incident.

Our new sign had slots on each side where I could place plastic letters that would spell out a message. On one occasion I thought it would be cute to place a message that just read, *Customers Wanted. Apply Inside.*

Believe it or not, we actually had several people come in and apply for the job.

PROVERB 59:
**Pursuing a goal is like buying a new automobile.
There are always many options.**

CHAPTER 13

GENEROUS MOTORS

My insurance business was going great until Peggy made an appointment for me to write an automobile policy for a minister who lived several miles from my office, on the edge of Grosse Pointe Woods, a very affluent area.

When I arrived and found the applicant was a black minister, I never dreamed I would have a problem insuring the man. I looked over every part of his completed application and couldn't find one single reason to decline his application.

We went outside to inspect the condition of his automobile and everything appeared to be satisfactory. By then it was very dark and there were no streetlights available, but I carefully checked the car inside and out and was satisfied that everything was in good condition. I bound the risk and submitted it to the home office.

About the same time a man came into the office to purchase automobile liability insurance. As I did with everyone, I read him a list of questions that he answered in a satisfactory manner. One of the questions I always asked

141

was if he was planning any trips in the near future. The question was important because certain people were known to take out a policy when they were planning a long trip, and when they got back home without an accident, proceed to cancel the policy. Obviously these risks were undesirable.

With the correct answers, I bound the risk and submitted the application to the company.

About two weeks later I received a letter asking me to report to the Detroit Insurance Company office for a review of my underwriting procedures.

I arrived for the meeting and noticed all the past cordialities were absent. First, there was the matter of me insuring a black man's car when it had been rolled over in an accident. I was stunned by the accusation. I couldn't deny that I insured a black minister, but I certainly denied there was any damage to the automobile. (I would later find out that while trying to avert an accident, the minister had swerved sharply and the car had been turned on its side sustaining minimal damage. A garage had repaired the automobile but I suppose a trained expert could see little ripples in the sheet metal that an untrained eye would never notice.) No blame for the accident was ever assigned to the minister nor was he ticketed.

Then they went on to the second case. This involved the man who had recently come into my office and purchased liability insurance. Apparently the man had lied to me and intended to purchase coverage just for an upcoming trip to Canada. While in Canada he had consumed a few beers and drove into an intersection striking a car carrying six passengers, all of whom claimed injury. The company was setting aside the maximum twenty thousand dollars for a settlement.

Under the circumstances, the company was reducing my commissions from twenty percent to ten-percent. Furthermore, commissions would only be paid when my annual loss ratio was reduced below fifty-three percent.

I had no option but to accept the terms.

Later, in reviewing an annual report of my loss ratio, I learned that all of the losses were reported as a setup and then restated when the loss was paid. Both amounts were then added together for a total loss ratio. In effect, they had doubled my reputed losses. When I phoned the company to complain, I encountered a great deal of enmity and no satisfaction.

There was one humorous incident Detroit Mutual neglected to add to their indictment. One day I received a phone call from the underwriting department demanding to know why I had insured a lesbian. I had to pause and think about it. I couldn't recall insuring any lesbian. In the '50s, it wasn't unusual for insurance companies to decline applications from homosexuals. Detroit Mutual made sure every agent knew where they stood on the subject.

I took out copies of every application I had submitted that week and found the problem. The entry on Mr. Abud's application read *lesbian* for nationality. The entire application was in Peggy's handwriting.

I called Peggy in and asked her about the man's nationality. The only help she could give me was that the man was an Arab.

"By any chance," I asked, "was he Lebanese?"

"Yes," she replied. "That's the word!"

One of the problems in "overselling" a product is that, if you change companies, you will never be able to switch your old clients to a different product. I would now be faced with that problem.

PROVERB 60:
**When you accept employment
with an unethical employer,
do not expect ethical treatment.**

As if things weren't bad enough, while driving to General Motors one cold, snowy morning, a driver failed to notice his side road was a sheet of ice. He was proceeding at a high rate of speed and skidded right through the intersection striking my car broadside. My car did two or three snap rolls and ended up in the median, a total wreck.

I was able to limp away, but not without the familiar headache I had experienced from the fractured skull I suffered in the merchant marines.

Once again I realized the virtue of working for a good company. The cost of my hospitalization and the hours and hours of rehabilitation were all borne by the other party's insurance company, but it was General Motors that continued my employment and continued to pay me my regular salary although I required a lot of time off for physical therapy.

One unfortunate result was that the doctors placed me back on a regimen of phenobarbital and I became addicted again.

Under the influence of drugs, my insurance business began to flounder. I would sit in a stupor unable to function rationally. I failed to renew expiring policies or to keep appointments for new business. One evening, I went to school and spent the night on a bench, never attending my class.

To compound the situation I signed away all my injury claims and subsequently sold the insurance business for a fraction of its value.

I existed this way for months. Fortunately, during a temporary moment of lucidity, I remembered what my goals in life were. The desire to accomplish something positive was the major impetus to quit the drugs cold turkey, and get on with my life. Over the years my headaches subsided and eventually stopped entirely.

Without the insurance business, almost the entire first floor of my huge home was not being utilized. I began searching for some kind of profit generating business I could put in there while I was still working for General Motors.

I found the answer right next door. The area where we were living was a workingman's neighborhood and the local independent Dixfield Market was like a magnet for the local residents. Dixfield sold every kind of product the public would want except liquor.

Before the Dixfield Market was built, a small group had established a storefront church just a few hundred feet from the site of the store. Because the church was within a hundred feet of the store, zoning would not permit the supermarket to sell liquor. Every request for an exemption had been denied.

I went over and asked Dixfield's owner how he felt about me opening a party store next door. Wisely, he agreed that it would actually be advantageous for his store. Most of his customers wanted to also buy beer and wine and many went to other supermarkets just so they could get everything in one location. Even though we were in a separate building, we both agreed it would be mutually beneficial.

To open up shop, all we needed was to start out carrying a thousand dollars in groceries and obtain a sales tax number and a business license. Within a few weeks we had everything that was necessary and on June 1, 1960 the Party Nook opened.

While it might not have been as unique as some of today's exotic markets, it was unique to Detroit in the 1960's.

In addition to most every brand of American beer, we also stocked beer from Austria, Australia, Belgium, Canada, Czechoslovakia, Denmark, England, France, Germany, Greece, Holland, Ireland, Italy, Japan, Mexico,

Norway, Philippines, Poland, Scotland, and a few other places.

Along with the most common foods, our shelves were stocked with canned and bottled savory snacks of octopus, herring, oysters, snails, shrimp, rattlesnake, crab, frog legs, chocolate covered ants, chocolate-covered-bees, grasshoppers, caterpillars, fried agave worms, eel, lobster, clams, quail eggs, rabbit, and other sundry delicacies.

From the beginning, we realized we were selling as many items for novelty gifts as we were for the buyer's consumption, but who cared. The idea was unique, but a survey of the industry would have told us that most small party store owners were only making a living. They weren't getting rich.

While business was good, it soon became evident that it would never develop into something that would propel us into the upper-class income strata. Besides, being a seven-day operation, it was too much like work. It wasn't long before we admitted there had to be a better way.

After only one year, we just closed the store and entertained our friends with the remaining inventory of the store. For months we would dine on exotic canned foods and quench our thirst with our fine wines and Champagnes. While the food and liquor lasted, it was the next best thing to being rich.

I continuously extol the virtues of owning your own business, but I certainly would never discourage anyone from first garnering the experience and education made available by many of the nations's leading corporations.

I still believe that two of the best things that ever happened to me were being fired by Ford Motor Company and being hired by General Motors.

Being fired made me a totally new person. I learned that I would never be indispensable and consequently became a more humble and compassionate person. These were two more important footprints on the trail to success. Being fired doesn't have to be fatal. It might be a crash landing, but it's one you can walk away from and any crash landing you can walk away from is a *good* landing. It also reinforced my conviction that I would rather be an employer than an employee.

PROVERB 61:
In an employment relationship,
there is a hierarchy of job security.
Only the employer is indispensable.

Providence was at work again one Sunday when, after church, Peggy and I went driving through the isolated back roads of Birmingham, Michigan. Birmingham was a Detroit suburb known as the "new money" area as opposed to the conservative "old money" area of Grosse Pointe, Michigan. It was fall and the pastoral scenery, with the leaves turning from green to various shades of yellow and orange, was breathtaking.

At one remote intersection we turned off onto a gravel road and ended up at a cul-de-sac. The entrance road was heavily wooded with only one house along this road. There, on a single two-acre site, was a brand new "For Sale" sign. I instinctively knew this lot was for us.

We immediately assumed that the property in this area would be too expensive, but what did we have to lose by calling and asking?

To our surprise, we learned that the property had just become available due to the death of the owner and the estate was willing to sell the two acres for ten thousand dollars. Comparable property in the area was selling for five times that amount. Our first offer was seventy-five hundred dollars and they accepted it. We bought the site.

In order to buy the property, we put a few hundred dollars on a land contract with payments of seventy-five dollars a month. We made payments for several years until we were able to build in May of 1965.

It took us seven years of saving before we could build and move into our new home in Bingham Farms. It was the first home I had ever designed and built exclusively for us. The total cost of the home and property was thirty-seven thousand dollars including the carpeting, landscaping, and a wide, circular concrete drive.

It didn't take long before we learned what we had done. On the next block lived the famous poet, Edgar A. Guest, and a granddaughter of President Franklin Delano Roosevelt. Our neighbors were the CEO's of Ohio Gas Company and several other multimillion dollar corporations.

In addition, our nearest neighbors were Jeanne Durand, society editor for the Detroit Free Press, and Simon Knudsen and John De Lorean, vice presidents of General Motors. We were awash in socialites and it was far more than we had bargained for.

One day we returned home from shopping and found a group of children in our driveway. We didn't pay much attention until one of the youngsters shouted out, "Are you the people with only one car?"

The next day I went out and bought a secondhand Henry J automobile. It came with an engine, four wheels, brakes, and a heater. One of our new problems was not suffocating during the hot summers when we drove with the windows closed so our neighbors wouldn't know our car didn't have air conditioning.

If you've ever thought of status, consider a community that's been accused of holding garage sales by invitation only and a fire department that didn't make house calls.

Surprisingly, it didn't take long for us to be accepted and get to know many of our new neighbors. Some of the introductions were not as gratifying as they might have been, such as my introduction to the Knudsens.

I was clearing some brush near my neighbor's six-foot high chain link fence at the rear of our property when a vaguely familiar figure approached. It was my immediate neighbor, Semon (Bunky) Knudsen, the man everyone expected to be the next president of General Motors.

After a mutual introduction, Knudsen admitted to knowing my son Marc and when I asked how they had met, I was immediately sorry.

Still smiling, Knudsen explained that his security guards had plucked Marc and his friends from his swimming pool on several occasions and banished them to our own property.

Of course I apologized, but Knudsen just smiled and threw his hands up. "Kids will be kids," he said.

About a week later he and his wife stopped by.

He being of Danish descent and Peggy being Finnish, they had a great time comparing notes. As they were leaving, Peggy fulfilled her ritual which was to pack some of her famous Finnish torte for them to take home. The following week, Mrs. Knudsen returned Peggy's dish filled with little Danish chocolate mints coated with a hard, sweet covering similar to our M & M's. It was a nice gesture but with surprising consequences.

PROVERB 62
If you are going to move, always move upward.

At work, I was temporarily assigned to the Plant Layout department to help plan a multimillion dollar expansion of Chevrolet's Spring and Bumper plant. Actually my task was quite perfunctory. Someone else made a decision and then I arranged the miniature scale templates on a floor plan exactly as specified.

On a certain date, all the big shots from Central Office would be meeting in our Plant Layout department for a presentation of the physical layout of the new facility and to review its costs and benefits. Although I was to be a spectator, I had no part in the presentation. In fact, my supervisor made it very clear that I was to "keep quiet and keep out of the way."

I should explain that office politics includes a hierarchy of visibility. It's the *totem pole* syndrome. The higher up on the pole, the more you must have access to visibility by those above you. I knew employees who would walk a mile out of their way just to go by some VIP's office in hopes they'd be noticed.

None of this was on my mind when the group of executives from Central Office walked in. At the forefront was the Vice President of General Motors, my neighbor, Bunky Knudsen.

Everyone of any importance was there, plus a few of us gofers who were expected to move the cutout templates on the aluminum grid boards if one of the chiefs requested a change. As protocol demanded, I was far back in the rear of the room with the other gofers.

The meeting had gone on for a half hour before Knudsen looked up and spotted me in the crowd. About forty onlookers watched in surprise as he interrupted the meeting and made his way to the back of the room and began talking to me.

"I didn't know you worked here," he said. "How long have you worked for Chevrolet? How are Peggy and the children?"

I smiled and answered him as briefly as possible. I could feel the glares of the plant manager, and the other people in the room. The questioning I got after the meeting convinced me my coworkers hadn't failed to notice the incident either.

He started the meeting again with a Central Office summary of expenditures for the buildings and equipment, as well as the return-on-investment General Motors could expect. These charts were on a series of slides that were projected on a large screen so everyone could visualize and understand the dimensions of the components.

After four or five slides and lengthy explanations, I became terribly bored. The next slide consisted of numerous columns and about forty rows of numbers. At the bottom of each column was a total. At the bottom of the last column was the grand total cost of the expansion project.

I can't explain why, but for some inexplicable reason, I began to add the last digit of the last number in the last column until I got down to the total. According to my calculations the last digit in the total should have been a seven. It wasn't. While the speaker droned on I added the digits again. It should have definitely been a seven and the screen showed it as a two. At the first pause in the speaker's presentation, I yelled out, "Those totals don't add up."

There was a deathly silence and then a great deal of pandemonium in the front of the room. Someone called out for a calculator and a ten minute adjournment ensued. I suddenly woke up to reality and realized what I had done. I tried to bury myself behind the people around me, as those in the front craned their necks to see who had challenged their financial credentials. Finally, someone announced that there appeared to be a few "minor" errors in the chart and that would be corrected while they continued with the presentation. It was a very lengthy presentation.

Unbeknown to me, most of the people in that room actually thought I had mentally tabulated all the hundreds of numbers in all the rows and columns in my head to determine the final total. In fact I had simply used an eighth grade arithmetic gimmick for rapidly checking column totals.

Two very wrong impressions were formed that morning. One, a lot of people thought I was a very close friend of the future president of General Motors, and two, a lot of people thought I was a mathematical genius. They were wrong on both counts, but I was not in a position to change what was about to happen to me.

A short time after the meeting, I was promoted to the Plant Layout department with a handsome increase in pay. Then, after another short period of time, I was called into the plant manager's office and told that the corporation had requested me to transfer to the corporate staff and become a member of their Team Study Group.

The Team Study Group consisted of several teams of consultants who traveled around the world to improve the profitability of General Motor's various divisions. The promotion to the corporate staff resulted in another raise in pay.

Consulting was a fascinating task. Every Monday I would fly to some location and on Friday I would fly back home. Evenings and weekends were all my own. Each team of consultants was usually comprised of about four men and each man brought his own special expertise to the problem. After work, we were free to pursue whatever form of entertainment we wished. To me it was a golden opportunity.

In one location, I resumed my flying lessons and obtained my private pilot's license. While Peggy wasn't enthused, I began renting an aircraft to fly back and forth between my assignment and Detroit. I'm sure it wasn't lost on the powers that be.

While working in Chicago at the Diesel Locomotive Plant, I studied art at the downtown YMCA and took organ lessons at Lyon & Healy's.

At the conclusion of my Team Study assignment, I was rehired by Chevrolet as the Supervisor of Methods Engineering with another increase in pay.

Shortly after that, to the surprise of everyone in the department, including me, I was promoted to the position of assistant department head of the entire Methods Engineering and Work Standards Department. This promotion included an increase in my classification to seventh level and another substantial pay raise.

Would this ever stop? Not yet!

A few years later, my boss died of a heart attack and was replaced by another General Motors Institute (GMI) graduate whom I will just refer to as Brice.

Brice was a man with an iron mind, impossible to influence or change. And, everything that he had to do, he delegated to me. When I gave him the completed report, he would have it retyped over his name and personally present it to the plant manager, along with the impression that he had done it all by himself. Brice really was a climber and the top of the totem pole was his goal.

Unfortunately, Brice had some bad habits. For one thing he was a compulsive fingernail biter. No matter where he was or who he was with, he would indulge himself with a fingernail entrée. To make matters worse, he was also a compulsive nose picker. It was a rare occasion when you couldn't observe Brice with one finger busily probing the uppermost reaches of a nostril.

Apparently, such distasteful habits were not an impediment to advancement, as long as you were a graduate of General Motors Institute. Brice possessed that piece of paper. But Brice also possessed another quirk that I had never encountered before.

In those days we didn't have computers. Every report, regardless of its length, had to be typed in triplicate using carbon sheets between the original sheet and the other two pages.

No matter the circumstances, when handed a report, Brice would call my assistant and me into his office. Then he would make me read the report from the carbon copy while he read the original and my assistant read the identical second carbon copy. During the reading he would hold up the original and make sure the wording conformed to the carbon copies. This was a man being groomed to be president of General Motors!

Unfortunately for Brice, I guess General Motors Institute didn't offer a course in ethics and he was unfamiliar with the word.

During the plush years, Brice would attend "important" seminars and trade shows all over the country. Fortunately, I was never invited to accompany him because someone had to remain behind to manage the department.

Over and over I would hear stories that Brice would take his wife along and never attend a single meeting. Instead, he and his wife would go shopping, to a show, or visit relatives.

There was one thing you didn't ever want to do in the corporate hierarchy: get a reputation as a snitch. I did not report these things only for that reason. On the other hand, I didn't discourage the knowledgeable parties from repeating their tales to others. If someone higher up ever did learn of it, apparently they didn't care.

In the end, something else would bring about Brice's downfall.

Whenever he was out of town at a seminar, he'd insist that I include him in the overtime authorization if anyone in the department worked overtime. He justified this by explaining that every employee had to work under supervision and, since he was the department head, it was logical for him to be considered to be supervising and included in the overtime.

Since we were almost always working overtime, Brice received payment for hundreds of hours of overtime that he never actually worked. If I had reported Brice, it would only have been a matter of time before everyone realized it, and my career would have been over.

Unfortunately for Brice, one day the general superintendent noticed Brice's name on the overtime report, when he knew that Brice was out of town that week.

Since I was the one who filed the Overtime Report, I was the one called down to the Superintendent's office to explain the contradiction.

It was impossible to justify the discrepancy without explaining that Brice had instructed me to always include his name on the overtime authorization. I knew there would be serious ramifications when it was discovered and I pleaded with the superintendent to keep me out of it, which he agreed to do.

When interviewed, Brice insisted he had never instructed me to place his name on the overtime list. Of course he could not explain why he had accepted the overtime pay for several years without reporting the "error."

PROVERB 63:
**Ineptitude, like cream, may rise to the top,
but it too will soon sour.**

A short time later Brice was transferred to Central Office and I was called into the plant manager's office and promoted to General Superintendent of Methods Engineering & Work Standards. In my new position I would have two secretaries and run the Time Study, Methods

Engineering, Plant Layout, and Appropriations Control departments.

The promotion to eighth level was accompanied by a host of creature amenities along with another hefty salary increase, and an annual executive bonus. Also included was the use of any new model company car I desired. After driving the car for 3,000 miles, I had to turn it in and choose another new model to drive. If I wanted, I could buy any of these cars at a substantial discount. Use included the gas and oil as well as all maintenance and daily carwashes.

Living a distance from the plant and with the extra miles I drove, meant I would receive five new cars a year. A mixed benefit was receiving the first prototype Stingray. Due to an undersized cooling system, the car overheated every time I stopped at a stoplight.

A subsidized lunch in the private executive dining room foreclosed forever the thought of carrying a brown bag lunch.

Being an executive with General Motors should have satisfied anyone. I was an exception. I found dimensions of ineptitude in some of my peers that challenged the company's reputation and diminished my own credits.

Although they finally did away with General Motors Institute, there were enough GMI graduates to sustain the "good ol' boy" philosophy. A common practice was for two managers arranging to have their sons work for each other. Then they would each advance the other man's son even though he lacked the brains to come in out of the rain.

What might have discouraged me the most was the resignation of three of the most competent men General Motors had; Semon Knudsen, Jim McLernon, and John De Lorean.

I figured if men of their stature could give up their positions to move on, there wasn't any excuse for me to hesitate.

The failures and petty performances by superiors were frustrations I wouldn't have to countenance if I was running my own company.

Besides, I wanted to be the Captain and not just another oarsman.

CHAPTER 14

ALMOST

The seventeen years I spent with General Motors provided me with the time and money to engage in a number of business opportunities, and I seized every opportunity I could. The one thing I was careful not to do was any personal business on company time or on the company premises.

One of my early enterprises was to capitalize on the public's insatiable appetite for magazines.

Long before anyone ever heard of the Publisher's Clearing House magazine subscription promotion, one of my million dollar ideas involved magazine subscriptions.

Back in the forties and fifties, eighty percent of America's households collected special trading stamps that were issued by stores and redeemable for merchandise. Almost every store and supermarket gave their customers green stamps, red stamps, or some other color stamps to paste in a book. It took twelve hundred stamps to fill a book and each completed book was worth one dollar and twenty cents when filled. You could take a stack of these filled books to a redemption center and trade them in for merchandise.

Of course the value of the merchandise was the full retail price so it would take months or years for someone to save up enough filled stamp books to get something of value.

I was standing in line with Peggy to redeem dozens of filled stamp books when I got a great idea.

Wouldn't it be nice if a person only needed two or three books to get a nice prize instead of twenty or thirty? Why didn't these stamp companies offer magazine subscriptions?

I sat down and did the calculations, weighing the advantages and disadvantages of such a program. It was a sure winner.

I designed an entire system for processing magazine orders and then contacted every major magazine publisher offering them thousands of new subscriptions in exchange for a sales agreement.

Every publisher extended me a fifty percent commission.

The next minor task was to contact the world's largest trading stamp producer and convince them of the merits of this program. Although there were a dozen similar stamp programs, Sperry and Hutchinson was the world's largest, producing over three hundred percent more stamps each year than the United States Post Office. I would offer Sperry & Hutchinson forty percent and I would keep ten percent for my profit and overhead.

Despite disparaging critiques from my wife and friends, I took off for the New York offices of S&H. I went straight to their fancy Fifth Avenue high-rise offices and asked to speak to Robert Patterson, Vice President of Marketing.

Patterson's first reaction was to automatically say "No."

Then I hit him with the charts and a list of advantages. All S&H had to do was redeem the stamp books and send me a form with the names of the magazines. I would process the orders and the magazine companies would ship the magazines. At the end of each month S&H would send me a check for the magazine orders less their commission of forty percent.

The beauty of the program was that S&H would not have any inventory, shipping costs, or loss from breakage and theft. I assured them the biggest advantage was that more people would seek out their stamps because they could get a gift in a short time without spending months or years collecting stamps.

Patterson still wasn't convinced, but he asked me to leave my presentation and return at three o'clock that afternoon.

I returned at exactly three o'clock.

I was ushered into a conference room where several other gentlemen had joined Patterson. The discussion was led by Donald Johnson, but there was no longer any doubt.

They all agreed it was a *good* idea.

There was only one stumbling block. They would not redeem stamps for any product unless they got a fifty percent discount on the item's retail price. It was a blow, but I still wasn't prepared to give up. I said I would get back to them.

Back in Detroit, I wrote again to all my publishers and explained the dilemma. To my delight, every single publisher told me to go ahead with the fifty percent commission to S&H, and they would still give me an additional ten percent. The deal was consummated. I could taste the money coming in.

A few weeks later I received a special-delivery letter from a vice president at Time-Life telling me to hold up everything because the Audit Bureau of Circulation (ABC) advised them that these were "giveaways" and not really sales. As such, they could not be counted in their circulation, and that meant they could not charge advertisers more money to cover the cost of printing all the extra magazines.

The next day the vice president from Time-Life telephoned me to say he would like to request a hearing before the board of the ABC, something I could not do because I was not a publisher/member of ABC. I readily agreed. I also reminded him that a federal court had ruled that these were actual sales and that states had the right to collect sales tax on all the products S&H sold when people redeemed their stamps.

The hearing took place a week later and the ABC refused to accept that the subscriptions were actually being sold. The whole project went down the tube.

PROVERB 64:
**For every great deal
   there are a hundred deal breakers out there.**

After all the work I had gone through to get my magazine sales contracts, I was reluctant to just let the subject rest. Then I got another great idea.

Christmas was several months away and, it seemed to me that magazine subscriptions would make a wonderful, albeit inexpensive gift. But how do you mass market the concept of giving magazine subscriptions as gifts?

My answer was an eight-page, four-color rotogravure insert in the nation's ten leading Sunday newspapers. The insert would offer coupons for forty discounted magazine subscriptions.

Now you're probably thinking, "Oh sure, that's what the world needed, another magazine insert in the Sunday newspaper!"

But let me enlighten you. Back in the early fifties magazine inserts were very rare. Even during the Christmas season Sunday papers had only one or two inserts.

I hired an advertising agency to layout an eight-page insert with ordering coupons for forty different magazines. The entire front cover showed a smiling Santa Claus dressed like a postman holding out several magazines. Above and below him read the blazing message, *"Christmas will be gone, but your thoughtful gift will go on giving."*

Inserting the catalog in the top ten Sunday newspapers meant a circulation of almost eight million homes. Unfortunately, the cost of printing the inserts and distributing them would run $119,000.

There was no way that I could afford to advance that kind of money, so I asked each of the publishers to prepay the cost of their ads. In exchange, I would only take a ten percent commission. After they had recouped their prepaid expense, I would start earning my normal fifty percent commission.

By the time the deadline came around I had sold all but eight ad spaces. I was twenty-five thousand dollars short and didn't have the kind of money to cover the shortage if the promotion failed. Neither did I have the courage to borrow that kind of money.

There was every indication that the promotion would have been a success and would have led to many similar ventures. It was the skepticism of those around me that convinced me I shouldn't gamble with our modest resources. I gave the promotion up.

PROVERB 65:
The greater the reward, the greater the risk.

This was an idea that might have worked fifty years ago because it was a novel use of newspapers. Last Sunday, my local newspaper had thirty-nine rotogravure inserts. I can expect almost double that number during the weeks before Christmas, further diluting the odds of even being seen.

In case you think this was a nickel-and-dime opportunity, let me tell you about Harold Mertz and his wife LuEsther. A few years earlier, in 1953, the Mertzes and their daughter Joyce started selling magazine subscriptions out of their basement in Port Washington, New York. Slowly but surely, they increased their sales until 1967, when they started a direct mail campaign that offered a ten thousand dollar prize to some lucky winner.

The results of their direct mail campaign were phenomenal. Before long they increased their grand- prize award to one million dollars. Over the years they made so much money they established a number of charitable foundations and still had millions for themselves.

It should also be noted that in 2001, their company, Publisher's Clearing House, paid a thirty-four million dollar fine to twenty-six states who claimed the Mertz's direct mail campaigns misled consumers into believing they had won or that they could increase their chances of winning a sweepstakes if they bought subscriptions.

Publishers Clearing House paid the thirty-four million dollar penalty and continues giving away a ten million dollar prize each year in their mass mailing subscription sweepstakes.

PROVERB 66
**There is more than one road to success,
but always obey the traffic signals.**

CHAPTER 15

GOING TO THE DOGS

I was looking through the business opportunities section of the *Wall Street Journal* early in 1966 when I came across an ad seeking parties to build a currency-trading network.

I have always been interested in collecting sets of newly minted coins and had subscribed to the US Treasury's coin sales for several years. However, I was unaware that the buying and selling of new and used coins by collectors was a speculative enterprise involving millions of Americans.

Out of curiosity, I sent away and requested more information. Enter Jody Shows, a long time speculator in rare coins and a walking encyclopedia of coin mintages and their current values. The amazing thing about him was his ability to tell you the "bid" and "asking price" of thousands of coins without the use of any reference book.

After many years in the business, Jody had come up with the idea of forming a national consortium of coin dealers that would operate like a stock exchange. His office would tabulate the demand and current sales price of every coin traded and disseminate this information to the member dealers in cities throughout America. It was up to the brokers to advertise and solicit customers but the ten percent commission was more than adequate to provide a good income.

A persuasive part of Jody's presentation was a comparison of coin investing against a similar investment in stocks. I was amazed at the difference. Historically, coins outperformed stocks by a substantial degree over almost any period of time. In addition, there were numerous cases where a single penny, nickel, quarter, or silver dollar would become so rare that it would be worth hundreds of thousands of dollars. You just had to be lucky enough to have one.

On March 5, 1966, I incorporated the "Currency Research and Investment Corporation" in Detroit. I was now an expert in currency investing.

Comparing historic coin and stock market investments made selling uncirculated currency not only easy, but also rewarding. My commission was only ten percent but professional people liked the status of having invested in such a unique commodity. It was very unusual, when I sold someone a portfolio of rare coins, that they didn't refer a friend or business associate to me.

Although the government mints millions of coins, they only produce a limited number of Mint and Proof coins each year. These coins are struck on special dies, given special handling, and sold as Mint Sets or Proof Sets. Lastly, they are enclosed in special packaging and remain untouched by human hands.

Ironically, one of the factors that most affect the market values is the ongoing disappearance of valuable coins. Coin collections are primary targets of theft rings that often just melt down the gold coins and use the silver coins in normal retail transactions. Once the rare coins enter the marketplace and are handled, they will never again reflect their mint value.

Another problem is the storage of these valuable coins. I found nothing wrong with keeping my coins in my dresser until one day I noticed a difference in my arrangement and found a number of tubes of coins missing. I would later learn that my son had been helping himself to a roll of coins whenever he wanted to buy some candy. One of the missing tubes contained fifty uncirculated 1865 dimes worth three hundred dollars each. It turned out that his school bus driver was paying my son just a little more than the face value of the coins. I wasn't able to do anything about the bus driver, but I did go out and buy a huge safe that I have since paid a fortune to move all over the country.

Things were really going well as Jody signed up more brokers and launched a wholesale newsletter detailing special opportunities in uncirculated coins. Each coin dealer had a Teletype machine so they could stay current with late fluctuations in the market. Within a few months other offices were opened in Long Beach, Los Angeles, San Francisco, Dallas, and Chicago.

Things were really going great for about two years. Then, in January 1968 the foundation of the business, Jody Shows, disappeared. His office was closed and no one could shed any light on what happened to him. There were no criminal charges or claims of malfeasance. Someone said he had had a stroke and someone else said he had suddenly died. Whatever the case, there was no longer any way to continue the business. Although I tried, I did not have the historical knowledge or the current skills to judge the condition of coins or to predict present and future trends.

Jody Shows was a one-man operation; a unique individual who had neglected to provide a means of continuing operations in his absence.

On August 14, 1968 I filed for the dissolution of Currency Research and Investment Corporation.

I still think it was a great idea and if you know anyone who wants to buy a huge safe and a ton of uncirculated coins, please give me a call.

PROVERB 67:
Building a business on another man's foundation can be hazardous.

Through my introduction into the investment arena, I suddenly became aware of the mutual fund industry. Mutual funds made a lot of sense to me when I was furnished with the statistics that out of every ten people who invest in stocks, one makes money, two break even, and seven lose money.

I realized that if I became a stock buyer, I was going to be competing with people who sit in front of a stream of current stock information eight or twelve hours a day. Which one of us is going to end up a winner?

But if I bought a Mutual Fund, I would be spreading my investment risk over hundreds of different companies who were chosen by those same experts who were studying the market minute by minute.

Of course, I could get lucky and be the one investor in ten who buys a share in some company and sees it grow to some fabulous value, or I could more likely be among the other nine investors who break even or lose money. I could see that mutual funds were the wave of the future and I was ready to go surfing.

My first try was with Investors Diversified Services. After reviewing my references they put me through their training program. Everything I would ever need to know about mutual funds was made available to me in training classes and manuals.

Unfortunately, some discouraging things about their investment programs were also made available to me. At that time, their investment program was similar to an annuity backed by an extremely conservative selection of stocks. It was originally designed to act like a savings program for farmers. The investors would put in small monthly amounts and be rewarded with a very modest return. As I recall, it also carried a front-end load which meant that the investor paid a fee each time they invested. In other words, for every dollar they invested, they only got eighty-five cents worth of stock. This was also true of every mutual fund at that time.

After going through the entire training program, the Detroit office submitted my papers to the home office. My application was declined. The company would only employ full-time employees. I was asked to choose between General Motors and them. I chose to remain with General Motors.

I had received a good education on mutual funds but I didn't have a way to sell them. Going back to the *Wall Street Journal*, I noticed an ad by William Jennings & Company of New Jersey, seeking mutual fund salesmen. Like everyone else, all of the funds they represented were front-end load funds but their funds had an excellent record of appreciation.

Mutual funds made it possible for anyone with a few hundred dollars to invest in a stock portfolio and the public was eager for the opportunity. The nice part of selling front-end loads was that I received my commission almost immediately. Even on a part- time basis my sales continued to grow and the opportunity to quit General Motors seemed close at hand. In a short time my broker's license was upgraded to division manager for the entire state of Michigan. Things were really looking up (again)..

It never dawned on me that some innovator would come along and introduce no-load funds. No-load funds were sold directly by the mutual fund companies without paying any commissions to salesmen. Almost overnight, no-load mutual funds were in and front-end load mutual funds were out. I was out.

Once again, a radical, unexpected change in an industry would foil my financial aspirations.

PROVERB 68:
Every upside has a downside.

Often the basis of a great idea is right in front of our eyes. Unfortunately, most of us aren't looking for something mundane. It has to rise up and bite us. This is actually what happened next.

In my case this would come about through the tragic loss of a pet.

Prior to going on a vacation in 1965, I boarded our five-year old ocelot in a typical boarding kennel.

We had the cat since it was six weeks old. It was tame as a kitten and bonded wonderfully with the entire family.

The day after we boarded it we learned that our cat had died due to the negligence of one of the children the kennel employed.

This episode awoke me to the conditions I had encountered at most of the kennels I had used. Most kennels were makeshift facilities with little or no heating or air conditioning. They were unprofessionally operated and as dirty and cluttered inside as they were outside. There were good reasons kennels refused to accept any responsibility for the pets they boarded.

After thirty-five years, I still know of only one pet-boarding facility that will give a pet owner a written boarding contract in which they accept liability for the care of the pet.

In fact, in the boarding agreement of the few animal kennels that offered a written agreement, it clearly stated that if your pet ran away, got sick, was injured, or died from any cause, they were not responsible. The pet owner was responsible. Worse than that, the pet owner was also responsible if their pet caused any damage to the facilities, or if their pet injured an employee, customer, or other animal in the kennel. It remains this way today.

What kind of legitimate business would even dare to take your money and deny every liability?

That was when I got the idea for a different kind of kennel, one that would be a real pet friendly facility.

Over the next five-years, while working for General Motors, I visited hundreds of kennels and animal research facilities all over the country.

In the end I came up with the *pet hotel* concept. In the United States there were already over fifty-six million dogs, and fifty-two million cats, plus nineteen million birds, rabbits, turtles, and other kinds of pets, and many of these pets needed a decent place to stay when their owners went on vacation.

My idea was to build a kennel similar to a human hotel with specially-designed accommodations for every type of animal. There would be large, private, fireproof, air conditioned accommodations and even a barn with horse stalls. The final design included kennels, an aviary, an aquarium, a serpentarium, a bunny club, stables, and special rooms for monkeys, apes, and other unusual pets. The lobby would resemble a hotel's registration area.

One major thing would set us apart from every other kennel in the world: our boarding contract. We would accept liability in writing for every pet we boarded. In bold type we guaranteed every pet would go home in as good or better condition than when it came to us. We even guaranteed that if a pet was injured or became ill from any cause, we would pay all of the veterinary treatment. If a death occurred while boarding, we agreed to reimburse the owner up to five hundred dollars. There was no need to establish fault. The only exclusion was for a preexisting condition. If an owner desired an autopsy, we would pay for it.

We would locate the facility on several fenced acres so the pets could be exercised. We also wanted a noise barrier separating us from our neighbors so we wouldn't have to keep the pets indoors all day.

The services we would offer would be even more unique. Included in the long list of services were afternoon and evening cookie breaks, exercising, yogurt parfaits, private playtimes with their own attendant, and of course baths and groomings. Soft "elevator music" would flood the facilities morning and night and special ventilation and sanitation systems would keep the facilities disease and odor free. In addition, dog and cat owners would have four options; Standard, Deluxe, Imperial and Regency suites.

All of the dog runs would have private indoor and attached outdoor runs, but the Imperial and Regency suites would be eight feet wide by eighteen feet long and furnished with miniature brass beds, and Poochie foam rubber mattresses with Snoopy sheets. Each Regency suite would have a television set and telephone with which owners could call and speak to their dog(s). The floor of every dog's inside room would be covered with a special perforated vinyl, antifatigue carpet, so no dog need ever lie on cold, rough concrete.

Having suffered the consequences, I would never employ children, and every employee, regardless of position, would be tested for drugs before they could be hired and then randomly during their employment. We would be the only certified "drug free" pet care facility in America.

There was one other industry misdeed I would address. It always bothered me that kennels and veterinary clinics would never permit me to go back and see where my pet was going to be boarded. I was very aware that many boarding facilities kept several dogs in the same room or placed them in small cages. To dispel any doubts, I would maintain an "open" facility, one that would permit every pet owner to take their pet to and from its room.

What I planned to do was contrary to everything that existed in the pet boarding industry at that time. Every veterinarian and kennel owner was quick to condemn the concept and predict its failure, but I was just as certain it would succeed. It would not only revolutionize the pet care industry, I predicted a chain of these pet hotels would be a multimillion dollar business.

PROVERB 69:
Sometimes a personal experience can create a financial opportunity.

All I needed was an additional $375,000.

It seemed the obvious way would be to just go to a bank and borrow the money. Forget that. Most banks rarely loan money to start-up ventures unless you indemnify the loan with marketable assets worth more than the amount you are borrowing. Even if you already have a successful business, your friendly banker usually requires substantial collateral before loaning you expansion funds. Banks don't bet on the come, they bet on sure things! If you have ever seen those huge billboards screaming, "Come to our bank for your next million dollars," let me assure you they aren't thinking of a start-up business or a novel idea.

Of course your relatives are always a consideration. Forget it! They are the ones who will give you one hundred and one reasons why your idea will fail. Even if an in-law does loan you money, odds are it will turn out to be the most expensive money you ever borrowed, especially if your business is successful and starts making money.

As a rule, the basic problem is not with who loaned you the money; it will be his or her spouse.

"Why should he make more money than you? He wouldn't even be in business if it wasn't for OUR money!" "Why is he driving a Mercedes and we have to drive around in a lousy Cadillac? He'd be walking if it wasn't for OUR money!" "Did you see Myrtle's new diamond ring? I can't have a ring like that because we gave him ALL of OUR money!"

I think I've heard every kind of recrimination there is and it's a sad fact that a number of good ventures have been torn apart by jealous family rivalry. The best advice is to stay away from relatives.

Another alternative is a Small Business Administration (SBA) loan. This is a wonderful sounding solution but rarely for start-up businesses that require substantial risk capital. One problem area is the SBA requirement of significant personal expertise and initial capital investment. The only exception today is if you are a minority. The trend toward political correctness has created an advantage for certain groups and it's too late for you if your luck was bad and you chose the wrong parents.

Well, how about going out for some of that "venture" capital? There are hundreds of venture capital groups out there with a purported objective to provide money for new or expanding businesses.

The trouble with the majority of venture capitalists is not that they want a piece of your business. It's that they want all of your business — like eighty or ninety percent of the stock. Without any specialized knowledge in your unique business, be prepared to have them tell you how you should operate a business that ends up having only a slight resemblance to your original concept. In addition, they will always know the "right" people to staff your company. Despite the extra financial burden, be prepared to add their accountant, their lawyer, and their public relations firm to your profit and loss statement.

If I sound pessimistic it's only because I've run the gamut of investment capital sources and have come to the conclusion that starting a business entails a great deal of risk when you have to rely on outside investors. If you have any doubts read my book, *Love Is A 4 Legged Word*.

PROVERB 70:
Venture capital is always more available in an advertisement than in cash.

There really is no easy way to raise capital for your next great idea, but it can be done. It's done all the time and it all goes back to the *inspiration* and *perspiration* factors. Get an idea and then don't give up when it comes to raising the capital necessary to bring your dream to fruition.

General Motors offered me more than most men would ever aspire to. But, for all that they offered, I would still be an employee subject to their whims and directives. The thought of building and running this revolutionary business overwhelmed my sense of gratitude. After seventeen years with the company and five years of dwelling on the pet hotel idea, I finally resigned my position and set out to raise the necessary capital to change the pet care industry.

Detroit didn't offer the financial climate that New York or Chicago did, so I packed up the family and moved to Chicago. I also figured that the sale of our home would help finance my new venture.

Changing conditions and new information necessitated the constant revision of my presentation and every revision cost more money.

The hiring of architects and engineers to design the buildings and equipment was only part of my expenses. There also had to be manuals detailing all the procedures, brochures, and a thousand forms designed. In addition, I had purchased an upscale home in the sedate city of Long Grove. The costs associated with a new home and three growing children were not insignificant considering that there was no longer any money coming in. To balance the equation, I took a job as a Managing Director of a consulting company headquartered in downtown Chicago.

CHAPTER 16

A DOGGONE
GOOD IDEA

AMCE wasn't just an ordinary consulting firm, it was owned and operated by a man I'll just call Peter, who was a friend of Mayor Daly. Apparently, while working as a consultant for another company doing work at city hall, Peter discovered a bad case of embezzlement by a department head. Instead of blowing the whistle, Peter went straight to Mayor Daly and related what he had found.

The mayor did not want his good friend (or himself) embarrassed so he asked Peter to cover up the matter. The culprit was retired with a huge retirement party, and the mayor replaced him with a crony who was as flawed as his predecessor. However, Peter also installed a very competent assistant, who really ran the department, so the new manager couldn't screw things up. In exchange for this service, Mayor Daly promised to take care of Peter by using him as a consultant. Peter immediately quit the company he was working for and opened his own consulting company. It did not take long for me to learn that the city of Chicago was the major source of income for AMCE. In fact it was just about the only client.

Whenever Peter needed work, he simply went across the street and came back with a *consulting* contract. When he needed money, he went back across the street and the accounting department interrupted their routine to cut him a check.

From what Peter told me, the mayor's consulting funds were really a personal slush fund holding millions of dollars to be doled out through an account called "consulting services." Not surprisingly, a great deal of the money always found its way back in the form of donations to the Mayor's election campaigns.

I knew nothing of this at the time. One of the main reasons I accepted the position was that, after telling Peter about my intention to build a chain of pet hotels, he liked the idea so much he offered to raise the money from his wealthy clients in exchange for a fifty percent interest. I agreed. After all, I had known this smooth-talker for several hours and he told me the things I wanted to hear.

Except for our affiliation with the City, I really enjoyed the little consulting I did. I saw a lot of trivial recommendations made, but also a few significant engineering improvements developed to improve products, processes, and returns on investments. Unfortunately, I saw many things that prejudiced my thinking about the majority of consultants.

PROVERB 71:
Consultants are the
"Preparation H" of commerce.

One of the perverse things about consulting is that someone will pay you thousands of dollars to solve a problem and then never initiate your recommendations. I learned that sometimes there is a hidden agenda.

I remember doing a study at the General Motors' Electromotive plant in Chicago. The plant would complete most of the diesel engine for a train and then ship the semi-completed engine to another location where it was finished.

The trucking door was on a street that led under a railroad overpass. Because of the height of the trailer and engine, it was assumed that the load would not clear the underpass. Consequently, the outside trucking firm had to travel several miles out of their way to a surface crossing, wasting time and almost doubling the transportation cost.

To confirm the problem, I decided to measure the height of the underpass. Surprisingly, I found the trucks could use the underpass with a full extra clearance of one foot.

My recommendation to change the truck route was never acted upon. It was explained to me that a long-standing arrangement existed with the trucking company, and the plant manager didn't want to "shake things up."

Eventually the plant was closed because it couldn't compete with General Electric, and the plant manager was *promoted*.

I also recall doing a study for Vacudyne Corporation, a company that manufactured vacuum chambers to condition tobacco leaves. The vacuum chambers resembled huge bank vaults. Two pallets of tobacco leaves were driven into the chamber, the door was closed, and a vacuum pump evacuated all the air and moisture from the leaves. The dried tobacco would then be stored. When needed, the tobacco would be placed back in the chamber and evacuated again. Only this time, steam was introduced into the chamber, which each tobacco leaf absorbed. When reconstituted, the tobacco leaves appeared as fresh as the day they were picked.

The steel chamber was manufactured out of several pre-cut, formed sections of one-inch thick steel plate that was assembled and welded in a very lengthy process. Because of its thickness, the steel plates had to be formed at the steel mill. All in all, it was a very expensive process.

There were several cost-saving ideas I came up with, but none compared with my proposal to do away with the steel chamber. This idea would stagger the president of the company.

My proposal consisted of a perforated steel deck and hinged frame to which would be attached a flexible plastic envelope. All the tobacco company had to do was to lower the frame and plastic over the pallets of tobacco; tighten the frame down over a large O-Ring to complete the seal, and draw the air and moisture out through a grid in the bottom steel plate. The flexible plastic envelope would simply collapse around the tobacco. The new design would eliminate the very expensive steel chamber.

When I presented the proposal the owner turned deathly pale. The meeting was abruptly cancelled and the owner took Peter into his office and closed the door.

When Peter reappeared he ushered me into a private office and ordered me to shred my proposal. Only then did I learn that the owner was in the process of selling his business and this new idea would severely diminish the value of his existing plant and patents. Peter even insisted that I swear a solemn oath to never tell anyone of my idea. The time just ran out.

The owner paid the consulting fees; Peter made a lot of money, and I got my regular paycheck. To this day I don't think any changes have ever been made to the processing of tobacco.

After a while, it became apparent that Peter had no intention of helping me find financing for the pet hotel concept. He had told me what I wanted to hear just so I would stay on as the Managing Director. Peter was a shining example of the "*Think big! Act big! Do big! Accomplish Nothing*" school.

However, this didn't mean I couldn't expend some effort to raise the funds myself, and one of my contacts resulted in an interview with a vice president of Quaker Oats. At that time they were located in the Merchandise Mart only a few blocks from our offices. Quaker Oats, in addition to owning many companies that manufactured consumer foods, also was a major producer of dog food. I reasoned that a chain of high-class pet hotels serving Quaker Oats dog food would certainly enhance their dog food sales. Apparently their management concurred.

After several meetings, Quaker Oats made me an offer. They would finance the construction of my pet hotel. If it were as profitable as I predicted, they would immediately build two additional hotels in the greater Chicago area. If these also proved viable they would continue the expansion and, at the end of ten years, buy us out for the sum of ten million dollars.

All I had to do now was give Peter the good news.

To my surprise Peter did not take the news pleasantly. In fact he became very agitated and almost belligerent.

"Ten Years? Christ, who knows if I'll be alive in ten years? I don't want my money in ten years. I want it *now*! Tell them they'll have to pay us the money up front or it's no deal!"

I was astounded at Peter's response. We were both still young and could have lived well with the additional income from the Pet Motel during the interim period. Peter would not listen to reason. I sat down and drafted the letter with Paul's demands to Quaker Oats. I was not surprised by their reply. They had reconsidered our proposal and were no longer interested.

A short time later I advised Peter that I was leaving and that I was taking 100% of the pet hotel concept with me. He signed off with the admonition that he had reevaluated the pet hotel concept and had concluded it wasn't a viable business.

PROVERB 72:
**It is a rare partnership that
doesn't contain the seeds of its own failure.**

I was back to square one and began thinking of what I should do next. The answer would arrive in an unexpected telephone call from the McDonald's headquarters in Oak Brook, Illinois.

From the time I started looking for investment capital, I figured I better change some of my routines. One of my changes was in my eating habits.

Did you ever run into Warren Buffet, Bill Gates, or the president of the World Bank in a fast- food restaurant? Did you ever find a *Wall Street Journal* or a *Forbes* magazine left behind on a table in Burger King? Don't expect to. You're not likely to find the captains of finance and industry in a fast-food restaurant.

It was 1972, while I was still at AMCE, that I changed my dining habits. There must have been two hundred eating places within walking distance of my office, but for lunch I decided to begin eating at the sedate (and expensive) dining room on the second floor of the Bismarck Hotel. I had heard that the mayor and many prominent bankers and business people always ate there. My goal was to meet the financier for my pet motel concept there. It certainly seemed more likely than where I was dining.

The dining room reeked of class and money. Mayor Daly, judges, bank presidents, and leading entrepreneurs dined there daily. A few even had special tables reserved just for them.

In fact, if they didn't show up, the maitre d', a middle-aged lady, refused to seat anyone at that table just in case the VIP arrived late.

PROVERB 73:
If you're looking for money,
look where the money is.

If you wanted lessons on how to run a hostess' job like a business, Dorothy was a classic case. I didn't realize how accomplished she was until a few days before Christmas when I opened a beautiful Christmas card and found her name at the bottom. On the rear of the card was a brief hand written-message addressed to "Mr. Leeds", which included a lovely personal wish for my health and welfare.

One of the ways I showed extra appreciation for service was to always round off the waiter's tip to the next higher dollar amount. This compensated the waiter, but not Dorothy's efforts. I had noticed several occasions when guests shook Dorothy's hand but I never realized what was actually going on. Now it dawned on me that they were passing Dorothy money as appreciation for some special effort.

The day after I received her Christmas card, I visited the dining room and wished Dorothy a very merry Christmas. When I shook her hand I left her with a crisp one hundred dollar bill.

Apparently I had underestimated the gesture because from that day on, Dorothy treated me like royalty. Even if there were a number of influential looking people waiting, she would step around them and ask me to follow her to my usual table. I reveled in the looks on people's faces as she adjusted my chair or stopped to exchange a few pleasantries. From that time on, I learned how important it was to patronize a favorite restaurant and to personally acknowledge the presence of the owner, the hostess, and the waiters. It's not just good business, it's *smart* business, and in this case it would pay a handsome dividend.

Except for exchanging nods with certain regular VIP's, three or four months passed without any success in finding a source of revenue. I received a lot of advice but that didn't count as collateral. I needed to find someone who could tell me exactly how to raise $375,000.

One afternoon, Dorothy introduced me to an elderly judge who she was seating at the table next to mine. The introduction was brief and not intended for anything special. While eating, the judge was glancing through a magazine and at one point lifted up the front section and I could make out part of the headline: "Ray — — — — Marketing Man of the Year". I immediately thought this might be the kind of person who could tell me how to market my pet hotel concept.

As the judge rose to leave, I excused myself and asked if I could read the headline of his magazine. As he raised the magazine up I read the full headline: "Ray Kroc Named Marketing Man of the Year."

"Who is Ray Kroc?" I asked.

"My God man, where are you from?"

"I'm from Michigan," I replied.

"Don't they have McDonald's restaurants in Michigan?"

I had heard of McDonald's, but had never eaten in any kind of fast-food restaurant and I couldn't recall ever hearing the name Ray Kroc.

The judge just smiled. "Kroc is the man who turned a ten cent hamburger into a multimillion dollar business."

I was speechless. This was exactly the kind of person I needed to talk to!

In 1980 I had coauthored a twenty-six-volume set of self-help books titled *Build A Better You – Starting Now!* edited by the famous lecturer, Donald M. Dible. My contribution was my philosophy, *"Ask And You May Receive."*

I know that many people proclaim they were self-made successes. While I don't doubt they were the driving force that made their dream a success, I really doubt that they did it entirely on their own. I am convinced that no one really succeeds alone. Somewhere at sometime, someone helped them along. It's like that old Dean Martin song, *"Everybody Needs Somebody Sometime."*

Look at it this way, if you need some help what is the shame in asking someone who has already been there? I'm not talking about asking for money or labor. I am talking about help in the form of advice.

In this case I felt I had a great idea, but none of my marketing efforts had brought about the desired results. Here was a man who had turned a ten cent hamburger into a multimillion dollar business. I figured he had the expertise I needed.

PROVERB 74:
You may be the architect of your own success, but the actual construction will involve many people with different talents!

When I got back to the office I started researching McDonald's and Ray Kroc. Then I sat down at a typewriter and composed a letter similar to dozens of others that had gone unanswered. Not every request will be answered, but you only need one reply to solve your dilemma.

"Dear Mr. Kroc, I have a revolutionary business idea that will be worth millions of dollars. I have followed your successful career and would appreciate the opportunity to ask you some questions about how you marketed the McDonald's concept."

I didn't even dream of Ray Kroc investing in American Pet Motels. The most I hoped for was a chance to get some leads on venture capital.

The problem with this approach is that most executives never see the majority of their mail. Their secretaries are trained to quickly scan the mail and dispose of what they consider *junk mail*. Except for the exceptional charitable request, letters like mine almost invariably end up in the trash basket. Requesting a personal interview with a prominent person is a turkey shoot with the secretary standing between you and your turkey.

A few days after posting my letter, my secretary told me I had a call on one of the phone lines. A raspy voice on the other end said, "Robert, this is Ray. How can I help you?"

I had several friends named Ray, so I paused trying to figure out which Ray was calling me. Finally the voice spoke out in a louder tone: "Ray Kroc from McDonald's!"

I felt like dying I was so embarrassed. As briefly as I could I told Ray Kroc about the financial merits of my revolutionary idea, but refused to tell him what the idea was. I did assure him that the concept was wholly viable and that I had the proformas, facts, and figures to prove it. I must have said something right because after a few moments, he gave me a date and time to meet with him at the McDonald's headquarters in Oakbrook, Illinois.

(Now, pay attention to this next paragraph!)

I didn't go in empty handed. I had every kind of proforma imaginable. There were monthly and annual profit-and-loss projections, statistics on the growing pet industry, complete architectural plans for the buildings, and most importantly, architectural renderings of the buildings drawn by an artist. I had spent hundreds of hours and thousands of dollars gathering the information. I never made a more impressive presentation in all my years at General Motors.

Kroc insisted that I open all my documents on his huge desktop, and then I proceeded with a persuasive explanation of the American Pet Motels concept. At the time, I didn't know that he and his wife, Joan, owned a small Yorkshire terrier that he was crazy about.

Kroc just sat there shaking his head in silence. He couldn't take his eyes off the artist's renderings. Finally he said, "Jesus Christ! This is the greatest idea since I thought of McDonald's!"

Turning his head he yelled out, "Fred, come in here." From a nearby cubicle, Fred Turner, the fry cook Kroc had chosen to succeed him as president, walked over at Kroc's command.

Turner stared down at the renderings while Ray tried to explain the concept. I could tell by the expression on Turner's face that he wasn't very impressed. After expressing his "Uh-huh," Turner turned and walked back to his cubicle. Right away I figured that Fred Turner had never owned a dog or cat.

"Listen," Kroc said, "I want to think about this for a while."

I interpreted this as the brush off so I reached down to pick up my papers. Ray reached out his arm saying, "Don't touch the papers. Just leave them with me and I'll get back to you." Then he looked at his watch and invited me to have lunch with him.

Over an extended lunch, Ray Kroc told me the story of his life and McDonald's hamburgers. I took away two things from that lunch;

1) Ray Kroc was worth $685 million dollars, and 2) a subtle, but ominous warning, "I don't get mad. I get even!"

PROVERB 75:
The wise learn from their mistakes.
The wisest learn from the mistakes of others.

I really thought that was the end of it. Instead, a few weeks later I received a call from Kroc's secretary inviting me to have lunch with Ray's attorneys at the prestigious Chicago Athletic Club. I accepted.

His three "personal" attorneys were members of Sonnenschein, Levinson, Carlin, Nath & Rosenthal, a firm that occupied an entire floor of 69 West Washington Street. The masthead of their stationery listed ninety-seven attorneys. I was impressed.

The first order of business was a round of martinis.

The second order of business was another round of martinis.

There was another round of martinis but I think we ordered some lunch somewhere in-between.

"Robert," an attorney began, "you are a very lucky man! Ray Kroc wants to invest in your pet motel concept. What kind of equity are you thinking of giving up if he furnishes all the money needed?"

I told the lawyer that it wouldn't be necessary as I already had about one-third of the money pledged by other investors. In reply, he just shook his head and said, "No! Kroc must be the only investor. The money won't be a problem for him. If he can't do it alone, he won't do it at all."

This stunned me for a minute, but I knew how far I would go.

If Kroc furnished all the capital, the least I could offer him was forty-nine percent of the stock. It was a lot, but I would still control the company and I instinctively knew I could work with him.

"No," the attorney answered. "Ray Kroc has certain agreements with McDonald's whereby he would have to own eighty-five percent of any business he goes into and under no circumstances can there be any other investors."

Then there commenced a scenario that totally blurred my resistance. (Maybe the three martinis helped.)

"Look, Robert, Ray really likes you. He wants to help you. He and Joan are going to make you and Peggy millionaires. Figure it out. Would you rather have one hundred percent of nothing or fifteen percent of millions and millions of dollars?"

Math was my best subject. "Fifteen percent of millions and millions of dollars!" I replied. (They must have really been impressed with my mathematical proclivities.)

**(Remember PROVERB 17
Matters of consequence should
never be considered while under the
influence of a mind numbing stimulant!)**

Another week and Peggy and I were in the Kroc's penthouse apartment signing the documents that made me a partner with one of the world's richest men. Every one of my concerns was included in our agreement. I would begin with a modest salary of twenty-five thousand dollars a year plus expenses, a Cadillac company car, and most importantly, a five-year employment contract as CEO.

PROVERB 76:
There is no offer, promise, or agreement
unless it is in writing and signed by all parties.

I had no doubt in the viability of the concept and knew the business would prove itself before the five-year period was up. How could I go wrong?

Well, one way I went wrong was to submit to Ray's insistence that one of his protégés, a young architect, be allowed to design and build our first pet motel. When the last brick was placed, my $375,000 motel ended up costing $1,250,000.

Foundations and walls were built in the wrong places and some of the customized equipment wouldn't fit in the designed space. In the kennels, eighty electrical outlets were unusable because metal gateposts were installed in front of them.

Underground water pipes and electrical conduit rusted out causing floods and electrical outages, and the air conditioning and heating facilities had to be doubled. I watched it happening and I pestered Kroc to fire the architect, but he refused to listen. He made it plain, "If Sal doesn't build the pet motel, nobody will!"

PROVERB 77:
When you divest yourself of more than fifty
percent of the interest in your company,
it is no longer your company.

Despite everything, with a brand new concept and not one previous customer, we lost only $12,000 the first year, were profitable the second year, and more profitable every year thereafter. If our revenue of $300,000 the first year was impressive, it was nothing compared to the $3,000,000 we eventually would be taking in.

It is quite likely that all of this came about because Ray Kroc's secretary was absent on the day my letter arrived and he opened his own mail.

One of the points that should not be lost in this story is that there are no unimportant people in this world. One way or another, the least expected person can affect your chances of success. The old adage *Be nice to everyone on your way up because you'll meet the same people on your way down*, will be as true for you as it has been for others in the past.

We can all learn important values and profit from the least expected source.

One of my favorite examples is the story that Sharon Nguyen tells about a small boy who was standing in line at an ice cream parlor. He waited impatiently until his turn finally came. Eyeing all the available items, the boy began asking the price of each selection. In response to each answer, the little boy opened his palm and counted the change in his hand.

The waitress displayed her impatience to the other waiting customers and finally told the boy that he'd have to make up his mind.

"How much is a Sunday? the boy asked again. "Three-fifty," the waitress snapped. Once again the little boy opened his palm and counted the coins.

"How much would it be if it didn't have all the toppings and the cherry" the boy asked.

A sign of exasperation crossed the waitresses face. "Two-fifty!" she said, shaking her head back and forth.

Again the little boy opened his palm and counted his coins. "I'll take the Sunday without all the stuff on it." the youngster replied.

Shortly after the boy had finished his icecream and left, the waitress went over to the his table and suddenly dropped into one of the chairs and started crying. Another waitress, who had witnessed the whole incident, rushed to her side and asked what was wrong. There on the table , next to the empty icecream dish, were a quarter, two nickels, and three pennies. Thirty-eight cents. Exactly fifteen percent of the cost of the boy's ice cream. "That little boy," the waitress replied, "he ordered the plain icecream so he'd have enough money to leave me the correct tip."

I harbor no doubts about that little man's future success. I am sure the waitress also learned something from the occasion.

PROVERB 78:
Success is never the province of one person.

CHAPTER 17

MCDONALD'S, THEY'LL DO IT ALL ~~FOR~~ TO YOU

Obviously, Kroc and his accountants were very impressed. They were so impressed that towards the end of the second year, I received a letter from Kroc's attorneys that included a series of predated demand notes totaling $150,000 with back interest at nine percent plus another $96,000 a year in rent. I was told to sign all the notes and return them at once.

PROVERB 79:
A bird in the hand is NOT worth two in the bush
unless you know what kind of birds
are lurking in the bush..

I was livid. Kroc's attorneys assured me the notes were just for income tax purposes but I was not convinced. I demanded a meeting with Kroc. It would take several weeks, but I finally got my meeting. When I reminded Kroc what our agreement was, he spoke up without any prompting.

"Hey, when I buy stock in a company they don't pay me rent for the buildings or interest on my investment."

One of his attorneys and his accountant jumped in and cut him off.

"Ray, you don't understand. Money has to earn money. Money begets money. Why, you could have put your money into tax-exempt bonds and earned a safe return."

On and on they went. Ray Kroc just sat there without uttering another word while his cronies tried to legitimize this act of fiscal piracy.

PROVERB 80:
The ultimate meaning of any agreement belongs to the shrewdest lawyer.

The lawyers had another trump card. I had made several requests to Kroc to begin building our second and third pet motels in the greater-Chicago area. Now his lead attorney warned me that if I didn't sign the notes, there would be no new pet motels.

PROVERB 81:
The "stick and carrot" approach works best with jackasses and minority stockholders.

In the end they reduced the rent to five thousand dollars a month. I signed the five notes plus a new note for $25,000 to cover the back rent from August through December and an additional $6,700 for interest on the back rent. It was the last meeting I would ever get with Ray Kroc.

With the stroke of a pen, American Pet Motels went from a very promising enterprise to one burdened by debt and only marginally profitably.

Fortunately, the outlook improved dramatically. As our services expanded and our reputation spread, our occupancy rate grew to the point where we would sometimes have more than a thousand pet owners on a waiting list for rooms.

It was business as usual until a few days before Christmas, 1976, when I received a telephone call from one of Kroc's attorneys.

"Bob, I wanted to let you know that Ray has decided to close the pet motel on December 31st. He wants you out of there not later than that date."

We had already booked over five hundred pets for Christmas and New Years. Many were already in the motel. The lawyer demanded that I not worry about the transition because someone else had been hired to run the pet motel.

In answer to my concerns, he told me they were not canceling the telephone services or changing the name of the company. I reminded the attorney of our contracts and my five-year employment agreement. It was then that I got a free lesson in law.

Kroc's attorneys had cleverly drafted all the agreements between American Pet Motels and me. With eighty-five percent of the stock, Ray could legally dissolve the company and thereby void all of our agreements. I was being forced out of my own company. My stock wasn't worth one penny. There wouldn't be the five-year severance pay or anything else.

The company would now belong one hundred percent to one of the world's richest men, the magnanimous ground beef baron, Ray Kroc.

PROVERB 82:
The meaning of any agreement will ultimately be interpreted differently by each party.

PROVERB 83:
Old age, lawyers, and treachery
will always vanquish youth and integrity.

It suddenly became clear. From the very beginning, American Pet Motels had been set up for exactly this scenario. I had allowed myself to be taken in by masters of deception.

Try to picture yourself at almost fifty years old losing everything you have. I was so depressed I didn't know whether to kill myself or go to a movie.

I didn't do either. Despite warnings not to do so, I hired a law firm. I think I found the only one in Chicago that would take my case. I wasn't too encouraged after having been turned down by a few hundred other law firms in the yellow pages.

To make a long story short, my attorneys drafted a suit charging Ray Kroc with stock fraud. The suit would be filed in a federal court. America's ground-beef baron would have to face a homesteader at the bar of justice.

One of the circumstances in my favor was that during that period McDonald's was trying to expand their company by raising millions of dollars through borrowing and stock issues. My lawyers felt a public lawsuit for stock fraud in federal court might sponsor a negative influence. Ironically, my lawyers informed me that even if we won the case, the most I could hope for was serving out the two remaining years of my five-year employment agreement.

PROVERB 84:
As a last resort, never overlook
an opponent's possible vulnerability.

Whatever the reason, the day before we were to file our complaint, I received a phone call from Kroc's attorneys suggesting that I had misunderstood everything, and if I wanted to buy Ray Kroc's shares they would arrange suitable terms.

Within a few days we signed the documents that obligated me to pay Ray Kroc $1.25 million over a ten-year period for his stock. The note would be paid in monthly installments of five thousand dollars plus fifteen percent of the profits at the end of each year. The interest rate would be a variable rate beginning at nine percent. Kroc would keep all the money he had taken out of the company but the notes for back rent and interest were to be cancelled. At the end of the ten-year period there would be a balloon note for $650,000.

PROVERB 85:
When you make a deal with the devil,
expect to get burnt.

No sweat. The first thing I would do would be to take out a bank loan and pay off Kroc. Right? WRONG!

The day after I signed the agreement, I received a call from my friendly account executive at American National Bank & Trust. In very plain language he explained they handled millions of dollars for McDonald's and that, under the circumstances they found it necessary to cancel our line of credit or extend any other service to us. He also suggested that I take our account somewhere else.

Hey, I didn't need American National Bank. There were hundreds of other banks, so I picked up my marbles and went across the street. Déjà vu. Of the nearly twenty different banks in downtown Chicago, not one would consider a loan or extend us a line of credit.

PROVERB 86:
A bank is just someone else's business.

PROVERB 87:
Avarice is the mother of failure.

The only thing left to do was find a small rural bank and then try to raise the money to get free of Kroc's stranglehold.

Since borrowing the money was out of the question, I came up with the idea of selling stock in American Pet Motels. After all, you always hear how people love to buy stock in some unique enterprise. APM wasn't weird, but I figured it seemed exotic enough to attract enough investors to pay Kroc off.

Now, if you're the average person with a business idea and thinking of starting out with a stock offering, think again. While this might be a valid method if you're some kind of high-tech company, it isn't something you wanted to try in a state like Illinois in the seventies.

Without knowing what I would be up against, I hired a law firm and a major accounting firm and began planning a stock offering to raise between $600,000 and $1,000,000. I planned to offer 200,000 shares of Class A stock at five dollars a share.

While the legal and accounting costs were high, another major expense would be the preparation, printing, and distribution of five thousand 40-page prospectuses.

I wasn't about to spend myself into bankruptcy so I decided that, with the technical help of a lawyer and accountant, I would write, print, and distribute the prospectuses.

I sent out and received a dozen or so different prospectuses for pending initial public offerings and studied them. Then I went to a typewriter shop and bought a used special IBM typewriter with various size and type fonts which would provide me with justified type lines. It wasn't easy to use, but it did the job.

While at General Motors, my Methods Engineering Section had its own printing press and I made a point of learning how to burn plates and operate the press while I was there.

The next thing I did was buy an old, used Multilith printing press for one hundred dollars and a plate burner for burning the printing plates. When I finally received the lawyer's approval of the prospectus layout, I cranked up the printing press and ran it night and day until all 200,000 pages were finished. After collating and stapling, it was time to present it to the Illinois Securities Commissioner.

Apparently there is a difference of opinion between political appointees and I had the misfortune of filing during a time when a Democrat was serving as the securities commissioner of Illinois.

Just glancing at the cover of the prospectus he looked up and said, "What kind of business is this?"

I explained what it was, to which he responded, "Do you call this a legitimate business?"

While my lawyer tried to confirm its legitimacy, the commissioner was shaking his head "no" all the time.

Finally he made his first ruling. American Pet Motels was not a regular business. It was a speculative promotion and as such, a different form of prospectus would have to be issued. Two-hundred thousand printed pages had to be thrown out, rewritten, and reprinted. Despite the fact that the prospectus stated that monies from the stock offering would be used to pay off Kroc's loan, the commissioner's second demand was that we include a boldface warning that Ray Kroc held a lien on the land, buildings, and business and in the event that he foreclosed on the loan, no stockholder would receive any money back.

When we challenged some of the additional warnings that had already been explained in the prospectus, the commissioner closed the meeting with the declaration that he was responsible to the people of Illinois and he wasn't going to let the people of Illinois invest in some "pie in the sky" promotion!

After including these and several other severe warnings in a new prospectus, I was doubtful that even I would have risked my money. It was the final nail in the coffin. The stock offering failed. During the term of this commissioner, not one IPO went public in Illinois.

The only alternative was to carry on and hope for the best. Unfortunately, hoping doesn't always pay the bills. I needed a second pet motel to bring in enough profits to pay the approaching due date of the $650,000 note.

While reading the *Wall Street Journal* one day, I noticed a display ad offering a beautiful dog food research facility just outside of Des Moines, Iowa. From the description I figured this might make an ideal second location, but I also assumed I could never afford it.

This building came on the market because a Fortune 500 company had sold their dog food business to another company that already had a research facility, so they wanted to get this one off their books.

Unfortunately, this opportunity appeared in the middle of my public stock offering and all my funds were tied up. Based on the description, I figured they would be asking at least a million dollars so I didn't bother inquiring.

When the ad appeared for several successive days, I decided to invest twenty cents in a phone call. An international banking company was handling the sale of the property.

"Make us an offer," pleaded the voice at the other end of the line. I decided to be upfront with the other party and explained my cash position.

"Mr. Leeds," the voice came back strongly, "would you give us $50,000 for the land, buildings, vehicles, and all the equipment and supplies?"

Of course, I figured there had to be something wrong. So, instead of saying yes, on Friday I flew to Iowa to inspect the property. It was incredible. There was a 10,000 square foot ceramic tile building, plus dog kennels, a late-model station wagon, and a tractor complete with all the apparatus to maintain the chain-link enclosed five-acre site.

Inside the modern research building were offices outfitted with computers, steel desks, and file cabinets. There was also a laboratory with Bausch & Lomb microscopes and other scientific instruments. It was a total turnkey operation that I conservatively appraised at being easily worth a million dollars. I accepted the deal at $50,000. I offered to pay the agent $35,000 on Monday and the $15,000 balance on the following Friday.

"No good," the agent replied. "We have to get the property off the books on Monday so our other deal can close Tuesday!" There was a short pause. "Mr. Leeds, if you can't raise more than $35,000 by Monday, we'll sell it to you for $35,000. I agreed and we shook hands on it.

You can bet that I had $35,000 in their escrow account on Monday morning. I couldn't obtain the money from our corporate account because of the stock offer, so I borrowed the funds from a physician and agreed to pay him $5,000 for ten days use of his money. The cost of doing business never bothered me as long as the end result was favorable!

PROVERB 88:

It is never how much you pay.
It is how much you profit.

What a great deal? Not exactly!

When I returned to Des Moines on Monday afternoon to sign the final papers, an embarrassed agent told me the property had already been sold to a local veterinarian. The Des Moines bank that had committed to giving me a $35,000 mortgage on the property was the same bank that loaned the local veterinarian the money.

I was told that another agent of the company didn't know that the property was optioned and had made the deal with the veterinarian. Furthermore, they had already signed the sales agreements and recorded the deed. The deal was irreversible.

I am still not sure that something dishonest hadn't happened, but the agent went out of his way to ameliorate my distress. He not only reimbursed me for my travel and financial expenses, his company also paid me a modest sum to soothe my sense of loss. In the end, this international banking company paid out more to sell the property than they received.

This is the way big business operates, so never presume any deal is impossible. Just don't trust anyone.

Despite all the setbacks, I would not give up trying to find a solution to my heavy indebtedness. If you think ten years is a very long time, just carry a note for $1,250,000 when nobody will loan you a dime.

Instead of giving up, I continued submitting loan applications to different banks and savings and loan companies. God knows how many I sent out.

Just prior to the $650,000 balloon note coming due Ray Kroc died. I was no closer to raising the payoff amount than I had been when I signed the note.

At the last minute, an aggressive, albeit greedy, Lyons Savings and Loan offered me a $500,000 loan for a $50,000 cash up-front fee. I still would have been $150,000 short.

As a last resort, I wrote to Ray's widow, Joan, and explained that I could pay her $500,000 immediately, if she would only carry the $150,000 for another ten years. To my surprise, she offered to carry the note for five years with a variable interest rate that had a floor of fourteen percent.

Apparently her financial advisors told her that it was worthwhile for the fourteen percent interest she would be getting. With no alternative, I accepted her offer.

I paid Lyons Savings and Loan the $50,000 cash fee and had the $500,000 check sent to Joan. Now all I had to do was to pay off the loan to Joan Kroc and I'd be home free. After all, what else could go wrong?

Let me tell you what could go wrong.

First there was an oil embargo. People stopped traveling which also meant they stopped boarding their pets. Then there was a little thing called inflation. Interest rates skyrocketed to twenty-one percent and our reasonable payment on our note went from five thousand dollars a month to eleven thousand dollars. The more money we made, the more money it cost us to stay in business.

The only way to make more money was to build another hundred room kennel on our site. Without being able to get the money from a bank, we resorted to some creative financing; we leased all the construction material on five-year leases. We leased the chain link fencing, the copper plumbing, the toilets, the concrete, and even the special epoxy paint. Everything we needed, we acquired on a five-year lease.

Obviously, I had to find a "special" leasing company who would exchange a high interest rate for the risk of giving us $250,000. Since there was no way we could return the leased "equipment" at the end of the lease, the leasing company suggested we substitute some discarded chain link fencing, conduit, and pipe, and turn it in at the conclusion of the lease.

As it turned out, before the five years was up, we paid off all the leases. It wasn't a dishonest agreement. I had no intention of stiffing the leasing company and they were overjoyed to receive a nice fat return on their money. We both got what we wanted.

With another hundred dog runs, we became so profitable that we soon added a million dollar lobby with a fourteen station grooming parlor, a retail store with animated talking animals, a television wall, and additional animal boarding spaces for birds and small animals.

While our competitors ridiculed us for building a pet supply store as part of the lobby when PetsMart and PetCo superstores surrounded us, we proved that the fifteen to twenty thousand annual visitors would take advantage of the convenience to shop at *The Safari*. The pet store became a lucrative profit center.

Shortly after acquiring our loan, the federal government forced Lyons Savings and Loan Company to close because they "made too many speculative loans with inadequate reserves."

The story of American Pet Motel's success was heralded throughout the world. In addition to being featured on the cover of *Time* magazine, articles about us appeared in almost every major publication in the world, from *Country Gentlemen* to *Penthouse* magazine. Our company appeared in travel books and was featured in most of the world's leading magazines and newspapers including in China, England, France, and Germany.

Whereas the Pet Boarding Association predicted our early demise, it took only a few years before their president and most of their members were trying to imitate us. Unfortunately, they changed their names from kennel to pet spa, pet motel, pet hotel, and others, but the changes were only cosmetic. Few really improved their level of pet care.

I kept the pet motel for twenty-seven years, but after two bad spells with cancer, I decided that because of the inheritance tax laws, it would be better to sell the pet motel and realize some cash for Peggy's future. Under the inheritance laws, if the government valued American Pet

Motels at four or five million dollars, my wife would have had to pay half that amount in taxes upon my death. There was no way my family could have raised that kind of money. Our wealth wasn't in cash or securities, it was almost all in the land and buildings of the American Pet Motel. The only option was to sell the company before I died.

The results of two appraisals by two different companies brought us to a horrible awakening.

Although we valued the Pet Motel at more than a million dollars, the appraised value came in at $200,000.

And, before you open a unique business, that requires an investment in single purpose buildings and equipment, you better consider how many people will be looking to buy your type of business. And furthermore, how many of the people who might like to own your unique business, would have several million dollars on hand to purchase it because a bank loan would be unobtainable?

In our case there were very few people looking to buy a pet motel and none of those who were interested could raise the money with which to purchase us.

The final appraisal was based on tearing down all of our buildings, leveling the land, and selling the real estate for residential lots. Two hundred thousand dollars!

Now let me tell you another story of how providence can play a part in a person's life. Just when the prospect of selling the pet motel seemed remote, I received a visit from a representative of an organization that was planning to build state-of-the-art pet hotels across America. According to him, his investors included the Merrill Lynch stock brokerage firm and the family that owned *National Geographic* magazine. They had over thirty million dollars and access to unlimited additional funds.

According to him, their company, XYZ Pet Resorts, had already bought dozens of existing kennels and acquired prime sites all over the country. In fact, they had acquired two prime sites at major intersections within a few miles of our pet motel.

Then the man looked at me and said, "Mr. Leeds, you run a phenomenal kennel. The one thing we don't want to do is wrestle a thousand pound gorilla. We want to buy your pet motel and your expertise."

Within a few days the terms were worked out. My son Marc and I were to be paid far more than we intended to ask for, plus almost 500,000 shares of stock in their company. We quickly figured that when their company went public, the stock would be worth another several million dollars.

One of the best provisions was a substantial upfront cash payment with the balance paid annually over a five-year period. The annual interest alone amounted to almost twenty thousand dollars a month.

I hired the best attorney I could find, and adequate safeguards were included in the agreement. One of these was that the name of our pet motel and its mode of operation could not be changed until we were paid out completely. Also, if the company became insolvent or was sold, we would be paid our full sales price or the pet motel would revert back to our ownership. This was strongly objected to by the buyer, but we remained adamant that there would be no sale without these provisions. When they continued to balk and threatened to cancel the whole deal, I told them they'd have to stand in line and walked out of the conference room and went home.

The ploy worked. They gave us everything we asked for and more. Marc was given a two-year employment contract at a higher wage than I had been paying him. Although I was going to retire, they insisted I sign a two-year consulting agreement. I would be paid $1,000 a day plus expenses with a minimum of $5,000 a year and first-class air transportation on my visits to their offices on the East coast. They emphasized their need for my expertise in their startup period and I believed them. I willingly signed the addendum thinking I really would be able to influence their planning. I still hadn't learned to distinguish manure from moon beams.

Now let me explain my main motivation for my agreement to sell American Pet Motels to these people. It wasn't because I thought they would be successful. It was because I knew they would fail. I was convinced they were a bunch of idiots and within a few years we would get the pet motel back and also have the money they had paid us.

While we were negotiating, Marc and I flew out to New Jersey and Connecticut to visit their prototype kennel and their headquarters. Except for a former dog groomer, they did not have one person on their corporate staff that had ever worked in a kennel or knew anything about the pet boarding business.

To impress visitors, one employee's sole job was to stick hundreds of different colored pins in a large map of America. The vice president stressed that they were going to bring kennels to main street America. Despite the zoning restrictions, he insisted on paying thousands and thousands of dollars to purchase land options on sites located at major urban intersections. "I can get past any zoning board," he boasted. Familiar with the zoning restrictions in Chicago and its suburbs, I found him a rare example of pompous audacity and bluster.

The pride of their efforts, a brand new prototype kennel in New Jersey, further convinced me they would fail. It was made entirely of untreated wood and knowingly violated major fire codes and handicap provisions. When they sought to demonstrate how the animal doors worked, the doors were so heavy that the executive guiding us couldn't open or close them. Everything they were advertising was misleading and significantly less than the whole truth. Their prototype was a roadmap to disaster.

I warned Marc that the place was a ticking firebomb contrary to everything I believed necessary for such a venture. A few weeks later we learned that on the day prior to the grand opening, the kennel burnt down.

There are some aspects of operation that kennels and pet motels share with the hotel business; they are both seasonal businesses. However, a pet boarding facility does most of its business during holidays and the summer months when schools are closed. This is when most people travel on vacations, especially people with children.

During a conference call with all of their kennel managers, an executive demanded to know why business fell off during the winter months. When told that the industry always experienced a slowdown when the children were back in school and families didn't travel, the corporate spokesman reprimanded the group and told them that they were going to change the way people took vacations in America!

Two years later they still hadn't called on me for any assistance, and had to be reminded that they owed me $10,000 for *non*-consulting. They just sent me a check. Apparently the stockholder's money meant nothing to these promoters.

Many of the kennels they bought were in deplorable condition. One didn't even have a well or city water and water had to be carried in by hand.

Unfortunately for us, the company's demise did not bring the results I had hoped for.

They did almost go broke, but at the last minute, in order to avoid bankruptcy and losing everything, they sold the company for pennies on the dollar to an investment company. The original investors got just what they asked for; they lost their shirts.

As for Marc and me, we made out quite well, but not as well as we might have. When the company was sold the transaction was structured as a series of mergers, which, through the manipulation of legal terms, precluded us from being paid out or repossessing the company. In addition, all of the common stock was cancelled and declared valueless which meant our dream of collecting extra millions of dollars disappeared in a cloud of fiscal shenanigans.

It is an unfortunate commentary on today's corporate competence that the new company has never sought the help of a proven kennel operator to guide them. They appear to be content with a return derived by continuously increasing prices to a declining customer base, and reduced staffing and service. With proper management, that company could have made American Pet Motels into a 780 million dollar a year company.

Now hear the lament of a man who sold his "worthless" business for several million dollars.

According to what I have heard, a major home builder bought up all the land and homes surrounding the pet motel. To complete their planned condominium development, they approached the new owners of American Pet Motels with an offer to buy only the land for more than twice what the XYZ company paid me for the land and the business. In addition, they included an offer to duplicate the pet motel on a nearby commercial plot as part of the deal.

Apparently the new owners thought they could wring more out of the tentative buyer. In the end, the home builder walked away from the deal. If only I had kept the pet motel for four more years!

CHAPTER 18

SO CLOSE. SO FAR.

I operated American Pet Motels for twenty-seven years, but that wasn't all I was involved with during those years.

The insatiable desire to continue creating successful new enterprises was never dormant, and some of my inspiration came from the most unexpected sources.

As a goodwill practice, I designed a special Christmas card each year that was sent to all the pet owners who boarded with American Pet Motels.

When I began in 1973, the cost of sending out a Christmas card was only eight cents for half an ounce. If the card and envelope exceeded the half-ounce limit the postage cost doubled. In 1975 the post office increased the cost of first class mail to ten cents for the first ounce plus another nine cents if you went a hair over an ounce.

As luck would have it, I designed a Christmas card for my patrons that weighed just over one ounce, costing me an extra four hundred and fifty dollars in postage. I was steamed.

Something had to be done and I figured out what it was: *The Airless Mail Company.*

I went out and bought the thinnest plastic obtainable and a hot wire sealer. Then I bought a large tank of helium that was really quite inexpensive.

With this equipment I fashioned an envelope-size insert that held enough helium to almost make a letter weightless. Goodbye overweight envelopes.

Now I was aware that the Federal Government might not like my idea, but according to their regulations, I couldn't find any existing restriction barring the mailing of an inert, nonpoisonous, nonflammable gas in the US mail.

However, I wasn't going to market Airless Mail as a gimmick to cheat the post office. I would use as subtle an approach as possible.

Just imagine the advantages to companies that do a lot of mailing or shipping (I also planned large envelopes for packages). My cases of helium envelopes wouldn't occupy any valuable floor space. They would just float up to the ceiling; a thought that caused me concern.

I went to bed one night and dreamt of a huge postal processing room with long lines of envelopes being transported along in conveyorized fixtures. All of a sudden the end of one file of letters started lifting into the air and soon the entire room was filled with floating letters. It was mayhem and I awoke abruptly with perspiration covering my forehead.

I knew the idea was sound as long as only one helium insert was used. But, I knew there were people who would not follow instructions, and one foul up would bring new postal regulations that would put us out of business. After due consideration and friendly guarantees that I would eventually run afoul of the law, I decided to give up on Airless Mail. In the end I bought a clown suit to cover the helium tank and began giving away helium-filled balloons to the children who came into the pet motel.

The following year I was far behind schedule in designing my Christmas card. After dinner one night, I rushed downstairs to my little office to create the verse for that year's card and an idea came into my head. I began writing and completely lost track of time until at 3:30 AM my wife called on me to come to bed. When I looked down, I was surprised to find that I had written over thirty pages of a Christmas story all in verse.

It was much too long to use as a Christmas card so I just set it aside not knowing what to do with it. Shortly afterward I received a letter from an old customer who informed me of her dog's death. Since my Christmas story related to the virtues of owning a dog, I decided to make a copy of my story and send it to her. After that, I began doing the same thing for other clients.

Apparently, people began reproducing my story and sending it all over the country. One afternoon, I received a telephone call from a man who identified himself as Orson Welles. I thought it was someone pulling a joke on me. The man insisted he was Orson Welles and I became convinced by the tone of his voice that it really was the great movie star and director. Someone had given Orson Welles a copy of *Christmas Tails*.

"Mr. Leeds," Welles began, "are you going to make your story into a movie?"

The thought of doing anything with the story had never crossed my mind. "No," I replied.

"Well I think you should," Welles responded. "This is a story that everyone should read. It's a story everyone should see. You should make this story into an animated feature!"

After a few minute's reflection, I realized that Welles was talking about something that would cost millions of dollars to produce.

There was silence for a few moments and then I said, "Mr. Welles, I operate a dog kennel. There's no way I could afford to produce an animated feature."

"You don't have to produce the movie. All you have to do is produce a storyboard and send it to Disney or some other animation company," he said sharply. "I guarantee you it will sell."

"How do you make a storyboard?" I asked him.

"Hell, it's simple. You just have an artist illustrate a section of the story. Then you add some music and get someone with a good voice to narrate the characters; put it all on tape and send it out."

I paused to digest his words. All I needed was an illustrator, an orchestra, some singers, and an animation company to put it on tape. Whether he realized it or not, he was still talking more money than I could ever come up with. On the other hand, if it did work, the money would be more than enough to pay off the Krocs and I'd be free of them forever.

Suddenly Welles voice boomed over the telephone once more. "Listen, I'll tell you what we'll do. I will record all the voices of the characters and send you the tape without any charge. All you'll have to do is get the other parts together. If you don't sell the movie deal, you don't owe me anything. If you do sell the movie rights, you send me $10,000. But remember, I'd like to be considered for the narrator role if the movie is made."

I was speechless. I felt more than a little intimidated and too embarrassed to say no. Instead I committed myself to the arrangement. At the time, Orson Welles was getting as much as fifty thousand dollars just to read a script. How could I turn down his offer? All I had to do was figure out how to produce an animated storyboard on my modest budget.

A newspaper ad for an illustrator brought a dozen replies and my decision was weighted toward the one who could produce an acceptable illustration at the lowest cost. My final selection was Marc Richards, an employee of Air France, who was trying to pick up some extra money by free-lancing as an artist. I think I paid Marc six hundred dollars for twenty-eight four-color illustrations. I don't believe anyone could have produced finer drawings.

Two or three weeks later, I received another call from that haunting voice. "Robert? Orson! It's in the can."

There was a long pause. What was he talking about? What's "in the can?" Was he talking about the garbage can? The proverbial s---can? Before I could ask, Welles responded with the answer.

"I recorded the entire soundtrack. The tape is in a can and being shipped to you."

I thanked him several times and hung up.

A new predicament arose. In order to be made into a full-length feature, I needed to grow the ten-minute story into one hundred and twenty minutes. The storyboard had to be at least twice as long as my original story. I began adding to the story. Although I had never written anything before, I even wrote some songs for the film and had them recorded.

Everything just fell into place. The artwork, the filming, the music, everything except Welles' narration fit together like a jigsaw puzzle. I would have to go back to Welles and ask him to record the new sections of the storyboard.

Remember what I said about providence? Before I had a chance to call him, I picked up the newspaper and there was an article detailing Orson Welles' death. It was the end of a grand dream.

I finished the storyboard using a different narrator to recite the added verses, but it wasn't the same. Orson Welles never portrayed Othello or Hamlet any better than he did Santa Claus, the dogs, and all the other animals in the storyboard of *Christmas Tails*.

I finally found an animation company in Ohio that wanted to produce a full length animated film of *Christmas Tails*. The company was actually an art teacher in Cincinnati, Ohio who was producing short animated features for several New York children's television shows. He got most of his artwork done by using his art students to draw the minor cels.

Although he had never done a full length movie, he was anxious to do this story because he felt it would be an opening into Hollywood for his talents. He figured he could do it in two to three years and agreed to absorb the costs for fifty-percent of the profit. It was better than nothing, so I told him to draw up a contract.

The agreement looked fine to me, but I took it to my attorney to review.

"Why would you want to take a chance on a third rate producer like this guy?" my lawyer scolded. "I have a friend with Mitchell, Silberberg & Knupp in Los Angeles who knows all the top agents that can get you into producers like Disney and Warner Brothers. You don't know if this Cincinnati guy would ever finish your movie. Let me introduce you to Hal Friedman."

A week later I flew to Los Angeles for a meeting with Hal Friedman. My lawyer was right; Hal knew the right people. That same afternoon we went over to the William Morris Agency and viewed the storyboard with Steve Konow, a William Morris agent. He liked what he saw. We agreed that the William Morris Agency would represent me and try to sell the story to a motion picture company. One of the world's largest agencies was going to represent me. A contract was to be sent to me by mail.

After waiting for months, I called the agents number and learned that he had left William Morris to start his own agency. When I finally reached his office, I was told they had no record of my story or me. Neither did the William Morris Agency. For this I had given up the sure prospect of having the feature produced. In addition, my lawyer charged me twenty-two hundred dollars for the introduction to Friedman and Friedman charged me another two thousand dollars to introduce me to Steve Konow. Add to this my airfare and hotel bills and I had a severe case of wishing I had signed with the Cincinnati producer.

I put the story and the storyboard in a closet and went on with my life. Another chapter closed.

PROVERB 89:
Lawyers are not deal makers.

They are deal breakers.

The operation of American Pet Motels required a great deal of maintenance that we located in a special tool room built as part of our garage. The tool room contained cabinets with every kind of screw, nut, and bolt we would ever need. In addition there also was every kind of washer, "O" ring, and tool any maintenance shop would have envied.

Of course none of these repair parts would have been of any use if we didn't have the proper tools for installing them and this often presented a problem. One of our major expenses was having to replace tools that were misplaced, broken, or stolen. Something had to be done to maintain a constant inventory of the tools. Another great idea.

Hanging tools on a pegboard rack was common, but no one sold pegboard with the tool outlines already silk-screened on the pegboards. Introducing another one of my great ideas; PEG-A-TOOL. On June 23, 1982 I incorporated the PEG-A-TOOL Corporation and registered the design.

Over a period of two months I laid every kind of hand tool sold by Sears on a four-foot by eight-foot sheet of pegboard and outlined them. Then I filled in the outlines with black paint. Next I bought an assortment of brackets and selected the ones that would hold each tool securely to the pegboard. It required fifteen different types of hooks or brackets to do the entire board.

My first two boards were all painted by hand. Every hole that held a bracket was identified with a letter denoting the type of bracket that went in that particular hole. It truly was a masterpiece of ingenuity and simplicity.

My next step (which should have been my first) was to figure out the sales price as well as the cost to ship the product. To my dismay, neither FedEx nor UPS would handle a four by eight-foot sheet of pegboard. It was back to the drawing board.

I cut the standard eight-foot long sheet of pegboard into four pieces two-foot by four-foot and re-laid all the tools out again. It worked fine and it was even better than having to handle a huge four by eight-foot board.

To ship the set of boards, I shrink-wrapped them in a transparent plastic envelope that also protected the boards during shipping.

Since I had used all Sears Craftsman tools it seemed logical to approach Sears and see if they would be interested in carrying the item. The minute the buyer saw the product he wanted it. However, because of its bulk and low price, he wanted it as a catalog item and asked if I could have several thousand sets available for Sears Christmas catalog sales.

Without hesitating, I assured the buyer the product would be available.

Now let me reveal some of the considerations in bringing a product to market.

I already had my source for the raw material, but now I had to buy a silk-screening machine. I also needed a heating tunnel with conveyors to dry the printed designs and again to shrinkwrap the plastic around the four-board set.

Of course it was impossible to move the pallet loads of pegboard, so I had to buy a forklift truck. When I finally had all the equipment and raw material, my pet motel's training barn was almost totally filled. I had to go out and buy steel racks so I could utilize the cube, and stack material on shelves up to the ceiling.

Naturally I purchased everything used, but I didn't always get the best price because I was racing to meet the anticipated orders from Sears.

To make matters worse, when I got my first truckload of pegboard and started silk-screening, no two boards came out the same. The holes never matched up. That's when I found out that pegboard is manufactured in huge sheets and just stamped out at random. The holes are never in the same place.

I called the pegboard company and explained the problem. Fortunately, in anticipation of the huge volume we would be using, the company agreed to take back all the cut pegboard and set up a special cutting section that would produce boards with identical hole locations. At last, all my problems were solved.

As Christmas approached, I still hadn't received a written purchase order from Sears. However, since we were going to ship for Sears, it seemed logical that they might be waiting until the orders rolled in and then issue a purchase order for the orders received. You know how it is. You have to make allowances for your BIG customers.

As we got closer and closer to Christmas, I dared to call their buyer again and was told there was something in the mail.

There was; a letter from H.C. Crittenden advising me that, because pictures of the product would take up too much space, the item had been deleted from the catalog.

The impact of the letter was a mortal blow. I sold off the pegboard sheets at giveaway prices to hardware stores and anyone else who would buy them. All the equipment, except the silk-screening equipment, went the same way.

PROVERB 90:
There is no such thing
as a verbal purchase order.

In retrospect, I should have developed a business plan and a marketing program that didn't rely on a single customer. I certainly should have introduced the product at the huge Hardware Show in Chicago but I didn't even think about trade shows.

Now, having a valuable piece of equipment, it seemed natural to me to find a way to utilize it. What more natural product could there be for silk-screening than T-shirts and sweatshirts. Enter another one of my better ideas, The Perfekt Company.

In 1993 I had just completed a new million-dollar lobby on my pet motel that included a large retail store. Instead of just carrying dog foods and supplies it was more of a boutique and stocked animal oriented items from expensive crystal and watches down to inexpensive greeting cards. Why not carry our own line of "T" shirts and sweat shirts?

I decided to have one design for almost every occupation and feature two cartoon characters modeled on the cat and dog robots in our store. Their names were Cecil, the dog, and Boo, the cat.

My first design was two railroad tracks coming across a desert. One was from the East and one was from the West. Instead of meeting, the two tracks ended six feet apart. Standing next to the tracks studying blue prints were Cecil and Boo. I had a similar design for a bridge and twenty or thirty other designs for other occupations. In each design there was a goof-up and underneath was the phrase "*So, who's perfect?*"

A clothing salesman who noticed our shirts immediately wanted to handle our line for sales to high-fashion clothing stores. He predicted they would be a sensation. He even had a better idea. Because we would need thousands of these T-shirts and sweatshirts we should have them made by a regular silk screening company. He also talked me into producing a line of sweatpants to go along with the sweatshirts. Down one pant leg was the slogan, *So, who's perfect?* As luck would have it, he had a nephew who had a silk-screening shop and was looking for business.

I went over and visited his nephew at his shop. I had really fallen into a great deal. He shared a huge building with a printing company and had the whole second floor for storage. He even agreed to warehouse the entire raw and finished product at no charge and just send the finished product to me as I needed it. I was also going to save expensive warehouse charges.

Of course, I had to advance him the money to have printing screens made and to buy the raw T-shirts, sweatshirts and sweatpants.

Now, in the clothing industry, you don't sell individual items, you package your products in certain combinations. In our case, each design was made available in a combination of two medium sizes, three large sizes, and one extra-large size. Small size, extra large, and extra extra large sizes could be ordered in quantities of three. Within a few months I had eight traveling salesmen covering almost the entire United States. Orders for the Christmas season started coming in immediately.

Items like T-shirts, sweatshirts, and sweatpants are very competitively priced with special offers happening all the time. Fortunately, I had a printer who was always finding ways to buy the best product available at thirty to forty percent off the regular wholesale price. All I had to do was keep advancing him money for the raw material.

As September rolled around we began packaging and shipping our orders. We had barely started when we found that we were short of certain sizes in every design.

When the printer kept stalling, I insisted on taking inventory in the warehouse. What I found was an almost empty warehouse. Despite all the excuses he gave, it was obvious the man was a swindler. Neither the state's district attorney nor anyone else could help me. I was told to sue the man in civil court. When I tried to seize his assets, I learned that the equipment, his car, house, and everything else was not in his name and could not be touched. The loss was sixty-five thousand dollars. There were a dozen things I could have done to prevent this swindle but hey, *who's perfect?*

RULE 91:
Failure to audit may cost you
the shirt off your back.

But wait. There's more bad news. About a thousand shirts and pants were still in the warehouse in brown cardboard boxes. I didn't want to waste any more money on storage charges, so I moved the boxes into the basement of my house and took off for a vacation.

When I returned home, I found all of the boxes under three feet of water in my basement. Chicago had received torrential downpours and both of my sump pumps had broken down. In order to salvage the clothing I rushed everything to a commercial laundry so they could wash them and remove the brown cardboard stains and the sewage smell. The brown stains didn't come out but the sewer smell did. Something else also happened.

Apparently, I hadn't asked the laundry to only use warm water, so they washed every cotton item in boiling water. Now an extra large size would fit a midget. I gave most of the items to Goodwill and saved a few for future gifts. Ten years later I still have hundreds of shirts and sweat pants stored in my closets. (If you're not over four foot tall, have I got an extra large sweatshirt for you!)

I've had my share of problems, but I realized that getting angry and trying to get revenge isn't the answer.

Temperament can be another detriment to success. I have encountered executives with horrible tempers but they were the exception. The majority of successful entrepreneurs are really very nice and, although they may insist on things being done their way, they do not choose to prevail in a disagreement by yelling and screaming.

A good example (or maybe he is a bad example), is my good friend Elliot. Elliot ruled his very lucrative business with an iron hand. He made every decision without benefit of counsel or compassion. To hold on to his employees he intimidated them with high salaries and cash reconciliation bonuses.

Late in his career Elliot sold a piece of property in a Chicago suburb for $800,000.

The following day he took the check to his bank in downtown Chicago. He strode up to the teller's cage and, even though he had no immediate need for the money, demanded the check be deposited in his account and the funds be available for an immediate cash withdrawal.

When the teller explained that the money would not be available until the check had cleared, Elliot began one of his tantrums. Not even the bank's officers could assuage his anger or loud use of expletives. Finally, Elliot threatened to withdraw all his money from the bank, picked up his check, and went across the street to the Superior National Bank, where he opened an account with the $800,000 check. They treated him like royalty and he liked that.

While his new checks were being printed, Elliot delayed transferring the millions of dollars he had in his old bank to the new bank. About two weeks after this incident, Elliot picked up his *Chicago Tribune* and read that Superior National Bank had failed. It was one of the largest bank failures in over a decade. Despite the employment of several law firms, Elliot was only able to salvage the $100,000 insurance offered by the Federal Deposit Insurance Corporation.

Now, this is something for you to think about. The Federal Insurance Depositary Corporation (FDIC) was established in 1933 after thousands of banks failed during the depression of the late 1920s and 1930s. Today, the FDIC holds over $44 billion dollars in earned premiums and insures more than $3 trillion of deposits. Before you bask in the light of these statistics, it is prudent to consider some other facts.

Out of the more than ten thousand banks, savings and loan associations, and credit unions in America, only 5,300 have chosen to carry the FDIC insurance. Many do not have any insurance for their customer's deposits.

The $100,000 insurance limit was established by the federal government in 1933 when $100,000 was what a million dollars is today. It has never been increased in the past seventy-one years.

In just the last three years, Americans have lost more than $128 million in uninsured accounts.

Face it! It is no longer extraordinary to go into business and accumulate more than $100,000 in working capital in a bank account. Many Americans sell a home or business for more than a hundred thousand dollars and place the money in a bank or savings and loan association assuming the institution is federally insured. Be aware. That friendly "hometown" bank that treats you so nicely might just not be insured. Everything you have may be at risk.

A warm presentation by a teller or loan officer is little compensation for losing all your hard earned savings because that particular institution does not offer the FDIC insurance! On the other hand, you can also end up losing everything you have in excess of $100,000 in an institution that does have FDIC insurance.

Now let me tell you what I would do if I were you. I'd go out and borrow a few million dollars and start an insurance company. I'd make arrangements with Lloyds of London or some other reinsurance company and I'd offer insurance for deposits of over $100,000. That $44 billion dollars in premiums that the FDIC has earned is probably peanuts to what you would earn.

CHAPTER 19

SUCCESS

CAN BE A GAMBLE

Over these many years I've come to believe that luck, both good and bad, runs in cycles. I have written much on acts of providence, but providence is just another word for luck. Some "successful" people might dispute this definition, but from my experience I remain convinced.

Luck or providence, whichever it is, for me the experience seemed to occur for sustained periods of time.

One of these periods occurred when Peggy and I were living in Farmington, Michigan. It started off with a local bank raffling off a brand new Chevrolet for their grand opening. All anyone had to do was to take the time to go into the bank and fill out an entry coupon.

I saw the sign on the way home from work, so when I arrived home I told Peggy to go down to the bank the next day and put in an entry ticket. She refused.

Peggy insisted we were so unlucky that we couldn't win anything. When I arrived home on the last day of the contest and learned she hadn't entered the contest, I stormed out of the house and did it myself. I made out one entry in her name and one entry in my name.

The next day, someone from the bank called Peggy and told her she had won the car. To this day she says she won the car and I insist that I won the car. You be the judge.

PROVERB 92:
When there is no risk, always take a chance.

A short time later a local supermarket had a free raffle for a side of beef all butchered and packaged for a freezer. Without telling me, she went down and entered a slip with the name Beef Aleana. The following Saturday they delivered the side of beef to us.

A few weeks later she entered a contest to name the stuffed buffalo toy that the Bank of Buffalo Grove was going to give out. She wrote down the name, *Count Buffy du Saver* and walked off with a one hundred dollar savings account and a huge stuffed toy buffalo.

Over the next several years it seemed we could do nothing wrong.

PROVERB 93:
There is no prize
　　　　　for the one who doesn't play the game.

While walking through a Sears' store, my eight year old son Marc noticed a huge jar of jelly beans on the Allstate Insurance counter and a sign offering a new television set to the person who came closest to guessing how many jelly beans were in the jar. Marc insisted on entering the contest. I gave him an entry form and he wrote in the number one hundred.

I looked at his entry and shook my head. "Marc," I said, "use your head. That's no way to guess how many jelly beans are in that jar. You have to use your head."

Then I continued with pure hogwash. "Now, that jar is about eight inches square and ten inches high. Each jelly bean is about a quarter-inch in diameter and a half-inch long so if you multiply sixteen times thirty-two and then multiply by the height of the jar you can get the exact answer. I did exactly as I explained and wrote down 4,960 and dropped my entry into the collection box. I was ten beans off and won the television set. I didn't do it scientifically. I guessed at every dimension as well as the final answer.

PROVERB 94:
Good fortune depends on good efforts.

In addition to these prizes, over the next few years we won a pig, a turkey, several thousand dollars in playground equipment, a pearl necklace, and four roundtrip tickets to Finland. We even won a modest prize in the Publisher's Clearing House promotion.

Except for the trips to Finland (We donated $2.00 to a Finish charity two years in a row and won each time.), we never bought a single raffle ticket. All we had to do was go a little out of our way or spend a little extra time to fill out an entry form.

But all these free prizes paled by comparison to a streak of luck I had in Las Vegas. I hesitate to include this in the book because it is so rare that I wouldn't give you any odds on anyone being able to duplicate it.

About 1960 Peggy and I took our three children and drove to Las Vegas for a two-week vacation. We stayed at a modestly priced motel called the Momart Motel. It had two outstanding features; it was cheap and it offered free babysitting service. We were on a very restricted budget, so we didn't do any gambling. We just went sightseeing, ate, and enjoyed ourselves.

On our way home we stopped on the strip at the Stardust Hotel to eat lunch. Afterward, Peggy wanted to take the kids to the restroom, so I said I'd just wait in the lobby for her. She left with a stern warning not to gamble.

As soon as they disappeared I sat down at an empty ten-cent blackjack table. I had never played blackjack and didn't know a single thing about the game. Relatively, my betting ten cents then was like my betting twenty-five dollars today.

I stayed when I had a fourteen against a dealer's ten. I hit on eighteen. I split tens. I probably did every wrong thing a blackjack player could do. To the dealer's bewilderment I kept winning. By the time Peggy returned with the children there were several pit bosses plus the dealer watching me play. They changed the deck and they changed the dealer, but it didn't help the house.

When Peggy got to the table she was ready to have a fit until I told her that I had run my ten-cent investment into over twenty dollars. She just scooped up all my money and went over to the jewelry counter where she bought a beautiful twenty-dollar simulated-pearl necklace. She still wears that same necklace when we dress up.

After that excursion and my employment with General Motors, we began visiting Las Vegas every three or four years. By that time I could afford to set aside a few hundred dollars to lose playing blackjack. I did just that. I lost every time.

About 1989 I was walking through a gift shop where I noticed a little booklet called *The Facts of Blackjack*. The price was one dollar. Out of curiosity more than anything else, I bought the book and slipped it into my luggage. When I got home I read the forty-eight page booklet.

Actually, I didn't just read it. I studied it. I studied it until I had memorized all the combinations and knew exactly what to do depending upon the dealer's face card.

I don't attribute what happened after that to luck; I attribute it to skill. I would never again play a hand of blackjack according to intuition. I play based on what I learned in a forty-eight page pamphlet that I bought for one dollar.

PROVERB 95:
Somewhere there is a book with all the answers.

Now let me tell you a few stories about luck, skill, and providence.

The next time we visited Las Vegas I sat at my usual five-dollar minimum-bet table. I don't like to play in a crowded casino, so Peggy and I would take in a show or do something else until midnight and then we'd go to bed. At 3:00 AM I'd get up and go down and play blackjack

By following the instructions given in that little book, I found myself almost four hundred dollars ahead when Peggy came down for breakfast.

The next night I sat down at a ten-dollar- minimum-bet table and when I quit I was ahead several hundred dollars. The following night I sat down at a twenty-five dollar table and by morning had another two thousand dollars. From that time on I would win one or two thousand dollars almost every night, and all of our room and dining charges were picked up by the casinos.

Before long I even stopped bringing money with me and just got a "marker" from the casino for the amount I wanted to gamble with. When I recently added up all the markers I had acquired, I found that I had borrowed more than $600,000 over a ten-year period. If you are impressed by this, you might consider that there probably are thousands of gamblers who borrow that much in a single night. You will always read about some celebrity winning thousands of dollars in a single evening. You will never read when they lose thousands of dollars more the next evening.

I've always said I didn't care if I made a million dollars, as long as I could live like a millionaire. In Las Vegas we lived like millionaires. You haven't lived until you get off a plane and find a liveried chauffeur holding up a sign with your name on it. The limousine whisks you to the hotel where you enter a private VIP room to register. You avail yourself to the fine candy, cakes, soft drinks, and liquors—all free, and the host treats you like you are a millionaire.

When you arrive in your suite there's a large basket of fruit, appetizers, and a bottle of Champagne wrapped in cellophane with a big red ribbon tied around it.

Although we could have behaved like gluttons, our expenses were quite modest compared to the behavior of some comped guests. For us it was enough just to eat a nice meal in one of their many fine restaurants after being ushered through the VIP line ahead of everyone else.

There are three outstanding memories that I have to relate. All of them took place in the MGM Grand or the Mirage Hotels.

I was sitting at a hundred dollar minimum-bet table. After playing all night I decided to quit and go to bed. At that time I had the habit of taking all of my winnings and betting it all on one last hand. Whether I won or lost, at least I wouldn't go home a loser.

In this game I ended up with $6,500 in winnings. Rather than risking it all on one hand, I decided to divide the amount and bet $3,300 in one hand and if I lost that, I would bet the remaining $3,200 on a second hand.

None of the other players got a spectacular hand, but I was dealt a seven and a four. Eleven. The dealer turned up a ten for her up-card. Now, according to my little book you always figure the dealer for a ten in the hole, which meant she probably had twenty. Unless you're counting cards, every book advises you to always double-down with an eleven because you have almost a sixty-seven percent chance of tying or beating the dealer. Everyone at the table stayed with their cards or drew additional cards. When it came to me, I didn't know what to do. I hated the thought of losing $6,500 in a single hand but I also hated the thought of missing the chance to win $13,000.

Since my bet of $3,300. was the largest on the table, everyone was waiting for me to do something. In addition to the players and the dealer, two pit bosses were also standing and waiting to see what I would do.

Despite my discipline, I wasn't sure what I should do. If I doubled down and didn't draw a picture card or a ten, I would probably lose $6,500. If I just played the $3,300 I would win or lose $3,300. However, if I doubled down and won, I would win $13,000.

The dealer and everyone else was waiting for me to make my decision. I had once promised myself that I would never play on intuition. I would always play according to the book. I turned up my two cards and hesitated. Then I took my remaining $3,200. and placed it next to my original bet. I had just wagered $6,500. on the turn of a single card.

The dealer asked if I wanted to borrow a hundred dollars to make my bet even, but I declined the offer. I didn't want to go home a loser.

The dealer dealt me my one card face down. When everyone's hand had been exposed she reached out and peeked at the face of my down card. Her smile disappeared from her face.

"I'm sorry," she said with a straight face.

Everyone at the table let out a groan and I felt my own heart sink. Then she flipped up my card. It was a queen.

I had twenty-one. The dealer only had twenty. I walked away from the table with $13,000 in winnings.

The second occasion was when I was playing at a hundred-dollar table inside the baccarat room behind the cashier's office at the Mirage. The maximum bet allowed was $10,000. There were three or four of us playing and I was going back and forth but still winning. A very neatly dressed Latin gentleman came in and occupied the seat next to me. He began by placing $2,000 bets and soon raised them to $5,000. When he felt comfortable with the table, he began betting the maximum bet, $10,000.

After about an hour of playing, the man asked the dealer to have the minimum bet limit raised to $20,000. The dealer refused, saying he couldn't raise the table maximum. The man then asked for the pit boss. The pit boss also refused the request, so the man asked to talk to the casino manager and was turned down a final time.

Then the man turned to me and said, "Excuse me. I've been watching you play and you're only betting a few hundred dollars on each hand, would you mind if I bet on your hand?"

I couldn't see any harm so I told him he could, but if he was going to bet the majority of the money, he should call the cards. He then handed me $10,000 in chips and I placed a $10,000 bet.

The game had stopped while this was going on. All of a sudden, the dealer told my new friend to take his money off of my betting area. Before my friend could reply, the pit boss stepped forward and ordered the man to take his money away from my bet.

I am usually very reserved and reluctant to engage in controversy, but I couldn't see what the big deal was. I looked up at the pit boss and asked him why there was a problem since it was my hand and I had no objection.

The pit boss paused for a moment and then laid out his rules. "OK, you can play with his money, but *you* have to play the cards. You can't ask him for advice. You can't even talk to him, and he can't talk to *you*. *You* have to play the cards!"

I looked over at my neighbor and shook my head. "I'm sorry," I said, "but they own the cards."

"I don't care," he replied. "You play the cards anyway you want. I'll give you the money."

I stared at him in silence.

"Look," he said, "I've already lost $70,000 today. I'm not worried. You just play the cards. We're going to win."

For the first (and only) time in my life I began betting $10,000 a hand. Even though it went back and forth, I never went below the original $10,000. The longer I played and won, the higher I raised my own bets until my portion of the bet was $1,000 a hand. We played until 4:00 AM when I realized I had to get up in a couple of hours to catch a plane. I looked down at the piles of chips in front of me and didn't feel at all guilty about quitting. When the dealer cashed me out I had $69,000.

I took the $19,000 that represented my share of the winnings and handed my new friend $50,000. He had been just as lucky and was probably up about $100,000. As I got up to leave, he took a stack of hundred dollar chips and pushed them over to me. I was flattered, but refused them. I figured that was the best evening's entertainment I'd ever have. It was.

There was only a small act of retribution from the pit boss. He neglected to give me credit for the evening's play. With that kind of betting I probably would have qualified for the penthouse suite. *Que sera, sera.*

The third occasion was to have a profound effect on my life.

It happened back in 1980.` I was once again playing at a twenty-five dollar table in the main casino of the MGM Grand. It was one of those nights when all the seats were filled with patrons who enjoyed exchanging jokes and stories, and the same people were at the table for several hours. Nobody seemed to be winning or losing very much.

It was about two in the morning when one of the players finally lost his last chip and stood up to leave. He was about 5'5" and must have weighed close to 300 pounds.

In excusing himself he remarked that it was time for him to go upstairs and work on his novel. This drew an immediate response from one of the ladies at the table.

"Oh," she exclaimed, "Are you an author?" To which the man replied, "Yes."

"What are some of your books? Maybe I've read some of them."

The man hesitated and then smiling he said, "Well, my best seller was a book on dieting for McGraw-Hill. It became a national best seller."

There was an embarrassing silence. As we looked at this rotund figure of a man. Nobody knew what to say.

In response to the silence, the man smiled and said, "Oh, I wasn't always this heavy. This is what happens when you write a bestseller and start living high on the hog." With that he turned and left a table full of smiling players.

I have to submit that I was especially impressed. I had never written or published a book before, but if a 300-pound man could write a best selling book on dieting maybe I could write something.

When I arrived home I looked up a letter I had received from the well-known lecturer and author, Donald M. Dible, asking me to write some chapters for his twenty-six volume book series titled, *BUILD A BETTER YOU – STARTING NOW!* Don's own bestselling book was titled *UP YOUR OWN ORGANIZATION.*

At the time I received his request, I didn't think I was qualified to write anything for publication. Now, after meeting a short, fat author who wrote a bestselling book on dieting, I wasn't quite sure. I submitted a manuscript to Dible and he published it just as I had written it. I was encouraged.

PROVERB 96:
Advice is plentiful.
   Experience and knowledge are rare.

Over the years I would write several more books; *How Santa's Best Friend Saved Christmas, Christmas Tails, All The Comforts of Home, Doctor Leeds' Selection of Epic Recitations for Minstrel and Stage Use, Love Is A 4 Legged Word, How to* almost *Make A Million Dollars,"* and I have three more books started.

By 1999, we were visiting Las Vegas five or six times a year. At the end of 1999 we decided to move there. We've never regretted it, but neither do I gamble any more. The one thing I've learned is that the casinos have an advantage.

The last thing I would want to do is to mislead someone into thinking they will have success handed to them if they just keep trying different things. Success is elusive and too seldom achieved only because most people won't persevere in a their objective.

It's much easier to give up when the going gets tough and pursue another dream. As for gambling, I've only told you about the times I won. No one ever talks about the times they lost. If you ever go to Atlantic City or Las Vegas take a good look around. Those billion dollar casinos weren't built by patrons winning. Losers build them brick by brick.

PROVERB 97:
**Remember, the poorhouse is full
of gamblers with systems, luck, and intuition.**

What you should learn from this book is that almost everything we enjoy today was improbable yesterday. This world abounds with opportunities for people who are willing to try something new or different. This was true yesterday. It's true today. It will be true tomorrow. Most of us have talents beyond our imagination. All we have to do is dust them off and use them.

If you want to succeed in life, you must first have a dream, and then you must pursue it.

PROVERB 98
The improbable is not the impossible.

CHAPTER 20

I LIED

Every word in this book is the truth except for two things. First, some of the names have been changed to protect the guilty, and two, I didn't *almost* make a million dollars. I did make it. In fact I made several million dollars. It may have taken me sixty-one years, but I made it. I made it and I spent it. I wanted to live like a millionaire and I did.

I'm not ashamed of the number of times I tried. In fact, I take pride in the fact that I never stopped trying. Except for a couple of youthful indiscretions, like diamond smuggling and taking liberties with a couple of loan applications, I never knowingly did anything unethical or unlawful. I blame those two questionable occasions when I strayed on youthful exuberance.

I certainly never intentionally did anything that resulted in someone else suffering a bad consequence. In fact, as I came along the way, I was overly generous to charitable causes and always sent in more money with my income taxes than was due. I felt a certain privilege in being an American and it pleased me to do it. I love and honor this country for providing me with so many opportunities.

For those of you who are just starting on the journey, let me tell you how I lived from the first minute I could afford it.

I had always joked that if I had a million dollars I would spend $400,000 on wild parties, $400,000 on wild women, and the rest I'd just spend foolishly. I didn't quite spend all of it that way.

When I was a little boy I used to go into the local candy store and stare longingly at the shelf that held stacks of these huge chocolate bars. To be able to afford a large Hershey chocolate bar in those poverty stricken times was one of my "impossible dreams."

As a child, I could accumulate a few pennies, but never quite enough to afford the price of that elusive almond studded chocolate bar. I promised myself then, that if I ever got rich, I would buy a supply of those giant sized Hershey's chocolate bars and eat them until I couldn't eat any more.

I will never forget the day I got my first paycheck from General Motors and was driving home. I drove past an intersection and my eye caught the location of a candy store. I didn't drive too far before I swung my car around and pulled into the parking lot of the candystore. I went in and purchased two huge Hershey chocolate bars complete with almonds. Then I went out to my car and ate both candy bars. If I recall correctly, I consumed two whole pounds of chocolate and almonds.

When Peggy served me dinner that evening, I dared not explain the complete absence of any semblance of hunger. It wasn't until years later that I would confess what I had done.

While not as dominant as it once was, I still accommodate a respect for this childhood obsession.

Among the fine wines in my thousand-bottle wine cellar is a special shelf holding an ample revolving supply of large Hershey chocolate bars (complete with almonds).

The second thing I did was buy some custom- made shirts with French cuffs and my initials embroidered on the cuffs. Unfortunately, I had not been endowed with a middle name, so the monogram would consist of only two initials, R and L.

The first time I purchased custom shirts with my initials monogrammed on the cuff, I looked at the two initials and realized that you couldn't get that fancy triangular design with only two initials. To remedy this, I just adopted the letter "N" to fill out the design. When my friends asked me about the new initial, I told them it stood for nothing. I just needed it to fill out the design. From then on my friends started calling me "Nothing" instead of Robert.

Out of exasperation, I had to make a change. Since I didn't have a middle initial, I chose the letter "X". I guess the X didn't provoke them, so little more was said. I went down to the county courthouse and had my name legally changed to Robert X. Leeds. Now you know "the rest of the story."

When I finally retired, I paid off all of my indebtedness and moved to that Disneyland of Blackjack players, Las Vegas, Nevada. Do you want to know the real definition of an optimist? It's a seventy-three year old man who takes out a thirty-year mortgage to buy a two million dollar home. That's what I did.

Along with buying the house and cars, I bought myself a birthday present. I took my family to Russia's flight institute at Zhukovsky air base outside of Moscow, where I rented a MiG 21 Fishbed all-weather-fighter, and broke the sound barrier just because I had never gone that fast before.

For my seventy-third birthday we went back to Russia and I rented a MiG 23 Flogger, MiG 25 Foxbed Strategic Interceptor , MiG 29 Fulcrum, and the new Sukhoi 30.

I flew two and a half times the speed of sound in the MiG 23 and took the MiG 25 up to 84,000 feet, the edge of space, and looked down through the blue sky below and could see the curvature of the earth. The MiG 29 and the Su 30 presented me with the opportunity to fly every aerobatic maneuver in the books, including pulling out of a loop at 8.5 G's. To top it off, I became one of the few foreign pilots to ever successfully perform the dangerous cobra maneuver.

In Moscow, we stayed at the famous Metropol Hotel and had breakfast every morning in the beautiful dining room where scenes for the movie *Doctor Zhivago"* were filmed. During the day we toured the museums and in the evening enjoyed ballets at the Bolshoi Theater. Wherever we went, the flight institute provided us with an interpreter and a chauffeured limousine. This was the style of life I wanted to experience, if only for a brief moment.

I'm not a multimillionaire anymore, not by banking criteria, but I still manage to live like one.

My house is filled with Bill Mack, Michael Wilkinson, Debbie Brooks, and Mirabelle sculptures and paintings. An original sculpture of General Custer by Todd Warner stands guard over my living room while a lifelike figure of a butler, complete in formal evening attire, by Mirabelle, greets incoming guests. A specially commissioned painting by Gary reflects the beauty of morning dew on a field of flowers from over our bed while the rare beauty of paintings by Dali, Martiros, Nechita, and Janice Cua compete for space on our twenty foot high walls. Added to all this are original etchings by Rembrandt, Renoir, and Goya.

Life is like a painting that takes a lifetime to complete. Nothing I have was acquired with one swift stroke of a brush. Despite many failures there were enough successes to permit me to acquire these luxuries over many years.

If I had given up at any time, I would never have achieved what I have today. In fact, if I had stopped after my first failure, I would probably have none of this. Perhaps I would still be working for someone else and saving brown paper bags to carry my lunches in.

While writing this last chapter, I received a telephone call from a motion picture company in Beverly Hills, California. They wanted to buy the motion picture rights to my last book, *Love Is A 4 Legged Word*.

Although the book had won two nominations for Best Book of the Year, it was impossible to achieve any sales volume because not one of the major bookstore chains would carry it in inventory.

While most authors would have given up, I continued to spend the money necessary to advertise the book in all the trade journals. I practice what I preach.

Just by chance, the president of the film company saw my advertisement and bought the book. He enjoyed it so much that he decided to make it into a movie. While I'll receive cash and a percentage of the gross, at my age it isn't the money as much as it is the thrill of succeeding.

In January all the contracts were signed and writers had begun the motion picture screen play.

Last month I signed a contract giving the Chinese government the right to publish this book in simple Chinese for the 1.25 billion citizens of mainland China. *Become an instant millionaire?* Heck, It's taken me sixty years of *inspiration, perspiration*, and lots and lots of luck! (Some good. Some bad.)

Perhaps I'll be able to add this one to my list of positive accomplishments. Maybe I'll even make some money on this one. Heck, who knows what providence will provide?

PROVERB 99:
Life is like a book. You never really know what
will happen until you reach the end.

If there is one thing wrong with the "Become An Instant-Millionaire" philosophy being touted in all these books and seminars, it is that you are only told forty-five percent of the story.

Recently I attended two of the nation's largest seminars. One was "How To Become An Instant Millionaire" and the other was on "How To Make Your Book An Instant Best Seller." While the speakers filled the audience with canned cliches and technical abstractions, in the end, a summary of each seminar appeared to be that the real way to make money was to go out on your own lecturing circuit.

Each expert told how he or she had achieved miraculous success and then offered to sell the audience a portfolio of monographs, tapes, and CD's for prices ranging from a few hundred dollars to thousands of dollars. In addition, for up to $25,000 more, you could receive "personal" instruction while staying in the speaker's home for a few weeks. (I'm sure the coffee is free.)

It made me wonder why we had paid thousands of dollars to attend these initial seminars in the first place. Apparently we paid to learn that we needed to spend thousand of dollars more to learn how to really succeed.

When you come home from these seminars you will carry with you enough phamplets, CD's, and impressive looseleafs full of instructions, charts and examples, to occupy your time for months to come. Few attendees ever play the sixteen hour-long CD sets, let alone read the hundreds of pages of peripheral data. They know it and you have probably found that out by now. Ironically, it's the few who actually do, that stand the best chance of becoming a millionaire.

I continue to read these "get-rich-quick" books and attend these seminars for only two reasons. If I can come away with one good idea that I might use, I consider my money well spent.

The second reason is that I'm one of those individuals who likes to be motivated. Reading these books and attending these seminars are like shots of adrenaline. They provide me with a burst of energy and a reinforced desire to pursue success.

Unfortunately, in a short time the effects begin to wear off. The path is longer and more difficult than was inferred in the advertisments. Reality clouds your sky and the rain of doubt begins to fall on your parade. The easily attainable goal that had been "guaranteed" begins to slip from your grasp. Now you have an option. You can give up, buy another "How To" book, purchase another seminar or, you can go back and re-read this book.

The truth is that most "How To" books are written and the majority of seminars are held, for only one purpose; for the financial benefit of the author or the company that conducts the seminars.That's not a crime. Every book and every seminar contains one or more seeds of wisdom. You just have to separate the chaff from the seeds.

Mark Victor Hanson, author of *Chicken Soup For the Soul* and his partner, Robert G. Allen, the preeminent guru of *Creating Wealth With Real Estate,* are probably the two most successful conductors of "Get Rich Quick" seminars in America. Thousands and thousands of aspiring entrepreneurs have paid millions of dollars to attend their seminars with the dream of becoming instant millionaires.

Paradoxically, these two men found it more profitable to tell others how to *almost* become millionaires, than it was with their Real Estate and Publishing activities. They recently were credited with making $60,446,286.49 from their seminar activities.

As corroboration of my thesis, at each of these seminars, I offered to hire several of the seminar speakers to take one of my books and make it a best seller (as they said they had done with their book or product and could do with anyone elses.) Not one "expert" would accept the challenge.

Now, let's just look at the rationale involved here. If they helped me sell 100,000 books, I would make around $500,000 and they could earn $125,000 as their commission. Who are they helping by turning down a $125,000 offer in favor of a $4,000 "consulting" fee? They're certainly not helping you or me and they're certainly not helping themselves . . . if they could do what they say they can do.

If their systems were so adequate, wouldn't they all be literary agents and churning out million dollar sellers one after the other?

Their "surefire" systems and "guarantees" that anyone can make their book into a bestseller overnight, disappeared when invited into the arena of performance.

There is a positive reward in reading "How To. . ." books and attending these motivational seminars, but don't plan on walking out and becoming that "Instant Millionaire." Most of us need that occasional jab of adrenaline. We need to hear of other people's successes. We thrive on it. It's a confirmation that "*it*" can be done. Yesterday it was him or her. Tomorrow it will be us.

Well, why not? Remember the other fifty-five percent of the story? Providence!

Fate has ordained that things will happen over which you will have no control. Bad things, but also good things.

That is why none of these "get-rich-quick-and easy" formulas can guarantee you success. Remember what I said about the odds of an entrepreneur becoming a millionaire? Seven out of ten will lose everything within three years. Another two will go out of business within ten years. One in 500,000 will reach their goal of becoming a millionaire. But, if you want to be that one, you have to do things that will improve your odds.

Just realize that your odds of success can be improved. They can be improved by what you have read in this book. Remember the stories and remember the proverbs. These can change your odds!

Instead of having one chance in 500,000, you will have a better chance of *being* the one in 500,000.

You can't do it by being a spectator. Life wasn't meant to be a spectator sport. Success is not for everyone, but the one sure way to avoid being successful is to not try! You've got to take chances and accept risks. You've got to participate. You've got to expect and experience failures in your life. Whatever your goal in life is, if you want to ultimately succeed, you've got to pick up the pieces when you fail and go on, and you're never too old.

If you think you're too young or too old to start now, think about Harland Sanders. He was sixty-seven years old when he lost his gas station and restaurant. He was penniless and living on a Social Security check of $105.00 a month. When Pepsi Co bought his company in 1986, they paid $840 Million for it.

Recently I had lunch with Mark Victor Hanson and by the time lunch ended he had convinced me that I was much too young to retire. After all, I'm only seventy-six years old and according to statistics, I've still got another twenty-one years to accomplish something worthwhile.

I could choose to spend this time in front of a television set, but why waste it when there are so many opportunities out there? I figure I could make another $21 million in the time allotted, and I'll still have time to write a few more books. Think of all the good I can do with that money. Think of all I can *do* with that money, period! I've got the experience, now all I need is a little more luck. I'm even thinking of giving seminars. I'm sure there are enough people out there who would pay good money to hear me tell them "How To <u>almost</u> Make A Million Dollars."

In summing it all up, the endeavors and hardships I endured were modest sacrifices to satisfy an unquenchable thirst to succeed in life and in business. After all that has happened, I'm still thirsty.

In conclusion, I hope this book will not only make you aware of the hurdles you may encounter in life, but also how you can overcome them or avoid them. Get out there and bring your dreams out of the closet. You've got to be a *"believer!"* Where there's a will, there's a way!

PROVERB 100:
Life is not a spectator sport.

In the meantime, always remember, *"Think big! Act big! Do Big!"* Hey, send me your address and I'll send you an oil well. . . in a minute.

Face it. We don't have a million years!

{ Portions of this book will appear in more extensive detail in Robert X. Leeds forthcoming autobiography, *WINDMILLS AT 12 O'CLOCK.* }

ACKNOWLEDGEMENTS

I wish I could claim credit for all the proverbs used to summarize the situations in this book. I cannot.

Over a period of more than seventy years, the mind accumulates a vast storehouse of phrases which, at the time, you say, "Gee, I wish I had said that" and you tuck it away in your memory bank. Unfortunately, for one reason or another, you fail to write it down, or if you do write it down, you neglect to credit the author. This is my present dilemma.

I can recall that I have read a good deal of Mark Twain, Oscar Wilde, George Bernard Shaw, Shakespeare, and Confucius, so I suspect I have used or paraphrased some of their artful characterizations. I don't expect any objections from them.

However, if you find your masterful locution quoted within the proverbs of this manuscript, please forgive me for not ascribing to you proper credit. Also, please do not call your lawyer.

Consider that I completed my Masters Thesis only by resorting to an emendation of a treatise done by Pliny the Elder in 50 a.d. In my limited capacity I have tried to paraphrase and otherwise disguise any semblance of plagiarism. Here it is my intention to acknowledge my obvious indebtedness.

I think it was Mark Twain who said that Adam was the only person who could claim everything he said was original. Whoever said it was correct.